For my girls:
Jennifer, Em, and Kate.

CHAPTER ONE

With each breath he sucked the plastic closer to his mouth. His teeth clamped down hard but missed the bag. He swallowed, trying to rid his mouth of the taste of blood and chemicals.

Miles always feared he would die from asphyxiation. Once as a child, he was pressed by a crowd from every side, making him unable to expand his chest to breathe. That feeling of air hunger haunted him ever since. What he didn't expect was how long it would take. By now he thought his mind would drift from consciousness. Instead, his thirst for air only increased, repeatedly bringing the bag flat against his face.

If only he could move his hands that were paralyzed beside him. They were being held down by The Void. Others may not see The Void, but the entity was real. The Void had followed Miles his entire life. It started as a thought, a fear of failure. This fear pushed him out of his hometown of two thousand souls to an Ivy League college. He was one of only a handful of Chambers men to ever graduate high school or stay out of prison.

When his fear grew from a thought to a voice and finally took shape—a black figure, darker than any darkness around it, like a skipped space in the air—he gave it a name, The Void. It was now behind him, pinning his hands to his waist and tightening a belt around his neck, cinching the plastic bag over his head.

His chest burned. Miles surrendered, hoping death would take him. His last project was meant to cement his legacy and be his crowning achievement: the creation of a weapon that would incapacitate a nation without firing a single shot. A weapon that would leave the enemy unable to organize a counterattack, or even a coherent thought. Everything was executed according to plan, but somewhere along the way he screwed up. The weapon was effective—the manifestation of The Void was proof enough.

He should have developed the antidote before he finished the weapon. There was a window when he could have. Now that window was firmly shut. Miles would be the first victim—surely the first of many with no antidote. He accepted his fate: the culmination of his worst fears—failure and suffocation. If only fate would accept him. A sharp breath slammed the plastic against his lips. His lungs felt like they would explode. How long would he remain in this purgatory of suffering?

CHAPTER TWO

CLAIRE

Her cool arm. That's what stuck with me. No living thing should feel like that. There were plenty of other signs that she was gone: how her head sagged, her vacant eyes, the gape of her mouth, even the empty pill bottles on the coffee table. But it was the feel of her skin that made it all real.

I couldn't rid my hands of that sensation. Sometimes I would wake up and have to look down to make sure I wasn't gripping my sister's bloodless arm. Even when the feeling would leave, touching anything lifeless brought it back in an instant. And most of what I touch in a day is lifeless.

No one seemed to enjoy living more than my twin sister, Amy. Her constant smile, energy, and endless optimism all grated on my nerves—something I feel guilty about. I'll never hear her annoying giggle again or her imitation of our mother until I laugh so hard I wet my pants. I'll never hear her defend our nosy neighbor or her creepy boss. No, she wasn't trying to irritate me; she was just a happy person.

But that all changed. Suddenly, it was as if all the good in her 125-pound body had been scooped out and its shell had been replaced with a sad, desperate girl. My sister, who had never been sick for longer than a day, was bedridden with all sorts of ailments. Headaches, stomach pains, nausea, dizziness—and those were her good days. After she had suffered in her body, her mind betrayed her. What started with sadness ended in madness. By the end, she literally tried to peel her own skin off, convinced it was poisoned. Our skin may be thin, but it's strong enough to withstand a few sharp nails. But that didn't stop Amy from trying. In places, she had clawed her arms down to the muscle.

I had pulled her body to the floor by her damaged arm, lacing my fingers together to pump her sternum. Thirty compressions, pausing for a breath, then thirty more. I repeated this until my arms burned. Until I heard sirens. But I knew. I knew she wasn't coming back. In truth, something had killed my sister long before that day.

My name is Claire Long, and I'm alone in the world. At least that's the way it has felt since my twin sister died.

I'm at work again. Not because I had to be and not because any patients were on my schedule. Mainly I went back to work because I couldn't stand staring at the same four walls of my home and hoping the next hour would be different. Now I'm staring at the four walls in my office and still feel horrible.

I made my way down the hall to Mia's office. Mia is my business partner and a fellow therapist. We met ten years ago in school. With my sister gone, Mia is my closest friend. I knocked on her door with the back of my knuckles.

"It's open," she yelled.

I turned the knob and entered her office. Mia sat by a far window, surrounded by tropical plants. Her face was obscured by a giant, pink hibiscus flower. From a corner fountain, water trickled over a set of stones. "In the jungle, I see?"

She stood up, her head cleared the plants. "My happy place," she answered. Mia walked towards me, away from her tropical oasis. Her office was basically divided into two parts, a therapy room for patients and a therapy room for herself. Something she called immersion therapy.

"Immerse yourself in an environment that brings you joy," Mia explained. "That's immersion therapy. It's simple. For me, it's the island of Kauai."

Why didn't she just move to Hawaii and really immerse herself? Or better yet, visit Kauai for the first time? That seemed more logical than a simulated jungle in the back of an Atlanta, Georgia, office. But I didn't push that idea. I needed Mia—now more than ever.

I took a seat on one of the two couches facing each other. Mia sat opposite me. We were separated by a round, glass coffee table. "Claire, aren't you back a little early?" she asked. Her eyebrows were raised, forming a set of wrinkles on her forehead.

"Don't worry. I'm not seeing patients," I told her.

"I know that. It's just—" Mia stopped talking. She looked up and down my body.

"Yep, I look terrible. You don't have to say it."

Mia gave me a maternal smile. Something she must give struggling patients. I hated it.

"No shower, no makeup. Going on...let's see...at least three days now," I answered.

"That's not like you," said Mia. More head wrinkles, another maternal smile.

"Neither is finding my sister dead," I answered.

Mia let out a heavy sigh. "Maybe you should be at home a bit longer. Or visit your parents."

"I've been at home. It's not helping being alone, without her." I leaned forward and asked, "Does it make sense to you?

What happened to Amy, I mean?" I didn't wait for Mia to answer. "She had no history of mental illness. Nothing bad happened in her life, at least nothing I knew about. But it was like this thing, this monster, overtook her. And she just couldn't shake it."

"That monster is called depression," answered Mia, "and it takes over a lot of people."

"Well, I'm a therapist and her twin sister. But I couldn't help her."

"Claire, it's not your fault. You know that."

I nodded.

Her voice sounded far away. "Why do you keep wringing your hands?" Mia asked.

"What?"

"Your hands. You keep rubbing them together. Is that a new habit?"

"Oh." I looked down at my hands in my lap. "I didn't notice. I... um... sort of have this feeling of her dead skin in my hand. When I touched her arm, it was—"

"Oh, Claire, it's okay." Mia raked her fingers through her black hair, pinning it behind both ears. Her own nervous habit.

"The thing is whatever Amy was feeling, I don't know, but I think I can relate to some of it."

Mia motioned for me to continue.

"Not all of it, of course. It's just... when she first changed." I followed Mia's eyes back to my lap to see that I was still rubbing my hands. "Right, in the beginning she had these body aches, nausea, fatigue, and headaches. She started complaining of feeling unsettled, anxious for no reason. You know, nothing like Amy." Mia nodded in agreement. "I'm feeling some of those things—especially fatigue and headaches. And I don't know, just hollowed out. I'm not picking my skin off or guzzling a bucket of pills, not yet anyway." I forced a laugh. Mia didn't smile back. "But something is off, and every day seems to be a little worse."

"Claire," Mia stroked her hair again, "you really need to get some help. Talk to someone."

"That's what I'm doing now, right? Aren't you a therapist?"

Mia said nothing. The room was silent, except for the trickling water from the fountain. She took a deep breath through her nose and let it out slowly from her mouth. "Yes, but I'm too close to this. To you."

"Even better. I don't think a therapist can know their patient too well," I told her.

Mia stood up and smoothed her cream skirt out against her legs. She walked back and forth in a tight line in front of the couch opposite me.

"You seem uncomfortable," I said.

She sat down. Another deep breath through her nostrils. "I am."

"So?"

"So I don't want to get into this with you," Mia said.

"Into what?"

"Your relationship with your sister."

I looked down and forced my hands to stop rubbing together. Maybe it was already a habit. "You might as well," I told her. "I am incapable of being offended at the moment." It was true. My emotions were blunted. I had skipped all the stages of grief except depression. Anger, denial, bargaining, guilt, well, maybe guilt. But mostly just sadness.

"Fine. I have often thought you and your sister were codependent. Don't get me wrong. Your relationship was beautiful. But I think the way she kept you from having to develop certain parts of yourself, and the same was true for her."

She paused—I guess to gauge my reaction. I didn't interrupt. "What I mean," she continued, "is that the natural tendency of your personality, to want to be in control, went into hyperdrive with Amy. Her free spirit made you double down on the need for control. I guess, for both of you. Like all codependent relationships, some areas in a person don't grow. In her case, responsibility, and in your case, spontaneity." Mia cleared her throat and leaned forward. "I'm not surprised you feel a little lost and confused. I'm also not surprised you believe you're sharing some of her same feelings. She was your twin sister; it's not just a death in the family. It's like a part of you died."

I leaned back on the couch, sinking into its cushion. "I thought you didn't want to give me any therapy." I let out a weak laugh. This new fatigue in my body was almost paralyzing. A kind of weariness where activities of daily living were a chore. "The thing is, Mia, I felt like this before Amy's suicide." I laid back, now flat on the couch. "The day she died I knew it before I opened the door to our apartment. I knew there was something seriously wrong behind that door." I looked up at the ceiling. "Do you remember that instructor, Neil, from school?"

"Dr. Vonn?"

"Yeah, Dr. Vonn. You remember that speech he gave about rose-colored glasses?" Mia nodded. Neil Vonn lecturing popped in my head—his bushy beard, steel-rimmed glasses, the faded jeans with a rope belt, his hairy chest pressed against a tightly buttoned shirt. "'You must have rose-colored glasses to live in this world,' he would say. 'The truth is we are born without a known purpose into a world where everyone we know is going to die. That inevitability draws closer with each day. If you can't find a way to see that with rose-colored glasses, if you see that the way it really is, you will go mad.'"

"Dr. Vonn was an atheist who used mushrooms during his therapy sessions," Mia countered.

"Yeah, well, I don't think I have any more rose-colored glasses," I said.

"Claire?"

"Mm-hmm."

"I never thought I'd ask this, but have you thought about hurting yourself?"

CHAPTER THREE

I flipped the card over in my hand. Javier Blanc, followed by a train of letters: MD, PhD, FAAN, FAPA. The card was thicker than any business card should be, like a formal wedding invitation. A cursive JB watermark faintly colored the background. His own logo. Well, that's a bit pretentious.

Mia had set an appointment already. I changed my mind twice in the past hour, something I rarely used to do. But now, even deciding on a grocery store run was difficult.

I took off more personal days from work. I wasn't doing well, which caused waves of distress. Other times I felt detached, like I was watching a sad person suffer from a distance. Mia had checked on me two days earlier. At least, I think it was two days ago. She cleaned a dirty dish pile, vacuumed, stripped the sheets off my bed, and made an appointment with Dr. Blanc. Not necessarily in that order. "The appointment is at two o'clock. Even you can't sleep past two," she had said.

For a while sleep seemed to be my only respite. Now, it was hard to come by. I watched the clock most nights. Too tired to get out of bed but unable to sleep. I placed the thick business card down, finally deciding to cancel the appointment when the phone rang. Mia.

"Hello?"

"Hello, Claire. I'm checking in. Making sure you are ready for your appointment with Dr. Blanc."

"Sure," I lied.

"Great. Do you need a ride?"

"Um, no, I can still drive, Mia." I looked at the JB watermark, the personal logo. "This guy is pretty strange, isn't he?" To have a reputation as a strange psychiatrist was difficult.

Mia laughed. "You know he is. But he's the best. No genius is normal. You know that."

"He's a genius now?"

"So I've heard," she answered. "I guess you two will have that in common. I mean the genius part. Just quit making excuses and go."

I looked at my watch, already one o'clock. I agreed and hung up. There was no use canceling; Mia would just keep making appointments.

My usual hour routine of making myself up was cut to ten minutes as of late. No longer did I straighten my hair or apply makeup. Now, a face wash would do.

Dr. Blanc's office was in a high rise building in downtown Atlanta. I parked at a nearby deck, then walked across a pedestrian bridge to the lobby. From there, I waited for a set of gold-plated elevators to bring me to the forty-eighth floor. Also waiting were two men and one woman, all dressed in power suits—she in navy pinstripes, the men in black. They looked me up and down without smiling. They were probably wondering what business I might have in their fancy building. We filed into the elevator. The three of them smelled fresh, expensive. I couldn't remember if I'd showered and just hoped I didn't reek.

One of them pushed the forty-eight button, another forty-nine. The elevator shot up so fast that I could feel my stomach drop.

The woman and I got out on forty-eight. A directory on a far wall showed two offices: a law practice and the office of Javier Blanc, followed by the same tail of letters—MD, PhD, FAAN, FAPA.

I turned to a set of frosted glass doors, each etched with Dr. Blanc's logo in the center. I pushed the door open to a gleaming marble floor. Two empty olive couches lined a cream-colored wall. A lone receptionist sat behind a modern white desk. In the center of the room hung a massive chandelier with long golden spikes. Each point was lit on its end like a giant firework.

The woman behind the desk looked up. She had blond hair spiked in all directions as if paying homage to the chandelier.

"Hello, I'm—"

"Ms. Claire Long," her high-pitched voice clipped. "Dr. Blanc is expecting you. You can wait in his office. First door on your right."

I nodded. Her sunken eyes tracked me as I walked by. She forced a brief smile, which quickly fell from her face. I pushed open the cracked door to the doctor's office. Once inside, I could see the entire Atlanta skyline. I stopped in the center of the room. The drop from forty-eight stories was dizzying. Just a pane of glass between me and the thin air.

Buildings of all heights stretched to the horizon. People the size of ants passed each other on the sidewalks below. Amy would have loved this.

"Not a bad view, huh?" a voice said behind me.

I turned to see the doctor in person for the first time. He was a small figure, no taller than my height of five feet seven, and dressed in all red. He had a black beard and mustache groomed to three fine points. He looked like a devil in a school play. "Yeah," I answered, "not cheap, I'm sure."

"Oh, family money," he said, waving his hand through the air as if the idea of money was trivial. "You look different from the picture on your website," he said.

The website. That was years ago. When Mia hired a professional hair-and-makeup team for our headshots. Whatever he meant, I'm sure it wasn't a compliment. I looked at the little man in the red suit with waxed mustache tips. "You aren't what I expected either," I answered.

He looked his red suit up and down. "Ha, right. It is striking. I dress for the mood I'm in or the mood I want to project. Red is about energy, action. Nothing we do is by accident," he answered, "unless you count that time I kissed my cousin."

Ugh, I looked at the door behind him, wanting to leave.

"Claire, please. That was no accident either. I wanted to gauge your reaction to a little humor."

I sighed. I was in no mood for games. I looked at a large screen mounted on the wall to my left. On it was a brain filled with brightly colored lines crossing each other.

He followed my eyes. "Beautiful, isn't it?" he asked. "The human brain. All those connections. It looks like madness, but everything is meticulously connected for a purpose. Do you know what plasticity is?" he asked.

"The ability of the brain to make new connections, to adapt, basically," I answered.

"Good for you," Dr. Blanc answered.

I'm a trained psychologist from Emory University with two credits short of a PhD, you condescending ass.

"It's the brain's plasticity that allows us to push through the hard times. To overcome problems and adapt a creative solution." He walked over to the screen showing the brain. "Do you follow monster trucks?"

What? "Do I look like I follow monster trucks?" I asked.

"Ha, me either. I'm Spanish and French."

This guy is stranger than I feared.

"Let me explain. When someone is dealing with a crisis they can't get out of, when they feel trapped—a learned helplessness—their brain digs a rut. I always imagine a car stuck in the mud. Its tires are spinning as fast as they can, but they only dig a deeper rut." He twisted the right tip of his mustache. "That's when I imagine a monster truck. To me, the monster truck represents an amplified signal between two neurons of the brain. With a monster truck, you can drive through the rut. You could even make a new path around the rut. That's neuroplasticity, the brain's ability to make new connections or to strengthen others."

I didn't answer. The idea of using monster trucks to dumb down neurochemistry for my benefit was just offensive.

He then cleared the monitor with a finger tap. After one more tap, another brain entered the screen. "So this," he pointed, "is a healthy brain. Well, at least a brain without depression." His little green eyes waited for some acknowledgment. I nodded. "Right, see these connections shown in pink and blue?" I gave another nod. He touched the screen again to bring in a new brain.

"Here's a picture of what's going on in a depressed brain. See how fewer pink and blue lines there are? That shows the activity in the hippocampus and prefrontal cortex. The connections are almost half that of a healthy brain." He paused, shook his head. "Amazing. But in this area," he thumped the screen, "in the amygdala, it's more active."

He walked away from the monitor to nestle himself in an egg-shaped, white leather chair. He tucked his feet under him, fitting his entire body inside the chair, like a little red ball. "That depressed brain has lost some volume. Lost plasticity. I guess the old adage, use it or lose it, is more than just a catch phrase. It turns out the brain circuits we don't use are pruned off." He looked back at the screen. "That poor brain has been cut worse than a five-dollar haircut."

Mia, why did you send me here? Genius or not, this guy—

"Look, I'm just going to—" I began.

"Claire, please, take a seat." He put his feet on the floor and motioned to another egg-shaped chair. "I know you think I'm pompous, maybe even crazy. Most people do."

Hmm, at least he's somewhat self-aware.

"That may be true, but I can help you. I'm sorry about your sister."

I sat down, emotionally exhausted. "Thank you," I murmured.

He nodded, causing the pointy beard to bounce. "Of course you've heard of functional MRIs and PET scans to evaluate blood flow. Well, here at J. Blanc's we use something more specialized."

Did he just use his name in the third person as an institution? Oh, boy.

"We use something called diffusion tensor imaging. This allows us to see how the brain is organized. By using this technique, we are able to construct a 3D map of the brain's circuits."

I was following, sort of. My concentration had been poor for weeks. Also his pointy beard was distracting.

"As I said," he continued, "I'm here to help. I'm a man of action. So," he tented his fingers together to make a steeple, "I'd like to run you through our scanners. See what's going on right now in your brain."

At the moment, all I could think of was my insurance company rejecting this barrage of tests. I saw myself at the kitchen table with a stack of medical bills or on hold for hours with Blue Cross. "I don't think that, um, my insurance would cover those tests."

He waved his hand through the air. "Don't bother. We have all kinds of grants for those machines. Besides, Mia sends me dozens of patients. I would never charge a colleague." He paused for a minute, waiting for my response. When I gave none, he answered, "Great, I'll have it set up by tomorrow. Linda!" he yelled out for his assistant with the spiky hair.

CHAPTER FOUR

I walked out on my tight balcony. Horns blasted from below. I could taste the exhaust from cars choked in a line of traffic. On the corner, a fat man yelled into a cell phone, his free hand cutting through the air. Across the street, the sun reflected off a new, shiny office building, blinding me if I turned my head to the wrong angle. Men and women dressed in pressed suits, ready to make money, funneled into the building's mouth.

Now that Amy was gone, I was reminded how much I wanted to be away from the noise of the city. My sister loved the energy of midtown. She had talked me into living with her in this high-rise building.

I watched as an older lady waited patiently for her little dog to pee on the base of each parking meter. The thought of going back to my bedroom twisted my gut. I had spent the last seven hours rolling over, fighting my aching joints, hoping sleep would find me at last. My phone rattled on the iron table next to me, making me jump.

"Hello?"

"Good morning, is this Claire?"

"Yes, speaking."

"This is Linda, from Dr. Blanc's office. I hope I didn't wake you."

Did I sound that sleepy? I cleared my throat. "No, no, of course not." I haven't slept all night.

"Dr. Blanc would like you to come into the office today to go over your test results."

I looked down at the traffic, now moving only in spurts. The thought of being in it produced a sharp pain over my right eye. "Can we, um, do this over the phone?"

I heard Linda take a breath. "I'm afraid not. Dr. Blanc wants to show you the results, personally."

"Why?" The question came out of my mouth the second it entered my mind.

Another sigh at the other end, this one quieter. "He doesn't share that information with me," she answered.

I agreed to be there at one o'clock. "Wants to show you the results, personally," she said. It had to be a brain tumor. Why else would he call me back into the office? The stabbing pain over my eye doubled in intensity. My head felt light, while the rest of my body felt heavy. A nauseous wave came over me. A tumor, so be it. At least it was an explanation for my failing body.

I had just over three hours before I needed to leave. I forced myself to get ready, pushing myself to complete what used to be an easy routine. If I was going to receive some terminal diagnosis, it was going to fall on ears attached to a made-up face and styled hair.

I traveled to Dr. Blanc's office in a daze, which was becoming a familiar feeling. Between bouts of fatigue, sadness, and anxiety, I had those strange spells of detachment, like watching someone else's life unravel. That's what I felt when I pulled open the door to the doctor's waiting room. From somewhere else, I felt my thirty-two-year-old self walk into the room and await her fate. Soon, I was sure I'd be looking at some sinister ball of cells eating at my cortex.

"Hi, Linda. I made it." The voice coming from my mouth sounded distant and stretched.

"You can head on back, Dear," Linda said.

I nodded. Dear? That sounded out of place for her. Was it her weak attempt at warmth for someone whose life was about to crumble? Maybe.

I opened the office door to find the doctor standing close to the monitor on his wall. Once again a monochromatic outfit, this time a teal blue.

"Claire, welcome," he said, spreading his arms out.

I worked the corners of my mouth up to muster a smile. "Teal today?" I asked and stood next to him, looking at the same screen that captured his attention.

"Yes, yes, today is a teal day, indeed."

"Calming effect?"

"Among other things," he answered. He tugged at the wax point of his beard.

To think of this caricature delivering some awful prognosis in this teal outfit suddenly angered me. That would be a difficult memory.

"So," the doctor popped his hands together, "how are you doing?"

I stared at him, said nothing.

"Right, dumb question. You recognize this?" He pointed to a picture of a brain on the screen.

"Should I?"

"I should hope so. It's your brain," he chuckled.

I shrugged and looked for something terribly wrong. Where was the tumor he was sure to point out?

He stood silent for a moment. "It's really stunning." He studied the screen, his eyes shifting back and forth.

"Stunning?"

"Oh, sorry. It's just I haven't seen too many scans like this."

"Can you just tell me what it is?" I snapped. "Like you said, it's *my* brain." For the first time in weeks, I felt like venting. He may be some genius neuroscientist, but this was no way to address a patient.

"Claire, I—"

"If you've found a growth, just let me know where and how big. If you found a stroke, tell me. If half of my brain is rotted beyond recognition, spell it out. For all things holy, just don't sit there and tell me it's a stunning piece of research!"

"Claire, there is no tumor. No stroke. And nothing is rotten. Just bear with me a minute."

I took a deep breath. "Sorry, I've been under some stress."

He nodded. "Let me show you a typical brain again." Dr. Blanc pulled up an image beside my brain. Okay, you see this area?"

I nodded.

"The hippocampus, of course. Stop me if you don't want any structural background."

"It's fine. My concentration has been terrible lately."

"I imagine that's right," he answered. "Not only has your hippocampus shrunk, but the size of your amygdala is seriously aberrant. And the prefrontal cortex," he pointed to my frontal lobe, "your circuits are very odd."

I opened my mouth to talk but suddenly was without any words. "Go on," I finally said.

"Okay, here is a patient suffering from posttraumatic stress disorder." He added another brain to the bottom left of the screen. "I'm going to add one more here." Another brain in the bottom right corner joined the rest. Now four brains made a square on the screen. "This patient has major depression disorder. So we have your brain on the top left, a 'healthy brain' on the top right, and on the bottom of the screen a brain with PTSD and one with major depression. Let's take a look at the brain with PTSD. We'll call her Pat. Pat with PTSD, for the sake of simplicity."

Dr. Blanc enlarged the brain. "You remember the amygdala, of course. That little area of the brain can be quite pesky in a trauma, sounding an alarm out to everywhere. So Pat here has definitely been sounding the alarm. Look at the areas highlighted in blue, showing elevated amygdala activity.

"Now let's take a look at this depressed brain," he continued, enlarging a different picture. "Let's call him Dan. Dan the depressed brain. The size and activity of Dan's hippocampus and prefrontal cortex are abnormally small. Check out the paucity of the pink and green colors there."

I nodded, mostly processing the fact he had just named two brains Dan and Pat.

"Well, your brain is a mix of problems. The activity in your amygdala suggests you have been through a traumatic event, but the other areas don't match up with that. You see these colors?"

I suddenly felt unbalanced. "I'm not feeling well. I'm going to sit down."

"Of course." He waited as I took a seat. "Have you been feeling anxious?" he asked. "Sort of," I answered. "But pretty wiped out as well."

He walked back and forth in front of my chair. "It's interesting. Your amygdala is overactive, while your prefrontal cortex and hippocampus are barely firing."

"Javier, can I call you Javier?"

"I've been called worse," he answered.

The area above my right eye was stabbing again. I was still

shocked there was no tumor. "This is, um, a little specialized. Or maybe it's just that my head is starting to ache."

"Looking at your brain scan, I'm surprised you can concentrate at all. And forget motivation. That area of your brain is almost mute."

"Yeah, that's not helping. What does this mean, practically speaking?"

He stopped pacing and looked at me. "Yes, forgive me, the meaning. This abnormal activity of your brain in these three areas all at the same time, it's like a perfect mental storm. The surge of stress response from the amygdala is generally regulated by the prefrontal cortex. But as you can see, that area is quiet. The part of your hippocampus that stores key memories is strong, but overall the region is undersized. Your brain," he made a low whistle, "shows the trauma of someone who's been in combat for a decade, but it's also similar to someone who's been severely depressed for a lifetime. These changes don't happen overnight." He looked up at the monitor. "These changes take a long, long, long time."

Maybe a tumor wouldn't have been so bad after all.

"This depression of yours, is it really just a few weeks old?"

"Yeah."

"Remarkable." He walked to the window and looked out to the city. "Have you been ruminating on any events? Unpleasant events?"

I thought of the feel of my sister's cool skin. "Yes."

The doctor spun his head around. "We don't have a lot of time."

"Excuse me?"

"If your brain has changed this much in a matter of weeks, then we have to act," he answered.

"And what do you suggest? Medicine?"

"Medicine? Yes, well, certain medicines can be effective. But the problem is they take weeks to work."

Weeks. How serious is this? He makes it sound like I'll be a vegetable in a matter of days. Truthfully, I couldn't imagine feeling much worse. Just having this conversation was painful. My joints were aching, my head felt like it was in a vice, and I was following only a quarter of what was said.

"You remember our conversation about plasticity?"

I nodded.

"Well, plasticity is what you need right now. Your brain needs to lay down some new tracks. Form some new circuitry to work with."

"And you don't think medicine can do that?" I asked.

"Medicine," he repeated quietly, gazing at the city skyline lost in thought. I waited for him to answer and was about to repeat my question before he finally spoke. "You ever wonder why antidepressants take weeks to work?"

I shrugged. The truth was I really hadn't.

"Take Prozac, for example. Like many of the first depression medications, it blocks the reuptake of serotonin. So you've got more serotonin hanging around between neurons. Increase the serotonin and voila—happy patient, right? Only that's not what happens. Nothing happens for close to two weeks."

Prozac. The name brought me back to Amy and all the empty pill bottles toppled over on the table. That lifeless stare of my sister popped in my mind, followed by the feeling of her skin. I rubbed my hands together in a futile attempt to rid the memory.

"Doesn't make sense, right?" He turned away from the window to look at me. I nodded slowly, still rubbing my hands. "Right. Well, research now shows us that serotonin has to work on another protein that ultimately leads to changes in the brain. So the plasticity takes weeks."

"So we wait a couple of weeks," I answered.

"Is that what you want?" he asked. I thought about the last two weeks and shuddered. Easily the worst of my life. "Two more weeks of this, and I'm afraid your neuroconnections, what's left of them, are going to look like a bird's nest." The doctor now looked at the screen.

"I could start therapy—I mean intensive therapy," I answered.

"Good, but still too slow. Have you heard of using ketamine?" he asked.

"I've heard of some doctors using it. I haven't personally had any patients try it."

"It turns out that ketamine, apart from being used in anesthesia, works immediately to change the brain's plasticity. It works by a different mechanism than the typical antidepressants. It blocks NMDA receptors, which leads to an immediate chain of events that increases plasticity of the brain. But unlike pills, this reaction takes place in minutes to hours."

"I don't know. Ketamine just sounds—"

"Like a party drug? Special K," he interrupted.

"Desperate," I answered.

"Hmm." He walked over to the screen and enlarged my brain on the monitor. "Claire, I think this may be desperate."

CHAPTER FIVE

JACK

"Jack Baker?"

I looked up. A woman in blue scrubs stood by the front desk. I walked through the packed waiting room, passing glares from those still waiting.

"Hi, Jack," the nurse said. "I'm Janet. Dr. Potts is ready for you."

"Thanks. Busy today?" I asked. That seemed more polite than pointing out it was an hour past my appointment time.

"Yeah, sorry, it's been crazy. We had an emergency." Her shoulders slumped, and her whole face looked tired. A mound of dusky flesh sagged under her eyes. Maybe in her late forties, I thought. Or a weary thirty.

I followed her, stopping in front of a digital scale. I wondered if they always said there was an emergency, even if the doctor was only late from lunch. But I imagine no one ever pushed for more detail. What did I know of emergencies anyway? There were no emergencies in the lab.

After I was weighed, the nurse led me into a patient room and took my vital signs. I scanned the table, looking at the doctor's family pictures. One was of a chunky kid with beet-red cheeks and a gap tooth. The other was the whole family: the doctor, her husband, the gap-toothed kid, and a little girl with red hair. The husband was a round man with a thick neck. The only thing defining his chin was a black goatee, centered on a pile of pink flesh. Janet said Dr. Potts would be right in.

I tried to gather my thoughts to present to the doctor. A toddler in the next room was screaming at full throttle while the mother tried to shush him in vain. My already aching head began to pound like a separate heartbeat. I attempted to organize my symptoms but couldn't concentrate. I knew I was about to unload a scroll of problems on the already late, overworked doctor.

Just when I stood up to stretch, Dr. Potts came thundering in the room. Her blond hair was loosely tied on top of her head, and she wore an ill-fitted cotton dress. She was slightly out of breath. "Did you hear that? What a battle."

"Sounds like it. Were you doing surgery without an anesthetic?" I asked. She let out a loud laugh. The doctor was a big woman with broad shoulders and thick wrists. Her deep laugh seemed only fitting.

"You would think so," she answered. "That, Jack, was just an ear check."

I nodded. She sat down on a stool and struck hard at the keyboard. After a few mouse clicks, she asked, "How's Andrea?"

"Anne?" I asked.

"Oops, yeah, Anne."

"Oh, we broke up a while back," I answered.

"Ugh, sorry. Zero for two."

"No worries," I said. "It was for the best." The doctor was always getting my family details wrong when she tried to be personal. It was something I'd actually come to like, being that I was also terrible at remembering names.

"So, Jack, can I call you Jack? I know you're also a doctor."

"Of course. I'm not a real doctor. Well, not a medical one anyway."

"It counts," she said loudly. "A PhD takes as long as a medical degree."

"Well, if they ask if anyone's a doctor on a plane, I'm not standing up."

She smiled and hammered a few more keys. "Fair enough, Jack. What brings you in today?"

"I just feel rotten," I answered. Her smile faded and the blood drained from her face. "Sorry, I mean more specifically, I've got zero juice. That is not like me. Usually I have to exercise just to burn off excess energy. Along with this fatigue, I'm nauseous. And headaches, constant headaches."

She worked the keys without looking in my direction. "Okay, so how long has this been going on?"

"A couple of weeks. Maybe three. I would have just tried to deal with it, but people at work are starting to notice. Every day it seems someone asks me if I'm okay."

"And how is work?" she asked. I put my hand out flat and rocked it side to side. "You work for the CDC, right?"

"Well, not really. More of a distant offshoot of the CDC."

"Testing new drugs, right?"

"Well, not exactly," I answered. "My division specializes in new ways to improve concentration."

She stopped typing and looked me in the eye for a brief second. "Go on."

"Right, so we've found certain areas in the brain that are more inactive in people who lack focus."

"And?" She took her hands off the keyboard.

"And we try to fix it."

"How?"

"Aren't you behind?" I asked. She shrugged her wide shoulders. "Right now we are using viral vectors to introduce proteins that can enhance connections in the medial prefrontal cortex."

"Fascinating," she answered. "I remember a case in medical school of a guy a long time ago who survived a huge metal rod that pierced that part of his brain. I think he survived, but his personality completely changed."

"Yep, Phineas Gage," I answered. "It was a railroad accident. Not exactly the same area of the brain but still the frontal lobe. But you're right—it was a huge metal spike, and he did survive. He was known as a mild-mannered guy, but after the accident most accounts say he became pretty vulgar."

"Interesting." The doctor looked over at one of her pictures. "Maybe you could accelerate the growth of my oldest child's prefrontal lobe. She's now thirteen. At this rate she's going to put me in an early grave. Anyway, back to your problems."

The doctor asked me a barrage of questions from every body part, stopping only to hammer at the keyboard. When she ran out of questions, she paused a minute, staring at her computer screen. She then turned my way as if something in her mind had suddenly crystalized. "Most of these symptoms sound like stress, Jack. Has that been a major issue for you?"

"Not really," I answered. The truth was every night I felt something leaching from my core. And each night the chunks got bigger.

"Really? No traumatic events?" she asked.

I thought for a second. "Well, I did have a friend commit suicide a few weeks ago. A coworker."

"Okay, were you close?"

"Yeah, I mean he worked in a different area than me. But

he did live with me a few months back while his place was being remodeled."

"Jack, that's a shock. No wonder you feel bad."

To be honest, I hadn't thought much about Miles. His suicide was disturbing but not something I ruminated on.

The doctor stood up, causing her ruffled dress to fall to her ankles. "I'm going to examine you now. And we'll run some blood work to see if there is anything behind your symptoms. But I really think this is stress. If everything checks out, I'd like you to see a therapist named Mia Yang. She's excellent. I'll get you one of her cards."

I left the office thinking of Phineas Gage and the massive iron rod impaling the front of his skull.

CHAPTER SIX

COLONEL STINE

"Patient Zero is the only patient?" A few grunts and nods. "And Patient Zero is dead?" More nods. "Damn well better be," bellowed the colonel. He shook his shaved, graying head. "What a cluster fuck of all clusters. How could you let this happen?" Colonel Link Stine glared at the businessman leaning against the rail in front of him. He had to fight against a primal urge to launch this pencil pusher headfirst over the deck. Let him get a closer look at his ten-million-dollar view.

"The package did what it was created to do, Colonel. Ultimately, it worked." Charles Stuart pulled at his sleeve and adjusted an Ivy League cuff link. He wasn't one to be easily intimidated, even by the grizzly Colonel Stine.

"The hell it did," Stine fired back. "You said we were moving forward with animal tests. Last I checked this guy was human." The colonel's face flushed, and an artery across his left temple bulged like a worm under his skin.

"Of course we didn't intend for this to happen," answered one of Stuart's assistants. "We were not certain Patient Zero was exposed until after he died."

Colonel Stine eyed the young-faced assistant. His obsequious nature irritated Stine almost as much as the arrogant Stuart himself. "Why in the hell did you bring us here, Charles? You know I've seen plenty of nice houses before."

"Perhaps you—"

"It's okay, Cam," Stuart cut off his assistant. "I know you're not overly impressed, Colonel. Even with half an acre of beachfront property on Figure 8 Island. But the truth is we need somewhere private to talk. Why don't we all just take a breath, go inside, and have ourselves some whiskey?"

Once inside, the colonel looked up at the cathedral ceiling.

"Good eye, Colonel. That's African mahogany wood, same as my house in Montana," Stuart said.

"Congratulations, Charles," Stine answered, and took a seat on a leather armchair.

"Yeah, I overordered. Seemed a shame to go to waste. Besides, Cindy loves it. Says it adds warmth." Cindy was Stuart's third wife. The other two were happy to replace his company with a handsome settlement.

Stine leaned forward in his chair. "I'm not here to play home and garden."

Cam soon arrived with a tray of short crystal glasses and a decanter of bourbon.

"Neat okay with everyone?" asked Stuart. After hearing no protest, he nodded to Cam who poured four glasses. Stuart took his glass, as did Stine. The colonel's man, Fox, refused.

"He doesn't touch the stuff," Stine told Cam.

Fox was born twenty-eight years ago as Grady Jones, a name he'd not heard in at least eighteen years. He was a man of few words. The colonel didn't know why he never drank, nor did he care to know. What he did know was that Fox was the best logistical man he'd ever seen. He had an uncanny ability to process, organize, and implement large amounts of information.

More importantly, he was discreet and fiercely loyal. His six-foot-five, 250-pound muscled frame and outstanding combat record made him different from other pencil pushers Stine had known.

Stine swirled his bourbon and took a swig. It burned but was smooth. Damn good, but he wouldn't give Stuart the satisfaction of a compliment. "Why don't you run through how we got into this mess, Charles?"

Stuart took a swig of his own drink. "That's a fine bourbon," he complimented himself on his choice of liquor.

He ran his hands through the sides of his perfectly styled salt-and-pepper hair. Everything about the man was polished, nipped, and tucked. A year-round suntan, manicured nails, and a gleaming, blinding smile. He probably even waxes his ass, thought Stine. Like Fox, Stine forged his reputation in blood and mud. He despised the blue blood in front of him.

"As I recall," began Stuart, "you came to me with an idea. You wanted me to take my research at NewGen and give you something that could steal the heart of a nation. So we switched gears. Everything we developed to block depression, anxiety, and all those intrusive thoughts we reversed. We even threw in a grand finale of psychosis." He stood up and looked through the high glass windows to the ocean. "We turned it upside down. We delivered viral vectors that bring hell itself. Once they latch on to the right receptors, a cascade of reactions wires the brain for failure."

"Right," answered Stine. "The part I'm missing is where you infect your own man with the product. Potentially exposing this whole operation."

Stuart walked over to the sofa. He sat down and crossed his legs. The colonel eyed his handmade Italian slippers worn without socks. "As I remember it, once we secured the contract, you wanted us to move forward 'without haste.' What were his exact words, Cam?"

Stuart's assistant read from his notes. "I want this to take away the will to produce, the will to plan, and the will to fight. It should ultimately steal the will to live and the mind itself. And it should be passed on easily from one person to another."

"Thank you, Cam. So there you have it, Colonel. You wanted a virus that would take away the will to live. Well, that's exactly what we produced."

Stine slammed his drink down, almost shattering the crystal glass. His jugular veins could be seen bulging under his wiry frame. "I didn't ask you to infect a subject. I was very clear that we needed an antidote. A working antidote before proceeding with any real subjects. So I ask you," he tightened his fist, causing the knuckles to crack, "do you have an antidote?"

Stuart uncrossed his legs and flashed Colonel Stine a smile. Perfect rows of white teeth. "Colonel, relax. Have another drink. We're all on the same side here. Of course we didn't start human trials. Patient Zero was an accident. We think he may have inadvertently been stuck by a needle trying to start animal trials. Hell," he put his hands up, "we didn't even know for sure until right before he committed suicide."

"Well, Miles Chambers', a.k.a. Patient Zero's, incompetence almost cost this whole damn operation," Stine snapped.

"It's not nice to speak ill of the dead," said Stuart. "That man gave his life in the service of this project of yours."

"Service? That moron almost started a plague on his own people."

"Gentlemen," Cam interjected. "Can't we work together to solve this?"

Stine wasn't sure who he disliked more, the arrogant Stuart or his lackey. "What isn't clear to me, Charles, is how someone can asphyxiate themselves with their hands free."

Stuart swirled his drink then tugged at a tassel on his Italian loafer. "The place was clean. No signs of another soul. Hell, even your boys combed it."

Stine shook his head. "I've been in some hairy interrogations. If you ever saw anyone bagged in plastic until their eyes bleed, then you'd know they'd break their own arm to rip their mouth free."

Stuart ran a free hand through his coiffed salt-and-pepper cut. "I'll admit, it's unusual."

"Damn near impossible!" Stine shouted. He could feel the blood rushing to his temples.

Charles laughed. "Not with the virus Miles created. Did I mention he was good?"

Stine could feel his head pound, causing his vision to slightly blur. He had been warned by a doctor of dangerous spikes in his blood pressure. Stine massaged his temples and fought the urge to rush Stuart.

"Colonel, we suspected exposure was a possibility. That's why Miles was working in isolation for most of the project, definitely his last month. We also had Miles remotely cross-train others."

"Isolation? Good." Stine took two measured breaths, and his vision cleared. "From this point on, I want you to cease moving forward with this until you find an antidote. Are we clear?"

Stuart nodded.

"And if I hear as much as a mouse fart about Patient Zero, I'm burning this whole operation to the ground. That includes all the money you're getting. Clear?"

Stuart nodded again.

"I believe that concludes our business then," answered Stine.

"Sir, one question to Mr. Stuart?" asked Fox.

It was the first time the man had spoken since they arrived. "Certainly, Soldier."

"What happens in the event that Patient Zero has not been contained?"

Charles Stuart looked at Fox and then down to his glass of bourbon. "Well, gentlemen, in that event, you've just unleashed your weapon on the American people. A cancer that will eat through the hearts and minds of all of us, one citizen at a time."

CHAPTER SEVEN

JACK

"Dr. Baker?"

"Call me Jack," I answered.

"Fair enough. I'm Mia, Jack. Follow me, please."

I walked behind the petite Korean woman. She couldn't be any taller than five feet and weighed most likely in the double digits. Two health visits in less than two weeks, I thought. That was more than the last five years combined. She led me to an office with two sofas facing each other. I could hear what sounded like a fountain nearby, trickling water. It appeared to be coming from a separate space full of all types of plants. I took a seat on one of the sofas, while Mia sat across from me.

She crossed her legs, throwing one black leather boot across another. She wore a hunter-green skirt with a white button-down top. Her jet-black hair was pulled up. "So where to start?" she asked with a warm smile.

I leaned back on the soft sofa, quite the opposite of Mia's erect posture. To my right was an ornate lantern with a rich, wooden frame. Inside the frame stretched on translucent paper were pictures of cherry blossoms in bloom. Behind the lamp hung an ornamental fan decorated with koi fish.

"My parents," Mia said.

I turned toward her, not understanding.

"My parents put that little corner together. My mother wanted the Korean patients she referred here to feel at home. Personally, I know nothing about Korea. I've never been there and have no desire to take the seventeen-hour flight."

"Yep, long flight," I answered. Not very insightful, but that was all I could manage. My mind felt as sluggish as my body. When I wasn't feeling drained of life, I had a sickening feeling something terrible was about to happen.

"You said on your intake form that your mother's alive but that your father died when you were twelve. That he died in a one-car accident."

I nodded.

"That must have been pretty traumatic for you," she said. Her voice was gentle. It was soothing, perfect for a counselor. I shrugged my shoulders. "Jack, this is therapy. You are going to have to talk if you're going to get anything out of our time together."

I thought of my father. His body crumpled in the seat of a folded Buick. "Not really. The world is a better place without him. He was mean. An alcoholic. A bully." I waited for the flash of anger to follow. The flood of adrenaline that usually followed any thoughts of my father. But nothing came. That seemed to be the way of things for the past few weeks—no sharp feelings, just fatigue, and a vague sense of impending doom.

"I'm sorry to hear that, Jack. And your mother?"

I grabbed my right arm with my left hand, massaging the bone. If I ever wanted to forget my father, my right arm would never let me. The old spiral fracture of the right humerus, courtesy of the old man when I was five. It pained me daily. Of course, he didn't take me to the doctor. At least not until almost a year later, after an abnormal healing process occurred. Any thought of repair by then would be worse than the actual injury. It didn't help that the family doctor was his golfing buddy.

You little dumbass, those were the last words I remembered hearing before a burning pain shot up my arm. That and the sweet breath. It would take me years to know the sweet breath was his favorite liquor. All I knew was to stay away from Dad when he had the sweet breath.

I ran my hand up and down my arm until the pain eased, sometimes a half minute, sometimes hours. All of that pain for marking up a wall when I was five years old.

"Jack, your mother?"

"Oh, sorry." My thoughts drifted to my mother, and the years of abuse she endured. All the while sober and silent. She didn't start drinking and popping pills until after Dad died. Ironic. I thought once he was gone she'd have another chance. We'd have another chance. "She's an addict. Still alive, but she hasn't been sober in years."

"Are you still in contact with her?"

I shrugged. "Not much. Some holidays, I guess."

At some point Mia grabbed a notepad and placed it in her lap. She scribbled a few words down. She tried to pry out more details from my upbringing. My laconic answers soon caused her to abandon my past.

"Your tests with Dr. Potts all came back normal?" Mia asked. This was after I ticked off a litany of physical complaints.

"Yep." I was starting to feel like a hypochondriac, but I couldn't deny that my body felt like it was shutting down.

Both of us were silent, waiting for the other to speak.

Finally Mia asked, "Why don't you tell me about your friend who died?"

"Excuse me?"

"The suicide of your coworker. It was one of the reasons Dr. Potts gave you my number, right? Were you close?"

Had I mentioned that in my patient history form? "Not particularly. Like all of us, he worked all the time. But he could never talk about the work he did. He worked in the part of our lab we called the Vault."

Mia scribbled in her book, then asked, "The Vault?"

"Well, that wasn't the official name, but it's what we all called it. Whatever happened in that section was locked up, like a vault. I always thought that was weird, seeing how we were all scientists. I thought he was doing the same work as myself, just a different part of the brain. But I believe he only reported to the top, Charles Stuart himself."

Mia lifted her notebook and crossed her legs in the opposite direction. "I thought he was your roommate."

I rested my head back on the sofa, staring at the ceiling. I had an urge to lay flat on the couch. "He was only with me a few weeks, while his place was being renovated. I wish he stayed longer. He was a great cook and quite a neat freak. A perfect roommate." I laughed. "Miles Chambers, he used to vacuum my floors like three times a day. Very fastidious, that guy."

"Miles Chambers?" Mia's eyes widened, and her mouth fell open.

"Yeah, you know him?" I asked.

She pulled her chin back to its resting position, cleared her throat, then straightened her skirt. "No, I don't think I do."

I smiled. "Mia, you need to work on your poker face."

"Well, at first I thought I recognized the name," she fired back.

That sounded like a poor coverup, but I let it go. "Anyway, strange he would bother to renovate a place only to kill himself a month later."

"And how did that affect you?" she asked.

At the time I didn't really feel much of anything. That sounded like a pretty callous, shitty thing to think, yet alone say. "Well, I guess I wish he had said something. Maybe then I could have helped him in some way," I finally answered.

Mia took a few more notes. "Perhaps your friend got used to hiding his feelings the same way he did his work. Maybe he learned to keep his whole life in a vault."

CHAPTER EIGHT

CLAIRE

"Take off that stupid hat." Mia's attempt to cheer me up by wearing a sombrero wasn't helping.

"Fine," she said and placed the blue sombrero on the table beside us.

"You don't even know where that's been," I warned her.

She shrugged. Mia had dragged me to her favorite Mexican restaurant, the one with dozens of sombreros on the wall for customers to wear. "Anything to get you out of your funk," she answered.

"Some therapy," I mumbled.

"Two house margaritas, no salt," a harried waitress plopped the drinks on our table. "I'll be back to get your order," she added.

"Part two of my therapy plan," Mia said and tapped her glass against my untouched drink on the table.

The place was starting to fill, which caused my chest to tighten. Lately, I found a crowd of over ten people to be challenging. Too many eyeballs.

"If I didn't pick you up, you wouldn't have left your apartment for another week."

I looked down at the drink, debating on picking it up. I wasn't opposed to anything to make me feel even slightly better. But the strange Dr. Blanc had me on a new concoction of antidepressants. I wasn't sure how they would react to alcohol.

Mia looked at me eyeing the drink. "It's not going to bite."

"That weirdo you sent me to, Dr. Blanc, has me on some new medications. I'm not sure how I'll react to alcohol. And he wants me to do a ketamine infusion in two days."

"Ketamine? That's intense," Mia said and took a large swallow of her drink.

"What can I get you ladies?" the waitress broke in.

"We're fine for now," Mia shot back. The waitress tucked a pen behind her ear and left. "Why do they always come at the worst times?" Mia complained.

The background music seemed to grow in volume. That, mixed in with dozens of surrounding conversations, was starting to feel overwhelming. "I didn't think you wanted to come back here after your last experience," I said.

"What?" asked Mia, dragging a chip through a bowl of salsa. "The food here is always good."

"No, the guy. The one your mother insisted you meet."

"Oh, that *experience*," Mia air quoted. "You must have man," she mimicked her mother. "You alone. No grandchildren for me." Mia shook her head. "What a nightmare. She failed to mention he still lived with his mother. Ugh." She took the final sip of her margarita and grabbed mine. "Every time she gets back from playing Mahjong, she starts up. 'Kim have new grandchild. Jin have three. You and your sister not married. You need man.'" Mia took a gulp of my drink. "And she still won't leave me alone about changing the spelling of my name from

Mai to Mia. 'You ashamed of name?' No, Mom, but now I don't have to correct people six times a week."

The tables surrounding us were now full. To our right was a group of women who looked to be in their twenties. One of them had a high-pitched squeal for a laugh. The squeal felt like it wormed its way into my ear and reverberated in my head. "Mia, I'm not feeling up for this," I complained. I felt weak and frayed. If it was anyone besides Mia, I don't think I would have had the strength to even assert myself.

"You're not going to hole back in your apartment." Mia flagged down the waitress. "Excuse me?"

The server stopped, withdrawing the pen from behind her ear. "You ready to order?"

"Actually, we want to know if we can move somewhere quieter. Over there would be great," Mia pointed to a dark area with empty tables.

"That section is closed," the lady said flatly.

"Well, can you open it?" Mia asked. The waitress bristled. "My friend has an auditory processing disorder," Mia added.

She clicked her pen and stared at Mia for a moment, then at me. "I'll see what we can do," she finally said.

"Auditory processing disorder?" I asked after she had left.

Mia smiled. "Don't mess with the Americans with Disabilities Act." She crunched on another chip.

"That's not cool, Mia. We're mental health professionals. And really, I'm ready to go."

A short man in a button-down and blue blazer strolled over to our table. He had thick, black hair plastered to his head. "I'm the manager, Carlos. I'm happy to move you ladies to a private section of our restaurant. Is there anything else you may need this evening?"

"No, Carlos. Thank you for the accommodation," Mia said in her professional voice.

"Certainly, and these drinks are complimentary. Thank you for joining us tonight."

We followed him passed empty tables to a far booth against the wall. The hyena laugh was now only a faint noise from the other room. Our drinks and a fresh basket of tortilla chips were placed on the table.

"See? I told you," said Mia.

I grabbed a chip, even though I had no appetite. I was dead tired but knew I wouldn't be able to sleep. I put the chip back in the basket.

"Are you not going to eat a single chip?" complained Mia.

"I have no appetite. Really, I know you're trying, Mia. But I'm just not feeling up for this."

Mia nodded. "Fair enough. Listen, I'll order to go for both of us, then drive you home. But while we wait for our food, I need to talk to you."

"Okay." What was she up to?

"You remember Miles Chambers?" she asked.

"Miles? You mean Amy's ex-boyfriend?"

"Yes, that's the one," she answered. "I need some water," Mia complained, looking past our empty room for someone to wave down.

"Well, good luck getting any service back here," I answered.

Mia took the last sip of margarita. "It turns out that he killed himself, like a month ago."

"What?" My hands rubbed together. "Around the same time Amy committed suicide?"

"Seems like it," answered Mia.

"How do you know this?" I asked.

"I have a new patient who worked with him in a lab. They lived together for a while."

I nodded.

"Now, get this. My new patient, Jack, is also depressed. He

has fatigue, a headache like a drill over his right eye, nausea, and no motivation. Does any of that sound familiar?"

"Very," I answered.

"Well, I don't think he has any history of depression or anxiety. It hit him out of left field. And from what Jack tells me, it was the same with Miles who also had no history of mental illness."

"Why are you telling me all this? Other than trying to violate about a dozen HIPAA laws."

Mia sighed and pushed herself back in the booth. "I'm going to get us some water and order from the bar if I have to."

She left the table. My mind wandered to thoughts of Miles —an odd, lanky man from a small town in Georgia. Always sweet, quiet. Quiet to a fault as far as Amy was concerned. I remember the day she decided to end it with him. "I'm just tired. Mentally exhausted," is what she said. "I can't guess what's in his head anymore. What he does at work. What he did in the military. I'm tired of guessing. This relationship won't move forward, because he won't let it."

Mia came back with two ice waters. "I ordered a chicken chimichanga to go for you."

I nodded. "Thanks."

"So did you figure it out?" Mia asked.

"Figure out what?"

"The connection? Aren't you a high school valedictorian, summa cum laude Emory graduate? There has to be a connection."

I stared at Mia to see if she was serious. "Mia, this isn't some conspiracy. There's nothing to figure out. You've met thousands of depressed people. How is this different from any other week you've had for the past ten years?"

"Well, Claire, let's see. Four people who have no history of mental illness all of a sudden wake up with severe depression.

Two of them have it so severe that it results in suicide. One of them, your twin, tries to peel her own skin off. These four said people have other strange symptoms in common like fatigue, nausea, joint pain, and some specific headache. Oh, and did I mention that these four people's lives intimately cross each other?"

I took a sip of water and forced myself to eat a couple of chips. My head was feeling light. "I was right. You've seen too many movies. Depression is not contagious," I said.

"I've been doing this for years. We've been therapists for years, Claire. How many well-adjusted people do you know who wake up one day and decide life is not worth living?"

I didn't answer.

"Right. None. Now, I'm not saying I know what it is, but it's weird," she said.

"Did you say that this patient of yours, Jack, worked with Miles?"

"Well, not directly. But they both worked in a research laboratory for a company, NewGen, I think."

I shook my drink, rattling the ice in my glass. "Maybe it's something they put in the water."

"I'm serious, Claire."

I sat the drink down. "What do you suggest?"

"I suggest you meet Jack. Next time he has a therapy session, I think you just happen to be at work that day." Mia raised her eyebrows and grinned.

"Yeah, and then what?"

"Then we figure it out. It's a start," she snapped.

I nodded slowly. "The game is afoot," I said under my breath.

"Damn right, Holmes," answered Mia. "And this is no game."

CHAPTER NINE

JACK

My next session with Mia was less than one week later. Five days to be exact. We were following up on any progress. Mia had suggested a few mindfulness exercises and other relaxation techniques. But if anything, I was worse. The only thing I was mindful of was how terrible I felt. Whatever was going on with me, it was going to take more than a few meditation sessions to fix.

Mia seemed distracted today. Maybe I was just being paranoid, but she seemed to be glancing at the clock over my head constantly, as if she were counting the minutes until our session was up. At one point I just flatly asked her, "Do you need to be somewhere?"

"Don't be ridiculous," she laughed and narrowed her eyes. Her fingers whitened as she grasped her pen. "Jack, I think we need to escalate your therapy. Medication is going to be an important adjunct. Your negative thoughts, even your physical symptoms, appear to be progressing daily. I'd like you to see a psychiatrist. I also suggest we meet three days a week."

I shrugged. I didn't care if they put me in a padded room if it made me feel better.

"Great," she glanced at the clock one more time. "It looks like our time is up for today. Let me follow you out. She shuttled me out of her office to the left. We walked by an open door of another office. A woman sat at a small desk alone. Her head turned toward us as we walked by.

"Oh, Claire, you're here," Mia said.

Although Mia acted surprised, it didn't seem genuine. The woman in the office also seemed to know we were coming.

"Jack, I'd like you to meet my partner, Claire."

"It's nice to meet you, Jack," she said with a brief smile.

"You too," I offered politely.

The three of us were silent for a minute. I was waiting for Mia to walk me out, but Mia waited on Claire, who in turn looked like she waited on Mia. "So," I started but didn't finish.

"Claire knew your coworker, Miles," Mia finally said.

That shocked me but not as much as it did Claire. Her fingers reached for her temples, rubbing them hard. "Mia, not appropriate," she snapped.

Mia put her hands up. "I'm sorry. You're right."

"It's all right," I said, more to Claire than to Mia. I watched Claire massage the temples of her head. She looked visibly uncomfortable. "How did you know Miles?"

"He dated my twin sister, Amy."

Amy—I vaguely remembered her. The image of a tiny firecracker blonde popped in my head. "Oh, right, Amy. How is she?"

Claire's fingers fell from her head. She turned in my direction, her gaze unfocused. "She killed herself."

"Oh, dear. Now I'm the one who's inappropriate," I answered.

Her eyes fell to the floor. "You couldn't have known," she said flatly.

"I guess you knew Miles committed suicide as well then?" I asked.

She nodded, then looked up. "Yes, I did." Her amber eyes studied me. "It must have been around the same time."

"I don't know," I answered. She looked pained, even before I brought up her sister. Something about her seemed familiar. And although I felt certain this meeting was no accident, she seemed ill prepared for it. For some reason, I felt drawn to her. "Would you like to have a cup of coffee with me?" The question fell out of my mouth, surprising even me. It was completely out of my character. I was used to calculating what I said. I took in a breath and was about to apologize before she answered.

"Yes, but I need something stronger than coffee. There's a pub across the street."

"Claire, do you really think—"

"Mia, I'll be fine," Claire shot back. "One drink is the least of my worries."

We walked to an Irish pub called the Dunberry. It was fairly empty, just a lone patron at the bar and two people throwing darts. A heavyset woman with tight curls worked a wet rag across the wooden bar. She threw the rag over her shoulder when she saw us enter. "What can I get you two?" she bellowed from across the bar.

"Popular place," I said under my breath.

"I'll take a black and tan," answered Claire.

The bartender nodded and looked at me. "Same," I said.

We waited while she poured the drinks. The layer of Guinness settled on the top of the two lagers. The woman pushed them roughly in our direction, spilling some of the top layer of

Guinness on the bar. She tugged the wet rag off her shoulder to mop it up. "Enjoy," she said.

"I'll get these," I said to Claire.

"That's not necessary," she answered.

I left a twenty on the bar, and the woman greedily snatched it. "Change?" she challenged after already tucking the bill away. I shook my head.

We took the drinks outside to a small section with iron tables overlooking the street. It was a crisp sixty degrees and a welcomed change from the stagnant, beer-soaked air in the pub. We sat down and watched a few cars shoot by before speaking.

"I'm sorry about your sister," I finally said, trying to make up for my earlier gaffe. I took a sip of the beer, then had to wipe the foam off my lip.

"It was quite a shock," answered Claire. "I'm the one who found her."

I let out a small grunt. "That must have been awful."

She looked down and shifted her beer. "It was. It is." She took a sip of the drink. "I'm sorry about your friend, Miles."

"Thank you," I answered. The truth was Miles and I were never very close. His work, his emotions, his life were all secret. We sat in silence for a few moments just watching traffic.

"Did Miles show any signs of depression?" Claire asked.

I thought back to what I knew of Miles, which was little. "He was kind of a closed book," I answered. "Nothing obvious, but with Miles I'm not sure I would know." The sun broke through the clouds, causing me to squint. "What about Amy?"

"Well, not at first," Claire answered and sighed. "I mean I knew she was feeling lethargic, which wasn't like Amy. I thought she was just fighting off some bug. But things got worse, a lot worse. So yeah, she became depressed, anxious, even delusional. She actually thought her skin was being poisoned and tried to peel it. Anyone who knew Amy couldn't believe it. Couldn't believe she actually—" her words trailed off.

I waited, thinking she may tear up. But she just fell silent, thinking. Finally I said, "I'm not feeling much better lately. I mean I'm not, you know, to that point, but I do feel terrible."

"Mia hasn't fixed you yet?" she asked. The corners of her mouth turned up in another brief smile.

Claire had rich, auburn hair that fell in waves. A handful of freckles spread across a pair of strong cheekbones and a soft, narrow nose. If I had a type, she was it. Her smile, however brief, was warm. I took a swig of the black and tan, this time a smaller foam mustache remained. I wiped it clean with a cocktail napkin. "No," I shook my head. "But no one else can either, for that matter."

"No one else?" she asked.

"Well, I went to my internist. I was sure there was something physically wrong with me." I let out a defeated sigh. "But all the tests were normal. Guess I should be happy with that," I added.

"But no answers," she said.

"Nope."

"Well, I can't imagine you feel any worse than me. I've been seeing this Dr. Blanc who's been experimenting on me."

"Dr. Blanc?" I asked and laughed.

"You know him?"

"Only stories. At NewGen we do novel treatments in the brain. Neuroscience is a pretty small community, really. He's not as research oriented as we are, but he's pretty out there. Kind of a maverick for a guy in private practice."

"Yeah, he's weird," Claire agreed. "I'm fresh off a ketamine infusion about a week ago. Never thought I'd be saying that."

"Ketamine?" I asked. "Like I said, he's a bit of a cowboy for private practice." I looked over while Claire finished the last of her pint. "Should you be, um, drinking?"

She held up her empty glass. "Probably not, but I'm up for anything to change my current reality. I was really hoping the ketamine would help. But it seems every day I feel worse. It was all I could do to get out of bed today. I haven't bothered to make myself up in weeks."

"But you made it out," I said. And you don't need any help with makeup, I almost added but caught myself. She was naturally pretty. Normally, I'd do my best to charm a woman as attractive as Claire. I would be doing everything in my power to get one step closer to bringing her home. But I lacked the energy. I hadn't felt any twinge of libido in weeks. "And all to meet me."

She smiled. "That obvious? I need another. I'll get this round." Before I could answer, she headed to the bar.

We were still alone among the half dozen tables outside. I hadn't seen a waitress since we set foot in the place, just the friendly bartender. I finished the last of my drink while I waited for Claire. I was a little nervous to see Claire drinking fresh off a recent ketamine infusion. But I was even more nervous that the drug didn't work. Ketamine was reserved for treatment failures, the worst cases. It was supposed to work within hours. If Claire had no improvement—and was in fact worse—then what therapy did that leave?

Claire came back, balancing two full black and tans. Fresh foam spilled from the top of the pints. I adjusted my seat from the direct view of the sun. She placed the drinks down, slamming a glass into mine. "A toast. To better days than these," she announced.

"I will certainly drink to that," I answered. I let her settle in her seat then asked, "Are you going back to Dr. Blanc then?"

She shrugged. "I suppose so. He wants to scan my brain again. He has some pretty expensive gadgets, specialized MRI scanners. I think the money is from a grant or a trust fund. Wherever it's from, money seems to surround that guy. His office is quite the palatial space in one of the top floors of a high-rise downtown. Seems excessive for a doctor's office."

"Didn't help you any," I murmured. She clenched her jaw. "Sorry, that wasn't necessary."

"No, it's true. Nothing has helped—the pills, therapy, even the ketamine infusion. In fact, whatever is going on with me, nothing is even slowing it down, which was one of the reasons that Mia set up our meeting. Well, more of a sabotage for you. Sorry."

There was a sad glaze in her eyes. Her mouth tightened, forming grooves around her chin. A single crease sank in the middle of her forehead. I could see faint laugh lines marking her better days. The current lines in her face seemed new and out of place. "Don't worry," I told her, "I'm not offended."

She forced a smile. "We do take HIPAA seriously. It's just when Mia met you and heard about all your symptoms, she—" Claire's train of thought trailed off. She picked it back up. "Well they were the same as mine. Then when she heard about Miles, it just seemed too much to be a coincidence. I can understand if you're angry. It is totally unprofessional. Unethical even." The line between her eyes deepened.

"Relax, Claire. I'm not bothered about our meeting. If we can help each other, by all means let's do so."

"That's too bad about your internist," Claire said. "I mean that he couldn't find anything wrong."

"She," I corrected. "And yeah, I was hoping I would get a course of antibiotics or something to kick this."

"Whatever I'm feeling, it's been weeks. If there's any

connection to Amy, she was sick longer, much longer. You're a doctor, right? Do you know any bugs that last that long?" Claire finished her sentence then began rubbing her hands.

"Are you cold?" I asked.

She looked down. "Oh, no, it's just a strange habit I've picked up. It's since... forget it, it's not important."

Her hands were now under the table in her lap. I didn't press the issue. "I am a doctor in biochemistry, to answer your question. This is not exactly my field of expertise." A trio came outside with glasses and a pitcher of dark beer. Two guys and one girl who held both of their attention. I looked back to Claire. "So what now?"

"Let's play a game," she answered. I winced. I didn't like games, especially in my current state. "A symptom game. We take turns naming symptoms. If you have it, you drink."

"Not the happiest drinking game but creative," I answered.

"Great, I'll start." She put her hands back on the table. "Nausea."

We tipped our drinks back.

"Very well," I answered. "Body aches."

We both drank again.

"Headaches," Claire said and rubbed her tight temple. "Specifically above the right eye, like an ice pick."

I tilted my pint back.

"Exhaustion," I said, "not improved with sleep."

She nodded. "We're going to need some more beer."

"I don't think that drinking is our answer." Even if alcohol numbed our pain, I knew technically it was a depressant itself.

"You're probably right. I just dread the thought of going back to my apartment, surrounded by four walls, and my thoughts. The place still smells like Amy." Claire bit her bottom lip. "It's nice to talk to someone who may understand a little of what I'm going through." She finished the last of her second black and tan, then stared into the empty glass. "Hopelessness. That was the final symptom Amy felt."

"Miles too, I would think," I answered.

CHAPTER TEN

COLONEL STINE

Colonel Stine waited in a small room overlooking the firing range. It wasn't his usual office. This was a hundred-square-foot box he used to oversee the cadets' marksmanship. It was cramped with poor ventilation. To reach it, he had to travel through a hundred yards of cracked red clay, or three inches of Georgia mud, depending on the rain. From there, it was up three flights of wobbly steps that would never pass code.

From below, a blast echoed through a slightly cracked window. Fox stood erect in the office corner, only sitting when asked. Stine peered to the left of the range to spot when Charles Stuart was coming. He wanted to see the man's Italian loafers caked in dust from the dry earth. The colonel knew the climb to the office wouldn't tax Stuart. He probably clocked twenty hours a week on a Stairmaster, Stine thought. But the steep planks of wood may not be the best surface for slick loafers. He may even experience a touch of vertigo, Stine mused in delight. The eighth infantry fired again in unison. The little office shook.

"He's coming now, sir," Fox announced.

Stine looked out to see Stuart trouncing across the dried clay. The man's hair was swept in a perfect coif, but to the colonel's pleasure, the businessman's face was beet red. His assistant, Cam, walked at his elbow. Stine waited in anticipation as the two closed in while the infantry reloaded. When they were just a few yards away, the squad blasted another round. Cam jumped and actually grabbed the right elbow of Stuart, who jerked it away.

The colonel couldn't resist a chuckle. He looked at the stoic Fox, who wouldn't allow himself a laugh, or even an obvious grin, in the current situation. But the colonel saw the hint of a smile form on the right side of the captain's mouth. They waited in silence. The footsteps of the two men could soon be heard coming up the steps. Their steps sputtered, taking frequent stops for either balance or breath. When they were close enough, Fox went to greet them. Seconds later he returned with Stuart and Cam.

"Nice spot for a meeting," Charles complained.

"Security is paramount," Stine fired back. He knew security could have been had in a half dozen more comfortable venues on base.

"Naturally," Stuart mumbled and looked at the two cheap collapsible chairs in front of Stine's desk. He sat down, crossed one dusty loafer over another. Cam sat in the next seat.

Stine stood as did Fox, who had no chair. "You want to tell me about the girl?" the colonel asked.

"What girl?" asked Stuart.

"Amy Long," Stine answered. "The ex-girlfriend of Miles Chambers. The ex-girlfriend who consequently killed herself."

"Oh, that girl," Charles answered. "Of course we know about her. She hadn't been in contact with Miles for weeks, even months. She was seeing a counselor and was on antidepressants." Another volley of gunfire caused Cam to tighten his grip on the side of the chair.

"I didn't go to an Ivy League school like you, Charles, but did it ever occur to you that she was on antidepressants because she was infected?" Stine choked back a series of expletives.

"Of course. We vetted her records. No reason to think it was ours."

Stine's fists balled. "No fucking reason? It's a suicide."

Charles Stuart flashed his set of white veneers. "Colonel, in the United States alone, there are over forty-nine thousand cases of suicide a year. That's about 135 a day. Just as we meet here, someone has committed suicide. Are we to panic in every case?"

Stine could feel bile rising from his gut. "Every case?" He inhaled two sharp breaths through his nostrils. Dressing down Stuart any further wasn't going to help his cause, he reasoned. "Well, do you think we may be able to trace some contacts a little closer? I mean we have millions of dollars in this."

"I'm aware of the money spent on this operation," Stuart answered. "Of course we have been tracing. Let me explain how this virus works. We designed how, where, and when the virus attacks by using data from TMS. That stands for transcranial magnetic stimulation, which targets electrical currents to precise brain regions. This information allows us to pinpoint, with astonishing accuracy, exact areas in the mind that cause fatigue, pain, depression, even delusions."

Stuart was talking with his hands. To Stine, the man seemed to relish the sound of his own voice. "Do I look like I asked you up here for a TED talk?"

"Colonel, if you'd allow me to finish, maybe you'll learn something." Charles Stuart waited. The colonel glared but didn't respond. "Thank you," Stuart finally said. "So the initial symptoms are both mental and physical, more like 30 percent mental and 70 percent physical. The physical symptoms are general—fatigue, headache, nausea, body aches. It's impossible to separate it from hundreds, even thousands, of other viruses. But as the weeks go on, the ratio changes. By six weeks, it's 70 percent mental and 30 percent physical. It's at that time the viral replication explodes, and the individual becomes more infectious. Once the virus hits a critical mass, the symptoms are almost 100 percent mental and intolerable. Madness ensues. Suicide would be the only release."

The men below released another round of gunfire. Stine loved this vantage point, watching the boys in action. It wasn't real combat, but it still got his blood hot. "What's your point?" he asked Stuart.

"My point, Colonel, is that if anyone is in the early stages, tracing it is going to be difficult, if not impossible. We designed it that way. It's a needle in a stack of needles. No medical professional is going to suspect anything other than one of a thousand bugs."

Stine eyed Stuart. The cocksure smirk on his face had returned. The colonel felt the bile rise a little further. "You may have some money in this," Stine said, "but my ass is on the line. The ass of the United States for that matter. Now we need to trace this better and harder. And we need to button it up."

"Button it up? Meaning?" Charles asked.

"You let me worry about what 'button it up' means," Stine shot back. Charles looked up and slowly nodded. His shoes may be dusty, but his nails were still manicured. And he didn't want any dirt underneath those pretty fingernails, thought Stine.

"Well, Amy's dead," Stuart answered.

"I'm putting Fox and a small team on it," Stine said. "We don't need any more eyes on this than what is absolutely necessary. These men will know little of our operational details, only enough to track. We've got men, like Fox, who can track anything and anyone, from a wild animal in the Amazon jungle to who impregnated an old porn star. Are we clear?"

"Yes, sir," Fox fired back.

Stuart turned over his right hand and examined a polished nail. "Sure, why not?" he answered.

CHAPTER ELEVEN

CLAIRE

I was on my couch lying flat, thinking of calling in sick to my appointment with Dr. Blanc. That was ironic, seeing how he was treating me for this very sickness.

Yesterday I repeated my second series of brain scans. Did I really need to hear that little man in another monochromatic suit tell me how screwed up my scans were? No. I didn't need a functional MRI, a diffusion tensor imaging test, or any other million-dollar machine to tell me the results weren't good. In fact, if he said the scans were better, that may even be worse. Because whatever was going on between my ears had clearly not improved.

As I lay flat, debating on making this call, my cell rang. Dr. Blanc's number.

"Hello?"

"Hello, Claire, it's Linda from Dr. Blanc's office."

"Yes?"

"I was calling you about your follow-up appointment to review your recent tests."

"Yes, I don't think—"

"Before you go any further, I regret to say that Dr. Blanc is unexpectedly out of the office today."

My heart dropped. "Um, is he sick?"

"He doesn't discuss his personal days with me, ma'am."

Ma'am, I hated that word. Being over thirty, I'd rather be called a raging bitch than ma'am. "I see."

"Right. So I'm not certain when the doctor will return, but he wanted to make sure you had access to our patient portal. I'll send you an email link in case you don't."

She waited. "Uh-huh, yes," I answered.

"Great," she said, drawing the word out with a hint of sarcasm. "On your portal he will send a copy of your results with a brief description. Any questions?"

I had plenty, but she wouldn't be able to answer them. "Tell the doctor I hope he's okay," I said.

"I'm sure that will be a comfort for him," she said in a flat tone. "Goodbye, Claire."

I hung up the phone and was immediately convinced the doctor must be experiencing my same symptoms. That is ridiculous, I thought. He could be out for just about anything. A family emergency, buying another colored suit, even going to Vegas. Or maybe he has one of another million viruses floating in the air.

I grabbed my laptop from the table and checked my email. I followed the link Linda sent to sign in to the portal. I wasn't surprised when an animated vault opened before accessing my chart. Was everything he did over the top? When I pulled up my personal message, pictures of my brain scans began to populate the screen. The following message was below the scans:

Claire,

Your latest scans are above. I know—shocking, right? Our current efforts have not produced the changes I had anticipated. In fact, some areas of your prefrontal cortex, and particularly your hippocampus, show decisive atrophy. The DTI scan in figure A is particularly disappointing. Not only were no new neuronal connections made, there has been a good deal of pruning. There's more pruning here than an introductory bonsai class.

I took a deep breath, failing to find any humor in this. I rubbed my eyes and read on.

The cerebral blood flow patterns seen are those typical in severe depression. But oddly, some of the scans, like figure A, look more like my schizophrenic patients.

I think we need to measure your neurotransmitter levels again as soon as possible. Finally, Claire, don't fret! We have plenty of other arrows in the quiver. We haven't used transcranial magnetic stimulation or a truckload of other new medications.

My best,
Javier
Javier Blanc, MD, PhD, FAAN, FAPA

I pushed the computer to the side. It sounded desperate, like throwing anything at the wall to see if it would stick. I can't say I was surprised. I didn't expect an improved scan. I pulled the computer back to my lap to look at my brain in figure A. It didn't mean much to me. I looked at the email again, making sure I hadn't misread it—like my schizophrenic patients.

I shut my computer. I could add this new disturbing nugget to my mounting pile of troubled thoughts. I lay back again on the couch, just praying I could get some rest.

CHAPTER TWELVE

JACK

I pushed my Subaru Outback up the dirt hill until the RPM gauge kissed the red zone. The scant gravel was nearly washed away, leaving a dusty six-foot-wide spit of earth. My all-wheel drive did its best to find a purchase on the loose grains of dirt.

I was in the rural hills of north Georgia, only a few miles away from the home of Miles's parents. Cell phone service was nonexistent. I looked down at the few directions I'd scribbled the day before. Four miles passed a sign Land for Sale, then take a left at the fork, my notes read. The sign in red paint, misspelling 5 Akres Fur Sale, had been exactly four miles ago. After cresting the dirt hill, my mileage now clocked at 4.3. The temperature outside was fifty-eight degrees. I wanted to ease the window down to enjoy the country air, but clouds of red dust surrounded me. Coming down the hill, I spotted the fork about a quarter mile ahead. Okay, now turn left and follow the fence to the river, I thought. I took a left and spotted the old wooden fence. It was in disrepair, missing several posts, but easy enough to follow. Once I made it to the river, I saw the trailer.

I pulled up near it, parked, and got out. A skeleton of a race car squatted over three-foot weeds with its guts scattered below. The lawn was littered with old wrenches and bolts, a spare battery, a rusted head gasket, and a leaky oil pan stained the earth black. The car's steel frame was wrapped in a red-and-black vinyl, peeling on the edges. A bright number 3 spanned the doors. The hood was propped open, showing an empty space where an engine should be.

I could hear deep-throated barks from distant dogs. The front of the trailer swung open to reveal a woman with a heap of dyed brown hair and a heavily wrinkled face. She wore a gray sweatshirt reading World's Greatest Grandma. The woman took a look in my direction, then cupped her hands to light a cigarette.

"You Bubba's friend?" she asked, blowing out a cloud of smoke.

I stood in front of the car for a moment. "Bubba?" I asked.

The door to the trailer opened again. This time a man with hair like black shoe polish stepped out, his face twice as wrinkled as hers. "Miles, she means." He cleared his throat. What sounded like weeks of phlegm rose to his mouth, which he spit on the ground. This left a dangling string of saliva, which he mopped up using the back of his hand.

"Right, Miles," the woman said and drew in from the cigarette. "Putting on airs." She blew another billow of smoke.

I nodded, not sure why, but tried to be polite. Behind the trailer through scattered hardwoods, the bright sun glistened off a gentle river. "Beautiful out here," I said.

The woman scoffed. "You hear that Earl? We're beautiful."

I mean the river, the words almost slipped out. The two

were perched on a wobbly deck leaning against the trailer. One of the handrails was missing.

"Not sure why you came all this way, Mr.—"

"Baker," I offered, "but Jack is fine."

Another tug off the cigarette. "Mr. Jack then. Not sure why you came. We hadn't seen Bubba, I mean Miles," she said, smirking at the man with the black hair, "in almost a year."

I walked toward the two on the makeshift deck. The smoke cloud drifted my way, leaving a sweet smell. Menthol, I thought. "I'm just trying to figure out what happened to him."

The man cleared his throat again. I waited for more phlegm to be expectorated, but nothing came. "He killed himself, Son. That's what happened."

I nodded and stepped a little closer. "I'm just trying to make sense of it. Did you know anything was wrong? I mean before it happened?"

"He don't talk to us," the woman said, pushing a puff of smoke in my direction.

"Shirley, don't blow smoke in the man's face."

"Better I dip snuff like you?" she fired back. "Spittin' and carrying on. Real fancy."

The old man shook his head. He looked at me. "It's true. We hadn't heard much from Miles before he died. I knew he was sick, but he didn't want us coming to visit. Said he didn't want us to catch nothin'."

I took a deep breath once the sweet smoke cleared. Maybe I was wasting my time.

"Not much left from my boy," the woman said. She flicked her cigarette butt using a finger and thumb. I watched it fly through the air and land in a graveyard of cigarette ends. "Most of what I had left the last group took."

"Last group?" I asked.

"Some group came up here a few days back. Said they

worked with Miles. Don't know what they wanted with my old box of memories. Said they just wanted to borrow it."

"Group," I murmured. "What did they look like?"

She pinched the beehive of hair on her head. "I don't know, like most city folk, I guess. Wearing fancy pants and fancy shoes, getting all dusty." She grinned at the thought of that, flashing a top set of dentures. "Putting on airs."

I looked down at my shoes, happy they weren't expensive. "Did they show any identification?" I asked.

"No, don't believe so," the man said. "But we got no reason to ask for identification here. They said they worked with our boy. Don't think they knew anymore why he killed himself than we did." The man glanced at the door to the trailer. "You want to come in?"

"No, thank you," I answered immediately.

The woman flashed the dentures again. "Them boys with the fancy shoes—I thought it was more real estate people coming. Saying they want to give us some million dollars for this here river property." She clucked her tongue. "I ask them if they want to dig up my daddy and my daddy's daddy first. My family's had this land as long as records go back. Got my kin buried up and down this land. Them real estate people, bunch of damn buzzards."

"Shirley," the man cut in, "leave it alone. He didn't come here to hear your stories."

"They can all leave, far as I'm concerned," she spat out, then lit another cigarette. "Even Bubba's fancy friends."

"They was nice enough, Shirley," the man said. "Except that big Black fella with 'em. He kept asking the same questions over and over but in different ways. Like he thought we were lyin'."

The barking from nearby dogs started up again.

"Your sister needs to shut them dogs up, Earl."

That started a round of bickering between them, which I let drown out along with the barking dogs. Who were these people from the company? And why would they bother to come all the way out here? "Mr. Chambers?" I asked.

"Mr. Chambers?" he chuckled. "That's my father's name. I'm Earl."

"Okay, Earl," I said. "What did this Black guy look like?"

"Like no one I seen from around here. Like I said, big fella. Tall and wide. Had a nasty scar down one side of his face. I do remember that."

"Can you tell me more about what kind of questions he asked?"

"Hmm, let's see—" His wife interrupted again to complain about the dogs, which he ignored. "Yeah, okay. This fella, he was real specific about the last time we'd seen Miles. Then he got right curious if we knew about what he'd been working on." Earl walked down off the porch and eyed the mound of cigarette butts. "Shirley, you want to clean up these butts?" That set her off on a rant about spit cups all over her house. He ignored her, kicking the cigarette ends into a pile. "I guess mostly he was real interested in the days leading up to Bubba's suicide. Kept wanting to know if he had told us anything or seen us. I told the man I knew less than he did."

"And that's when they took most of what we had left that was Bubba's," Shirley said. "Should have given 'em nothing."

I looked out to the river. The Toccoa River, I believe it was called. I watched the sunlight dance on the ripples in the water. I imagined a cabin with cathedral ceilings and long windows overlooking the slow-moving current. The thought was snapped from my mind when Earl cleared his throat once more. This produced another massive glob of phlegm that he spit on the ground.

"Why don't you ask your new friend here what's worse?" the woman asked. "My smokin' or your spittin'?"

Earl looked up and paused, as if considering the question. My eyes fell back to the car laying in parts on the patchy grass. "Yeah, you got a good eye. That's going to be a champ someday." Earl ran his arthritic hand over a fender.

"Yeah, someday I'm going to Bora Bora," Shirley spat out from the porch.

"It is going to be a champ," he yelled back. "And you keep talking about Bora Bora. Go ahead and drive there if you want."

She blew out a puff of smoke and laughed. "You hear that? Drive to Bora Bora. Don't think your Chevy is going to fare well in the Pacific Ocean."

Earl scoffed. "Last and only time that woman got on a plane, she had a two-hour panic attack." He knocked his knuckles against the frame. "Just need to drop the V8 in here. End of story." He cut a hand through the air.

"Yeah, you just need an engine," yelled Shirley. "I'd say that's a pretty important detail, what'chu think, Jack?" I didn't answer. "By the time he gets an engine, that car's going to be nothing but rusted scraps. Kind of like Earl himself."

Earl shook his head. "Aluminum don't rust," he yelled back. He turned to the empty hood. "Besides, nothing goes in here less than eight hundred horses."

I was worn thin and anxious to leave. "Listen, thank you for—"

"Bubba may have helped you with the engine cost, if you didn't put that big number 3 on it."

"Everyone likes the Intimidator, even Miles," he shouted. The effort resulted in a coughing fit that ended with more phlegm on the dirt.

"If you'd've paid attention, you'd know he was a Jeff Gordon boy, through and through. Even had the bedsheets."

Earl wiped the sides of his mouth. "Pretty boy, that Gordon," he murmured.

"Don't much matter now. Bubba's dead, and you've got your rust bucket."

Earl balled his swollen knuckles into fists. He narrowed his eyes and took a sharp breath, which made a low whistling noise. "Look now—"

"I'm just teasin', Earl." She threw another cigarette butt from the porch. It rolled on a hard patch of dirt, still smoking. "I'm sure you'll be champ." She snickered before pulling the front door open and added, "You be careful driving home, Mr. Jack."

Earl opened his balled fists and began to pet the car fender again. Fearing a handshake with his saliva-soaked palm, I eased back toward my own car. When I was a good ten yards away, I turned and said, "Thanks for meeting with me. Sorry about Miles. Is it okay to call back if I think of any more questions?"

Earl nodded and cleared his throat again. He moved to spit but thought better of it and swallowed. "Sure thing. You be careful going down that dirt road. Lots of turkey and deer out here that don't steer clear of it."

CHAPTER THIRTEEN

I was careful to reverse the directions to drive back to civilization. I had an urge to clean my hands, my whole body for that matter. But my hand sanitizer was out of reach. I mentally cataloged what I touched, or didn't touch, from the past hour. Normally, I wasn't worried about germs, but my failing health, and the sight of another man's phlegm, had put me on edge.

Once I hit a paved road, I stopped at the first gas station that was open. I reached in the back seat and grabbed the hand sanitizer. I greedily rubbed it onto my hands, pumped some gas, then applied a second coat. Next, I cleaned my phone for good measure. It was a relief to see at least two bars on my cell phone. I dialed Claire and waited three rings before she picked up.

"Hello," her voice came through, tired and flat.

"Hey, it's Jack. You okay?"

There was a pause on the other end, then a sigh. "Sure," she answered.

"Yeah, I feel like garbage too," I said. "I just met with Miles's parents. Or should I say Bubba."

"What?"

"Never mind," I answered. "His parents are, well, country, to put it nicely." I merged on a highway ramp back towards the city.

"I remember Amy said he was from a small town, and that he had nothing in common with his parents," said Claire. Quite an understatement, I thought. "Did you learn anything?" she asked.

"Maybe," I answered. I spent the next few minutes describing the guys who came before me, looking for Miles.

"Why would guys from your office come to his parents' house?" asked Claire.

"I don't know," I answered, "but I'm not sure they were from NewGen."

"Why is that?" she asked.

I put the phone in a cradle and switched to Bluetooth. "I talked to Ken Hendrick, who's above Miles, actually a few job levels above Miles. Anyway, he said they scrapped whatever Miles was working on. When I pushed Ken on exactly what Miles was working on, he had no idea. Ken thinks Miles reported to only one man, Charles Stuart himself. Also, they described one of the guys. A huge Black man with a long facial scar. I haven't seen anyone like that at NewGen."

A red car pulled out in front of me and suddenly hit the brakes. My heart jumped. I swerved in the next lane. "Son of a bitch," I blurted.

"You okay?"

"Yeah, yeah." I looked in my side mirror back at the car. "Sorry, some guy just cut me off." I let my adrenaline fade.

"For a second there, I thought you were in danger," Claire said.

"No danger," I answered. Earl's voice came into my mind, *Right curious if we knew what he was working on, real specific on the last time we seen Miles. Nice enough, except that big Black fella.* Something about that guy had spooked them.

"Jack, hello?" Claire said through the Bluetooth.

"Oh, sorry, what?"

"I said I guess we're at a dead end." I said nothing. "Are you there?"

"Yeah, I just remembered something Miles said before he died."

"What? Did he mention anything about hurting himself?"

"No, not that. It was something about his job. This was weeks before he died. The way he was talking, it's like he knew something bad was going to happen."

"How so?" asked Claire.

I thought back to that night. Miles was on his third scotch. "I don't know. Maybe it was just the alcohol. Miles didn't usually drink." That much was true. The only thing more rare than seeing him drink was hearing him talk. At the time it seemed like a rare moment of babble before he passed out. A string of verbal vomit.

"What did he say?"

My head began to throb at the temples, then focused like a laser above my eye. I pictured Miles rambling, stretched out on my La-Z-Boy chair. A rare moment of vulnerability. His head tilted as he stared at the ceiling. "You know, I used to say I'd die to have my job. Of course that was a metaphor. I never thought it might actually come true." The pain in my head intensified. Suddenly, the vision in my right eye became hazy. I pulled the car into the right side emergency lane and stopped.

"Jack? You there? You sound funny, like you're breathing hard."

"Yeah, I, um, just had a little scare." My vision cleared, and the throbbing started to ease for a moment. "Listen, can we talk about this later? I think I should concentrate on driving." Black clouds loomed on the horizon. A lone, fat droplet of rain smacked the center of the windshield.

"Sure, maybe I can come over when you get home. Help you remember more," Claire said. "I'm not trying to be forward," she added quickly. "It's just, there's no one who really understands what I'm going through. And," another sigh, "honestly, I don't want to be alone with my thoughts."

I was exhausted. When, and if, I made it home, I craved sleep. But her voice sounded raw, even fragile. I wanted to help her. "Okay, I'll be home in a couple of hours."

"See you soon. Be careful, Jack."

I eased the car back on the highway. A few isolated drops of rain were soon followed by a steady rhythm on the windshield. Minutes later it was pounding to the point the wipers couldn't keep the glass clear. I thought of pulling over, but Claire was coming soon.

I hadn't seen this much rain since—my mind drifted back to when my father wrapped his Buick around the old oak tree. It was a turn at the end of our road he must have known by heart. One he had done hundreds of times before. But the rain must have blinded him. That and the booze.

Help her? Like you helped your mother? Ha, said a voice inside my head. Just your subconscious, I tried to reassure myself. But even though there was something familiar in the voice, it was definitely not my own. It was shrill, cold, and critical. A gravelly voice with a slurred, Southern twang. I tried hard to place it but could not.

Thought you two would live happily ever after? Then the snicker. A chill shot down my spine. My heart accelerated. How I hated the voice. I almost told it to shut up. The truth was I didn't feel guilty about that night twenty-five years ago. I'd left the house to bike in the pounding rain. Anything to get out of hearing my old man berating my mother once more. I couldn't take it. Ever since I could remember, he screamed at her, belittled her, even battered her. It's all my twelve years on the earth had ever known. So I left in the downpour.

Not long after, I saw red lights blinking miles down the road, like a blur. Something lured me there. Curiosity, boredom, I couldn't say. The rain stung my eyes as I rode toward it. I had to steer with one hand, constantly clearing my face with the other. The lights in the distance came into focus—taillights from a car. There were headlights too. They looked funny, angled wrong toward the sky. The closer I got, I could see the folded, crushed metal of the car. A little closer, I could make out the color. Closer still, I heard the moaning of a man.

I had to wipe my eyes twice to make sure. Yep, it was Dad's Buick, no doubt. Its front was destroyed, hugging the oak on either side. I could see a wrist hanging limp from the driver's side. It was hairy, all the way to the back of the hand. The long fingers had two rings, a green one on the pinky and a gold wedding band. I knew those rings. Those rings had cut my mother's face dozens of times.

I had hopped off my bike and trudged through puddles of water to the wreckage. The moans grew louder. Moans followed by weak coughs. I got close enough to see the back of the head—and blood. Lots of blood. Even the sheets of rain couldn't wash the blood away. I walked closer, wiped my eyes clear, and looked into the driver's eyes.

"Jack," my father moaned.

I could smell the sweet breath. Even through the smell of the rain and blood.

"Get help," he moaned. "Oh, Jack, hurry. Get help."

One of his legs was twisted. His foot was at an unnatural angle. I took a few steps back, and then a few more. His moans cried out in the distance. "Get help, damn you. Get help. You dumb little shit."

I jumped on my bike and started down the road again. No other cars were coming. No people were out. Just a dark, rainy night with my father slowly dying at the end of the road. Minutes later I was home, showered, and silently eating a snack.

My car hit standing water, and I momentarily lost the feel of the road. It snapped me from the past. The rain was not slacking. I punched my hazard button. Up and down the highway, cars were pulling over to wait it out.

But your plan never worked out, did it? Murderer. "Shut up." This time I actually did speak out loud. "I was protecting her. I didn't kill him. And she didn't either."

How was I supposed to know she kicked him out that night? He could have slept it off, as usual, on the couch. *And now your mother is riddled with guilt. Forcing Daddy out in the rain, too drunk to even stand straight.*

CHAPTER FOURTEEN

CLAIRE

I lowered my car window despite the light rain. A few drops flew into the car but not many. Not even enough to wipe my face. Just enough to feel something. And I was desperate to feel something, anything different from my current feeling.

During the twenty-minute ride to Jack's house, I realized how little I knew about Jack. It had been a long time since I'd been to a man's house. What was I doing? A better question was this: What did Jack think I was doing? Sure, Jack was attractive. Everything I would normally look for in a man: smart, witty, caring, great hair, and those impossibly long eyelashes. But I didn't feel attractive. And I had no desire to turn this into a romance. The truth was he was a kindred spirit in suffering. Someone to confide in, to commiserate with. There was comfort in not being alone.

A strong breeze shot more rain onto my left cheek. I closed the window. I looked at my face in the rearview mirror. My eyes were red and puffy. Still, my face didn't reflect the hell I'd endured the past few weeks. How could it without being hideously disfigured?

Once outside Jack's place, I parked and studied myself in the mirror. I applied some balm to my lips and smacked them together. Now taking a closer look, I could see how recent events were taking their toll on my face. *That face needs a pound of powder*. My inner dialogue, once a source of inspiration, was now a bully I couldn't control. "Whatever," I said, shifting my eyes from the mirror. "Jack's just a—" I stopped. I shouldn't have to explain myself. I got out and slammed my car door, hoping to trap that awful voice inside.

Jack stood under the front awning wearing a T-shirt and jeans. His hair was disheveled, and his face held a three-day stubble. He looked better than I remembered, despite no effort to groom himself in days. Just another thing in life that's not fair.

"Hey, Jack. Thanks for taking me in," I said, making myself sound like a stray.

He smiled, but his eyes looked sad and tired. "Sure. As you can see, I'm very busy."

I looked around the place. It was picked up, but I wouldn't say clean. The baseboards were a little dusty, as well as the corners of the ceiling. Little details that were overlooked. It had a slight musty smell but not overwhelming. Altogether it lacked any sign of female life. To my surprise, this came as a relief to me.

We walked into his kitchen. There were two lone pictures on the refrigerator. Jack was in both. One with an older woman, about a foot shorter. The other with two friends wearing backpacks in front of a mountain range.

"Can I get you some wine?" he asked. "Or I've got beer, water, um, milk."

"I'll have a beer," I answered. "Is that you and your mother?" I asked.

He followed my eyes to the picture on the refrigerator. "Yeah, about ten years ago."

"Where's your father?" I asked.

He didn't answer. I wasn't sure if he heard my question, but I think his jaw clenched. I pointed to another picture. "And this, is that you with your brothers?"

"No, I'm an only child. That's with some college buddies in New Zealand." He pulled two beers out of the fridge and opened them. After passing me one, he took a long swig of his own. Looking at his phone, he asked, "Are you hungry? You want to split a pizza?"

I'd only eaten half a bagel all day. For the past few weeks, I'd had no appetite. I was afraid to even check the amount of weight I'd lost. "Sure," I answered, knowing I'd be lucky to finish one slice.

He ordered a large pizza with everything. The thought of that much food caused a sudden wave of nausea to come over me. After Jack hung up the phone, we made small talk about his neighborhood and restaurants nearby. The conversation slowed, finally coming to a halt.

"So," I said, breaking the silence, "tell me about Miles."

He shrugged and took another swallow of his drink. "Not much to tell."

"You mentioned he was acting strangely."

Jack nodded. "Yeah, the night before he left. He had more than a few drinks and let his guard down. A rare moment for Miles."

I nodded.

"He was rambling. Going on about how his job was killing him."

"Hmm." Not very helpful, I thought. "People tell me that in therapy almost every session," I said.

"True. But it seemed more than that."

"How so?"

"Well." Jack sat in a wooden chair at his small kitchen table. He closed his eyes, then rubbed them hard with two fingers.

"Jack?"

"Yeah," he answered, opening his eyes. "I was just trying to remember exactly what he said. 'They're going to bury me with their damn secrets, Jack.' That's what he said."

"That's telling."

"Yeah, for a guy who doesn't show any emotion, he was all over the place that night. He was angry, then sad."

"What else did he say?"

Jack took a drink and looked blankly at the wall. "I don't know. My mind isn't too sharp lately. I was drinking that night too."

"Take your time," I said.

Jack chewed on a nail. "He said something about how he used to be proud of what he did and where he worked. He got pretty worked up, saying, 'I'll do some burying of my own, either in my office at home or in plain sight.'"

"What does that mean?" I asked.

"I don't know. I asked him that question the next morning when he was nursing a hangover. I don't think he remembered half of what he said."

"He didn't admit to saying it?"

I shrugged. "He was back to the old Miles. Stoic. Said it was just work stress, nothing serious. That I shouldn't listen to a man after his fourth drink."

"Anything else?"

"He wished he could go back to being one of the good guys. But how did he put it? He was 'trapped like an animal.' And like an animal, 'One day they will put me down.'"

I winced. "Yikes."

"Yeah, whatever happened, he felt trapped for sure."

"Sounds like someone more likely to be killed than kill himself," I said.

"Yep," Jack murmured softly.

"How close were you? I mean you had no idea what he was doing for the company?"

"Miles kept to himself. Even those few weeks he stayed here. Besides that one night, he never talked about whatever was happening with him. As far as NewGen, I knew he worked on cutting edge treatments for mental health. Mostly depression and anxiety but also more serious issues, like schizophrenia. They used some of the same therapies we did, like transcranial magnetic stimulation. You know of it?" I nodded. "The weeks before his death, he was completely inaccessible. Not only to me but to the rest of the company. I spoke with Ken, and even the people brought in to help Miles can't be traced. There's no record of them. His work, and Miles himself, were always private. But those last weeks, he seemed to sever completely from the rest of us. And like his drunken prophecy, ultimately the whole thing *was* buried. Including him." Jack got up and rubbed his tousled hair. He opened and closed the refrigerator without taking anything out. Filling a glass with tap water, he said, "Your sister may have known more than any of us."

"I doubt it," I said. "Miles was a mystery to Amy. She used to get excited to find out any little detail about his life. I think it was like a game for her." I sighed. "But in the end, even Amy got frustrated. Too many secrets."

"Yep." Jack chewed on a fingernail. I caught myself rubbing my hands again.

"You think he was killed?" I asked.

Jack turned his face toward mine. "What? No, I didn't say that."

He seemed to be ruminating on a thought. "Then what?"

Jack shook his head. "I don't know. Something happened to him. Whatever it was, there may be a connection to us. We need to go to his house and look around. Who knows? Maybe we'll get lucky. Maybe he really did bury some secrets to find." The doorbell rang. "Ah, pizza."

I reached for my purse. "Let me give you some—"

"Really, I got it," he interrupted.

Jack returned with a large pizza box. He placed the box on the table and opened it. The smell of hot cheese and sausage gave me a jolt of nausea. "You okay?" he asked.

"Yeah, sure. Excuse me for a minute." I dashed to the hallway bathroom. I thought I may be sick, but my nausea faded. I splashed water on my face and dried it with a hand towel. I looked in the mirror. Small capillaries filled the whites of my eyes like baby spider webs. Loose flesh now sagged underneath them. My entire face was puffy and worn. I pulled a tube of red lipstick from my purse and applied a light coat. Now my face looked puffy and worn with a coat of lipstick. *Homely*, said a voice followed by an ugly, high-pitched laugh. *Like lipstick on a pig*. The voice belonged to someone else, but I was alone. Another high-pitched laugh. I balled my right hand into a tight fist. I had to stop myself from punching the mirror. Instead I closed my eyes, took two deep breaths, and splashed more water on my face. I heard a few soft knocks on the door.

"Claire? Everything okay? I thought I heard something."

Was I talking out loud? "Yes, everything's fine," I lied.

I walked out of the bathroom to the kitchen. The top of the pizza box was closed, and a bottle of white wine sat near it on the table. "I opened some wine if you want."

I want, I thought, to drown this voice. "Thanks." I poured myself a generous glass.

"You sure you don't want any food?" Jack asked.

I shook my head. "Not yet. Maybe later. I still have these waves of nausea."

Jack nodded. "Yeah, me too."

I looked into his eyes. They looked tired—and bloodshot like my own. Besides the weariness, I could see kindness in his eyes. Why couldn't I have met him when I felt like a human being? I was never perfect, but this version of me—

"So where were we before the pizza came?" asked Jack.

"You were talking about going to Miles's house. You think that's safe?" I asked.

"I don't see why not. As far as we know, his death was a suicide." Jack opened the pizza box. This time, thankfully, I felt no wave of nausea. He grabbed a slice. "I tell you what's not safe: doing nothing. I don't know about you, but every day I'm feeling worse."

I thought of the disturbing voice in the bathroom with the high-pitched laugh. I caught myself rubbing my hands. "Yeah, you could say that."

Jack must have sensed my unease. "Hey, maybe we should take a break. You like *CSI*?"

"The TV show?" I asked. He nodded. "I do," I answered.

"Let's take a break, watch some *CSI*. Maybe we will get some ideas about Miles."

I looked at my watch. It was getting late. I should probably go.

Jack looked at me. "I don't really want to be alone," he said.

I thought of myself alone in my apartment. Hearing that voice all night. I shuddered. "Me either."

"It's settled then. You sure you don't want some food now?"

I had to eat. Despite my waves of nausea, my stomach grumbled. "Maybe." I walked back to the kitchen, thinking of the voice from the bathroom, trying to place it. I used all my therapy tricks. I analyzed my thoughts and challenged the validity of them. Logically, there was no separate voice. There was no outside attack. Situational stress and fatigue have manifested in a negative inner dialogue, Claire. You are safe, sane, and whole. I poured another full glass of white wine. Safe and sane, I repeated to myself. I didn't believe either word.

Jack was already on the couch. The beginning of a *CSI* episode was paused on the television. I sat with my wine and pizza. I ate and drank. For a moment it was quiet. I only heard Jack's soft breathing and voices from the television. Even the ache in my joints eased a bit. Somehow, I knew it was only a moment. Everything was waiting to return with more intensity. The pain, the voice. I finished my wine and rested my head on Jack's shoulder. He laced his hand in mine. I tried to enjoy whatever reprieve this was. I tried to focus on the moment, something I have never been good at doing. I took a deep breath, taking in his scent. I closed my eyes. Maybe the only good thing was that Jack was with me.

As if reading my mind, he said, "You are not alone, Claire."

CHAPTER FIFTEEN

I woke up bathed in sunlight with a strange blanket draped over me. I breathed in a musty smell. My mind clicked. I was still on Jack's couch. Wow, what time was it?

Jack walked out of his bedroom, fully clothed. His hair was still wet from the shower. "Good morning. Coffee?"

I swallowed to clear the terrible taste in my mouth. It didn't help. My mind raced to remember. I ran my hands down my clothes. What exactly happened last night?

"Don't worry. Nothing untoward happened," Jack answered. "You fell asleep on the couch. You looked worn out, so I threw a blanket over you and let you sleep."

I nodded. I pictured myself asleep on the couch, snoring or drooling. Was he watching me sleep? I winced.

"I didn't watch you sleep either," he said.

I cleared my throat. "Did I, um, say that out loud?" My grasp on reality was fading.

"No, I just saw the look on your face," he answered. "I was pretty worn out too. I started out with four strong hours of sleep, but that was it for me." He cracked his back. "You, on the other hand, got a solid eight."

"That's more sleep than the last three days combined," I said. My tongue felt thick. Despite sleeping through the night for the first time in weeks, I still wasn't refreshed.

"You want some coffee? Or maybe some breakfast?"

He sat down beside my feet stretched on the sofa. I kept my distance, assuming my breath was toxic. "I think I should get home."

"Yeah, listen, I was thinking this morning. Insomnia has given me plenty of time for that. Anyway, I still have a key to Miles's place. He gave it to me a while ago to get his mail, water his plants, or whatever. Maybe we could head over there this morning. See if we can find anything useful."

I ran my tongue over my teeth with my mouth closed. I really needed to clean myself up, I thought. "You sure that's a good idea? I mean you think the police might be there or something?"

"Police? No, it's not a crime scene," he answered.

"Well, what about his parents or siblings?"

"I don't know. I think Miles was an only child like me. And his parents? Well, they are in their trailer."

"You think anyone might be living there?"

"Maybe," he answered.

"Or watching the house?"

"Maybe."

"That's a lot of maybes," I said.

"Maybe it is a lot of maybes," he answered. "Look, all I know is that I'm not feeling any better. No one seems able to help. I'm not sure if we have the same thing, but if so, then ketamine won't even help. I have a hunch it has something to do with whatever Miles was working on."

"I need to use your bathroom," I said.

I looked at myself in the mirror, the one I almost punched yesterday. The whites of my eyes were slightly more clear, but my face was still puffy. The weight of the past few weeks had literally pulled my face down, as if I had aged ten years. I took a deep breath, ran water over my hands, and splashed my old, saggy face. I popped my cheeks with the palms of my hands. It was no use; I looked haggard.

I walked to the kitchen where Jack handed me a cup of coffee. "Everything okay?" he asked, staring at me.

"Oh, yeah. I've just, um, been rough on myself lately. I'm not usually like that," I answered.

"Yeah? Me too," he said. "Just last night," his face went slack. "Never mind," he said, seeming to purge the thought. "How do you like your coffee?"

"Black," I answered.

"Not fussy," he said.

"My dad is military. And yes, I'll go to Miles's house with you. First let me go home to shower and change."

* * *

Jack picked me up, and we drove to Miles's house. It took just twenty-five minutes. Anything less than thirty minutes in Atlanta was close. I was nervous to enter the house of someone deceased, key or not. Somehow it felt wrong. But after weeks of being a spectator to my declining mind and body, taking any action felt right.

Jack pulled his car into a subdivision. He slowed as we passed neatly trimmed lawns, a child on a bike, and a man walking a shaggy dog. We stopped at the end of a cul-de-sac in front of a large brick home with an American flag hanging on a front column.

"Miles lived here?" I asked.

"Yeah, you surprised?"

"Hmm. Just seems a little suburban for a bachelor," I answered.

"Yeah, well, you know Miles, always a mystery."

We walked toward the house. I made an effort to look casual, as if we'd been invited. As Jack tried the key, I glanced from side to side to see if anyone was watching.

He swung the door open. To my relief the place felt empty. The air inside was hot and stale. Once past the foyer, the floor plan opened up. I could see a kitchen and a great room. Drawers in the kitchen were pulled out, some removed from the cabinet entirely. Their contents were spilled onto the counters. Cans of food and dried pasta were strewn in front of an open pantry. A line of Cheerios was scattered across the tile floor. In the great room, sofa cushions were turned over and unzipped. Their feather stuffing had been pulled out and dumped.

"Guess we're not the first ones here," I said.

"Yep, this place was tossed. Someone came here searching hard."

"Wonder when they left?" My voice cracked. I could see my hands shake. I didn't want to be here if they came back.

"I'll have a look downstairs. You want to go up and take a look?" Jack asked. I swallowed. My throat felt dry. "Don't worry. They're not coming back. They did their worst."

I looked at the feathers covering the living room floor. "Suppose you're right. Not much to come back to."

I walked up the stairs. I entered the first bedroom, the master. Something from the corner of my eye moved. My heart dropped. I whipped my head around to face it head on, but nothing was there. I froze, then took a deep breath. There's no one here, I reassured myself. But something moved. A faint whiff of something sour, something dead, hung in the air. I sat on the bed. A wave of vertigo came over me.

"Anything?" yelled Jack.

I steadied myself and stood. "Not so far," I yelled back. I took another deep breath. The smell was gone. Get it together, I murmured. Most of the drawers to a bedroom dresser were pulled open with clothes strewn on the floor. I really didn't know what I was looking for, so I looked for anything out of the ordinary. But nothing looked ordinary. As Jack put it, the place had been thoroughly tossed.

I walked into the bathroom. The counter was littered from whatever was in the medicine cabinet—Band-Aids, a razor, hair gel, prescription bottles. I read the prescription medications. Zoloft, antidepressant, no surprise there. I picked up another label I didn't recognize. Then a third bottle, mostly full, was labeled clozapine. That's an antipsychotic. As far as I know, it's only intended to treat schizophrenia. I wasn't aware of any off-label uses. I didn't know Miles well, but I was a mental health professional. Surely, I would have noticed if he was schizophrenic.

I pocketed the clozapine and left the other pills where I found them. I walked to another upstairs bedroom, which yielded nothing of much interest. I stopped to listen. The house was quiet, too quiet. Did something happen to Jack? "Jack?" I yelled out. No response. My heart accelerated. "Jack?" I called out again. I ran down the stairs, breathing heavily.

My hand shook the banister. "Jack?" I shouted.

"In here."

I followed the voice to a home office. "There you are. I thought I was alone." I clutched my chest, still heaving. Something crunched under my foot.

"Careful, there's glass there," he said.

I looked down. Jagged shards of glass were scattered on the

floor. Two picture frames had been ripped off the wall and shattered. "Did you not hear me?" I asked.

He looked up at me, still scanning the room. "Yeah, I called back. You didn't hear me?"

I shook my head. The room, like the rest of the house, was trashed. A massive mahogany desk filled a third of the room. Underneath it was a small oriental rug. A steel file cabinet was dumped over. Bits of glass and loose papers covered the floor. A small palm tree, badly in need of water, sat next to a window. I picked up a few loose papers that looked like bank records. "Anything of interest here?"

Jack shook his head. "Not yet."

"Did you know Miles was on clozapine?"

"No. But I don't know what that is."

"It's an antipsychotic."

"Oh."

"Right. I mean I knew he was likely depressed. But clozapine is used for schizophrenia. Was he—"

"No," said Jack. "I mean Miles was eccentric. Mysterious, right? But he was brilliant. Highly, highly functional." Jack looked over the floor and let out a deep sigh.

"What is it?" I asked.

"If we found anything, I thought it would be here. All the talk about burying something."

I looked over the ransacked room. I didn't know how we would find anything in this place. I wanted to leave before someone returned. "Did you check under the rug?"

"Yeah, I did. Not under the desk, but that must weigh four hundred pounds." I nodded, about to suggest we leave. "I think we need to move the desk." Jack pushed his sleeves up and tried shoving the desk. Glass crunched under his feet as he dug them into the wooden floor. After a few grunts and curses, he moved the desk about six inches.

"Need some help?" I asked.

"You think?" he smiled, breathing heavily. I walked over to the side of the desk to join him. "On three," he said. "One, two —" We pushed the desk together. It moved, maybe a foot. Then again, another six inches. We kept it up until we were both gasping for air and starting to sweat. But we managed to move the wooden beast across the room.

"Now what?"

Jack shrugged and peeled the rug back. "Well, no trap door." He kicked at some glass, then sat down on the floor, defeated. "Damn it."

I got on my knees and began to run my hands over the wooden planks.

"What are you doing?" Jack asked.

Just as I heard his question, I felt the slightest little gap in the wood. "Ha, I think I found a cut."

Jack bent down and ran his fingers over the wood. "Yep," he agreed. "I can even see it," he said, staring down.

We tried unsuccessfully pulling and prying at the wood. Jack slammed his fist onto the floor in frustration. The far end of a wooden plank popped up and down. "Aha, you see that?" he asked. I nodded. He firmly pressed where his fist had been. The end of the board lifted up, and I removed it. Then another plank. After removing two more, we looked at a hole in the floor. "Bingo," Jack said.

"A safe."

We tried to lift it, but it was useless. "I think it's bolted to a floor joist or something," Jack said. He stood up and dusted his pants off. "I'll have a look underneath."

I nodded. He left, and soon after my head began to throb. The excitement of the moment faded, and I felt the ache in my joints again. *You're going to end up dead or in jail.* My heart raced—it was the voice from last night. The high-pitched laugh returned. A wave of nausea came over me. I tried to ground myself with reassuring facts. You're not in danger. You're safe. You're sane. The voice scoffed.

"You okay?"

I looked up to see Jack had returned. I nodded, taking some deliberate slow, deep breaths. I looked down to find I was wringing my hands. "What's below?" I asked.

"Nothing. We would have to tear down the ceiling just to see the bottom of the safe. And then, who knows, it still might be bolted, or welded, to something."

"We'll just have to crack the safe," I answered.

He looked to the safe and popped his knuckles. "Right. I guess the obvious one would be his birthday. Jack's forehead wrinkled.

"But you don't know his birthday, do you?" I asked.

"Yeah, I know the day, December 8, just not the year." He punched some numbers into the safe. A red light came on followed by a beep. "Fail. What would the year be?" Jack drummed his fingers on the wood, thinking. "He was close to my age."

While he ruminated, I held my phone up to him. "What's that?" he asked.

"Miles Chambers's obituary—died age thirty-four."

"Great, good thinking. Okay, now let's try the month and year." I waited. Another red light, another beep. He cracked his knuckles and punched in a different combination. Same result. Then another attempt followed by the same red light, the same beep. He pushed back from the safe and groaned. "Son of a bitch, it's useless. What's nine times nine times nine times nine?" I shrugged. "Not going to happen, that's what. Too many possibilities."

"Don't you know anything more about Miles?" I asked.

"We've been over this. Miles was a closed book." Jack

leaned back, shifting his weight onto his hands. "Ouch, umpf." He picked his right hand off the wood. A small shard of glass cut into the meat of his palm. A slow trickle of bright-red blood followed. "Hmm. Got me." He sucked the wound.

"What are you doing?" I asked. "Do you need help?" He shook his head, his mouth still on the cut. "I don't think that's the best way—"

"I'm going to look for a towel," he said. Jack came back with a paper towel pressed against his palm.

"Did you learn anything on your visit to see his parents?"

He took the towel off his hand. Blood slowly returned to the wound, and he pressed the towel back on, then blotted at the cut. "Come to think of it, maybe. You know Jeff Gordon's number?"

"No," I answered. "I don't know him or his phone number."

"No, no," he shook his head. "He's a race car driver. Seems Miles was a closet NASCAR fan, or at least he was when he was a kid."

I entered Jeff Gordon's racing number into the search engine on my phone. "Twenty-four," I said. "Between me and Google, we know everything."

Jack smiled, punched in more numbers, and once again heard the disappointing beep.

"Worth a shot," I said. "What did you use for the other two numbers?"

"Dale Earnhardt, his father's favorite." He rolled his neck in a circle. "Last shot, let me try reversing the numbers."

His hands went back under the gap in the floor. I heard him punch in four numbers and waited for the familiar rejection chime. It didn't come. "Did you not—"

"Brilliant," he said. "We're in!"

CHAPTER SIXTEEN

JACK

Inside the safe was a manila folder stuffed with cash, a passport, a thumb drive, two notebooks, and a loaded gun.

"What kind of gun is that?" asked Claire. I picked it up. It felt cold and heavy. "I wouldn't play with that," she said.

I shrugged and put it down. "I don't know anything about guns."

I removed the contents from the safe until only a plastic lining remained. I used the flashlight on my phone to shine into it. The steel square was roughly the size of a large glove box.

"Why does Miles have a gun?" asked Claire.

"I don't know. But I've got about a dozen more questions." I dropped the gun back in the safe. It landed with a clunk.

"Careful," Claire hissed behind me. "You don't want that thing going off."

"Oops, sorry," I murmured. "Like I said, I don't know anything about guns."

"I feel like this is a movie. It doesn't seem real," Claire said.

I looked back to the safe, empty except for the handgun. Claire was close enough I could feel her breath on my shoulder.

"Well, it's definitely not a comedy," I answered. I stood up and opened the envelope. I pulled out a stack of one-hundred-dollar bills and thumbed through them. "There must be over twenty thousand dollars in here."

Claire had the passport open. "At least his passport is real. If it had another name, I really would think this was a movie."

I flipped through the notebooks. It was Miles's handwriting all right. I could picture his left hand scrawling the squatty letters. The pages of one notebook were full, front and back. The second notebook was filled with more diagrams and pictures. A few blank pages were left at the end. I heard a mechanical noise behind me. I turned to find Claire holding the gun from the safe. I saw her push something into the handle of the gun, making a clicking noise. "Like you said, maybe we shouldn't touch that."

She examined the steel barrel. "I think it's a .45. My dad has a few guns."

"Well, this one isn't registered to us," I answered. "Besides, who knows where that gun has been." I feared the worst. I'd watched enough detective shows to know the barrel of a gun left a pattern on a bullet like a fingerprint.

"Don't worry. The safety is on," she said and placed it on the floor.

I heard a distant dog bark and a thump overhead as if something landed on the roof. "Shh," I said, putting a finger to my lips. We went silent. A few more barks followed but nothing more. The only other noise was my own heartbeat and Claire's breathing.

"Maybe it was a squirrel on the roof," said Claire.

My pulse picked up speed, and my mouth felt dry. I walked to the window and parted the blinds. The street was empty. "I think we should get out of here."

Claire nodded. "What about all this stuff?" She pointed to the gun, passport, money, and notebooks.

"I think we should just take the thumb drive and notebooks," I said. I could hear a tremble in my voice. I looked at the money, the gun, the passport—something felt seriously wrong.

"Okay," Claire answered. "Let's go."

We kept the notebooks and the thumb drive. Claire put everything else back in the safe while I waited to replace the boards. Then came pushing the massive desk again over it.

It was a relief to finally get in the car and put some distance between us and the house. If they had come before, they'd come again. And just who exactly were *they*, I thought.

Claire wanted me to take her home, but I wasn't sure. "You think we're in danger?" she asked.

"No, nothing like that," I lied. The money, the passport, the gun, our declining physical and mental health. Of course we were in danger. "I'm just getting used to having you around is all." That was true enough. The last twenty-four hours or so had been like having a partner in hell. I'd never felt worse, but she had been there.

"Why don't you take some time and look at Miles's notebooks. We can touch base later, and you can tell me what you found," Claire suggested.

I agreed and dropped her off at her apartment. Once home I dug into the notebooks. I drank four cups of coffee, trying to keep my focus. I was interrupted constantly by my wandering, negative thoughts, as well as a constant need to urinate. The coffee was going through me so fast I thought of grabbing a makeshift chamber pot.

Despite my wandering mind, the disturbing material held my attention. The answers to all my questions for the past weeks were finally in front of me. As I flipped through the notebook, I couldn't believe what I read. Miles did report directly to

Charles Stuart, that much I had already figured. But the person pulling the strings behind Stuart was a shock.

The operation was labeled Universal Madness. That's cute. A Colonel Link Stine in the United States Army was behind it. As to who was behind the colonel, it appeared Miles didn't know. Just Colonel Stine, over and over. One thing was clear: by the amount of money spent on the project, it must have reached far up the chain of command.

I knew Miles had been working on new ways to treat mental health, but this project actually *induced* mental illness. It was an ingenious and horrific creation. A virus that started with vague symptoms: fatigue, nausea, headaches, and muscle pain. Everything I had experienced in the past few weeks. As a weapon it was beautiful. It hid in plain sight. Once its hooks were firmly in its target, the nature of the virus changed. Miles designed the virus to hit different receptors in different areas of the brain as it replicated. During its early stages, the virus would stimulate certain NDMA receptors of the brain, leading to depression. As the virus grew in number, other NDMA receptors would be blocked, leading to psychosis.

I realized I had been reading in the same position for so long that my arm felt numb. I shifted my weight to bring blood flow back to it. As the feeling returned, a stinging sensation ran from my left shoulder to my fingers. The next section of his notes covered the neurotransmitter glutamate. Once again, depending on the area of the brain or the stage of the virus, this neurotransmitter was either high or low. High in areas to cause depression and low in areas to cause delusions. The more I read, the more angry I became. The fact that Miles could create something like this at all was mind boggling. If he could do this, he could have made something to cure 99 percent of mental illness. Instead he created a weapon to destroy mind, body, and spirit.

As I read on, my anger faded. The journal became dark. Miles scribbled a litany of physical ailments, ones very familiar to me: headaches over his eye, throbbing joints, crippling fatigue, nausea. This was followed by a dash and the word "exposed." The next pages went down a rabbit hole into his disturbed mind. *In bed for two days. The colonel knows.* I could feel drops of sweat forming on my brow, pooling under my arms, and trickling down my spine. His writings began to ramble. Paranoid bits of personal warnings. *They're coming. They sent him.* I flipped the page to a series of haunting sketches—a tombstone with the word "failure" etched on the face. A man with what appeared to be a bag over his head, his eyes bulging, tongue protruding. The image of a shadowy figure drawn over and over in different shapes and sizes, filled with black ink so heavy it leaked through the page. The word "void" written under each one. Miles, what the hell happened to you?

There was a shift in his writing. The tone, the slant, the aggression of the letters all changed, as if someone, or something, possessed his hand. "Sent?" was written beside the word "void." Always there beside it. The journal—turned graphic novel—ended in one final word, "goodbye."

I closed the book and felt an intense pressure grip my chest and head. My heart thundered warnings into my brain through quick bursts of blood. Feeling trapped, I had an urge to run outside, but that seemed too open, too vulnerable. Plagued by waves of claustrophobia mixed with agoraphobia, I stumbled to the bathroom and splashed cold water over my face.

I stood frozen, staring at a hunted man in the mirror. Questions flooded my mind. The US military? Did this colonel know Miles was infected? Did he kill Miles? Who, or what, is a void? One thing was certain: Miles hadn't finished an antidote. His final ramblings made that clear enough.

I returned to the desk to write down a few ideas in the notebook before I left. Ideas that Miles started before he slipped into a delusional state. I quickly read over my page of added notes.

I had no more time to waste. I had to warn Claire. It had been nine hours since we last saw each other. And I spent at least eight and a half of them learning what was happening to us. I didn't want to tell Claire anything over the phone. Not that I believed our phones were hacked, but then again, anything seemed possible.

I drove to Claire's apartment. When I arrived, the lights were off and the blinds drawn. "Can I turn on some lights?" I asked when I walked in.

"Oh, sorry, I thought it might help my headache," she answered.

"And did it?"

"No," she said. "But vomiting helped. At least for about ten minutes."

I flipped a light on. I told her what I knew—things I'd read from the notebooks and the thumb drive. I left out the parts about the void, drawings of tombstones, and bags over faces. Partly because I didn't want to freak Claire out any further, and partly because I had no idea what they meant. Before I was done talking, Claire had to redirect me three times. My anxious words were coming out in spurts of muddled fragments.

"A virus?" she asked. "By the military?" Claire shook her head. "This is nuts. Why wouldn't the military just create a virus that killed everyone? Why go through this whole rigamarole?"

"Rigamarole?" I asked.

"You know what I mean."

"Well, think about it. A virus that kills a population is obviously effective. But a virus that steals the will to live is something entirely different. People can heal from a deadly virus. They can come together and rebuild. But this virus rapes the mind, makes people question their own reality. It crushes the spirit of a nation. Generations without hope. It's diabolical."

Claire took in a deep breath and let out a heavy sigh. "I guess so." She rubbed her hands together. "And Miles had no cure?"

"He was working on one," I answered. "It seems the virus shifts its protein structure on the surface all the time. I got the impression from his notes that it was even programmed to shift after so many days. As it replicates, its structure changes to target different receptors in the brain." Claire's face looked more troubled than usual. "What is it?" I asked.

"Nothing." Another sigh followed, this one weak and shallow. "The way you describe what happened to Miles. The negative thoughts—the targeting of NDMA receptors leading to psychosis." Her breath seemed to quicken, and her hands shook. "The eventual atrophy of the prefrontal cortex." Her voice trembled. "And this virus just keeps shifting while our brain wires itself into a spider web of doom." She stood up, balled her fist. "Jack, we're fucked."

"Hold on," I said. "Calm down." I couldn't argue much against her logic, but I felt like I had to. "Miles wouldn't have created something like this that couldn't be cured."

"Okay, then why did he kill himself?" Claire asked in a high and shaky voice.

"Look," I answered, ignoring the question, "he alluded to some ideas."

"Alluded?"

"It means to suggest to or hint at."

"I know what allude means," she snapped. Her mouth tightened, and her brows turned down.

"Right, sorry. Anyway, the key may be to attack something

in the virus that's more permanent. Something that doesn't shift. Like a core protein."

Claire sat down. "And you think you can do that?" she asked almost in a whisper.

"Yes," I lied. But I wanted to believe. I needed to believe. Not just to save me but to save her. To save Claire and whoever else may come into contact with this thing.

CHAPTER SEVENTEEN

FOX

Fox waited until Jack Baker walked to his car. He watched seven minutes drain from the clock. In his experience, if something was left at home, a person would return within seven minutes or not at all. Fox was alone. For the rest of the team the colonel assembled, Fox sent on a different lead.

He preferred to work alone. Not that Fox couldn't work with a team, but this group he didn't know. Any mission could get him killed, whether in suburban America or the deserts of Afghanistan. These men he'd yet to see in action. Fox knew from experience that it was impossible to predict how a soldier would react in combat. He'd witnessed some of the toughest marines in their class freeze at the sight of their first live round. That was his litmus test. Until he saw this crew in combat, he preferred to work alone.

Fox started in the back of the house, in the garbage. This was where he got nearly half of his intel. It always shocked him how careless people were with their information. After sifting through meaningless junk mail, empty packages, and take out, he was satisfied no answers were coming from the outside cans.

Coming in the back was exceedingly easy. The only lock was on the doorknob. Fox took a quick assessment of the place. The colonel wanted information. He had no orders to subdue or eliminate the threat. The best course of action was to keep the target at ease and leave no trace of his visit. Fox swept the place to make sure it was empty. Satisfied, he tucked his standard issue M18 service pistol in the small of his back. Fox knew he didn't need the weapon. His hands were deadly enough. They had killed more enemies in close combat than he cared to remember. But sometimes the sight of a weapon commanded more respect. With his weapon he could direct from a distance. His hands—he looked down at them—were less predictable. They were heavily calloused and as thick as his feet. Once engaged, they were more likely to snap a neck or break a bone than the distance the M18 afforded him.

He took his time sifting through bedroom drawers and closets. There was nothing of real interest. It wasn't until he entered the office that he found anything worthwhile. And there it was in plain sight: two notebooks of data and a thumb drive inserted into a desktop. So transparent that Fox thought it may be a trap.

After a quick analysis of the notebook contents, Fox had no doubt found what he came for. The colonel will be pleased, he thought. These must be the records from Miles Chambers that concerned his boss. He zipped the notebooks in a small black bag he carried.

Fox left the same way he entered. He didn't let his mind wander to alternative plans. Gather information and get out were his orders. Following orders was baked in his DNA as much as his will to survive. He was a highly trained, efficient tool with surgical precision. But ultimately a tool for the US military. It wasn't for him to ask why. *Why* was a question for civilians. *Why* caused hesitation. *Why* got you killed.

Once home, Fox assimilated the confiscated material quickly. If he wanted, Fox could have been an academic. The written word always came easy to him. He was able to digest and regurgitate massive amounts of information in short periods of time. Not only regurgitate but comprehend and analyze. He had attained the highest possible score, ninety-nine, on the ASVAB, the Armed Service Vocational Aptitude Battery test. For these reasons, the colonel was always trying to use him to run logistics.

To Fox's credit, he was loyal and completed each mission, even logistical ones, with swiftness and professionalism. But the idea of being cornered in a role outside of battle concerned him. He liked to get his hands dirty. It was true that Fox had an outstanding mind, but he preferred to use it in combat by creating solutions that others thought were impossible. He had never asked to move up the ranks. If his ambition had been rank climbing, he never would have stopped at captain.

When Fox was satisfied that he had read enough, he put the notebooks down. He did his twenty pull-ups, one hundred push-ups, and two hundred crunches—a daily ritual since boot camp. Missing was the six-mile run, but it was getting late.

He then dialed the colonel on an encrypted phone. "Sir," he began.

"Do you have an update, Captain?" asked the colonel.

"Affirmative. It seems subjects gamma and delta are aware of Universal Madness. My reconnaissance further shows they are infected." Miles had been labeled subject alpha or zero. That made Amy the potential beta, and Jack and Claire were gamma and delta. Fox could hear Stine chewing a cigar.

"Roger, Soldier. Plan on elimination tomorrow," he responded.

"There may be a line on a cure," Fox responded. The

added information was not exactly insubordinate but certainly unsolicited. It wasn't Fox's style.

"Come again?" the colonel asked. "You say there is an antidote?"

"No, sir, he seems to be close." Fox had read the few notes added to those of Miles. Writing that seemed organized and coherent after a series of strange sketches and rambling thoughts. He couldn't say for sure if it was Jack's, but the writing was distinctly different.

"Close doesn't work, Fox," the colonel responded. Anyone else ranked under Stine would have received an additional earful, but he respected Fox. "Assemble the team by tomorrow, 1800 hours. Proceed with elimination. Clear?"

"Yes, sir."

The line went dead. The instructions were clear enough to Fox. He knew what elimination meant. He didn't need to know how, where, or least of all why. The order was clear, and he wouldn't dwell on it.

Death had been a part of his life since Fox was a boy. The first time he killed a man, Fox was thirteen. He had two older brothers. The oldest, Nate, was the most impulsive of the three. He had a hot temper with a short fuse easily lit. That's what ultimately led to a gun being aimed at his head in an alley behind their dilapidated apartment.

Fox looked up to Nate at the time. His older brother was the only one bringing home any money for groceries. His old man was absent, and his mother was using. The fact that the money came from petty thefts and small drug deals didn't bother Fox. He only saw Nate come home and confidently slap a wad of bills on the kitchen table. "Ya'll get something nice," he'd announce. "Courtesy of old Nate."

Well that night, old Nate was in a bad spot. Fox sensed something was wrong. Nate had promised to meet him in the park to shoot baskets on the rusted, netless rim. When he didn't show, Fox went looking for his older brother. That's when he heard him in the alley. Nate was trying to talk his way out of a bullet to the forehead. He wasn't begging; Nate would never beg. It was that same smooth, commanding tone Fox was used to hearing at home.

It was dark, so dark that Fox had to rely more on his ears than his eyes. The only sliver of light that touched the alley cast on the man with the steel in his hand. Fox worked his way behind the gunman. He could hear Nate's deep, confident voice. Fox took his time as he closed in. Once close, he crouched behind a dumpster just ten feet from the man. He ran his hands along the filthy ground until they brushed something cold and hard. He picked it up. It was heavy in his hand, maybe an old tire iron or lead pipe. While the man still spoke of how Nate was going to die, Fox swung the pipe. It struck the right temple. The man fell down without breaking his fall. The gun scattered on the pavement.

"You did what you had to do," Nate told him later that night. His older brother spoke about his first kill. "Man, I couldn't sleep for a week," he said. "Had nightmares, felt too sick to eat. Now," he let out his low chuckle that Fox loved, "it's like brushing my teeth when I gotta put someone down."

Well, Fox never had nightmares or felt sick. He slept fine and ate fine. In fact, after that night, his fear was gone. Days of tiptoeing around the corners of the projects were gone. No longer did he feel stalked. His heart no longer jumped in his throat when the sun dropped. In the park and alleyways of his neighborhood, you were either predator or prey. Fox was no longer the prey.

That night was mere duty—Nate was family. Fox poured himself his nightly glass of whole milk as he remembered the details from fourteen years ago. Seven years later, Nate would be shot in that same alley. Fox's other brother died two months after Nate, courtesy of two bullets to the chest. Then his mother overdosed six months after that. Fox learned of it all only after returning from a mission to Kuwait.

Now an orphan, the US military was his only family. And Fox didn't question family business.

CHAPTER EIGHTEEN

Fox woke up and vomited. His head pounded, and his joints throbbed. It was worse than the first, and last, time Fox drank alcohol. At age fourteen he had split a fifth of liquor with his brother Nate.

He ran water over his face and looked into his bloodshot eyes in the mirror. Fox couldn't remember the last time he was sick. Besides a bullet he took in the shoulder in Afghanistan, he hadn't seen a doctor in a decade. No, Fox didn't get sick, and he didn't drink alcohol. There was only one explanation. It was one he pushed in the back of his mind but knew the minute he woke up—he was infected.

Damn, that was fast, he thought. And he hadn't even had any direct contact with the subjects. Fox felt the urge to go back to bed but knew his aching body wouldn't allow any sleep. It was rare for him to sleep past 0500, and it was already 0800.

Fox mentally recalled the course of the virus he reviewed the day before—the virus that was now pumping through his bloodstream. He could expect more headaches, nausea, dizziness, and fatigue. Soon would come depression, anxiety, and paranoia. Finally, he could expect to become so hopeless, so psychotic, that his own death would come as a relief. That was the weapon that had exploded in his face.

Proceed with elimination. Clear? Fox could hear the colonel's voice in his head. *Close doesn't work, Fox.*

Despite his head pounding in pain, Fox's brain was working just fine. He knew, even before his stomach contents hit the toilet, that he would be part of Stine's elimination. Why wouldn't he? If the virus stopped with him, Fox may consider eating his M18. But it did not. Miles had thought that and accomplished nothing. Even if Fox was the last one infected, he didn't know if he had it in him to eliminate himself. The only thing stronger than Fox's commitment to duty was his will to survive. Forged from the projects of NYC and chiseled in the hills of Afghanistan, Fox's survival instincts ran deep.

It was true that Fox had never disobeyed an order from a superior. The only exception to that rule may come if that order resulted in his own destruction. True, he was a tool for the US military, and a deadly one. But first and foremost, Fox was a survivor.

You say there's an antidote? He heard Colonel Stine's voice again. *No, sir, he seems to be close. Close doesn't work.* Well, it will have to be, thought Fox. His life would depend on it.

CHAPTER NINETEEN

JACK

Even before I saw the missing notebooks and thumb drive, I thought something was wrong. Paranoia was building inside me for weeks. With every turn, I thought I was being followed. Every noise made me practically jump out of my skin. But seeing the notebooks suddenly gone validated all that paranoia. I stared at the empty desk, frozen with fear. Were they in the house now? The only sound I heard was my shallow, rapid breathing. These were trained professionals. If they wanted me dead, I wouldn't be breathing at all.

Once Miles was infected, he must have known his time was short. Either the virus would kill him or those behind it would. As it turned out, he died by his own hand. At least I think he died by his own hand. Why had he given up before finding a cure? There must have been something he feared more than death. The thought sent a chill through me.

I tried to gather my thoughts and steady my breathing. I hadn't moved since seeing the notebooks gone. I mentally cataloged what I needed to pack. Then I made myself move. Slow at first, then at a frantic pace.

Dead man walking. Damn, that voice. I tore through the cupboards, packing anything edible that wouldn't perish. I stuffed the back of the car with everything I could think of to survive outside: sleeping bags, tents, lanterns, batteries, medicine, blankets, and cash. By the time I finished, I was sweating so badly I stripped to my undershirt.

I thought of calling Claire but decided against it. One of the first things I needed to do was disable my phone. That seemed the easiest way to be snared. No calls. I would drive to her house and hope she was there.

I left with all the lights on. I didn't want the impression my house was empty. Driving to Claire's I took several side streets to see if I had a tail. *You are out of your depth.* Hmm, that much was true.

I went through three rounds of knocks before Claire answered.

"What's wrong?" Claire asked.

I let myself in and scanned the apartment. I had a sudden fear that the place was bugged. "We're in danger," I blurted out.

She laughed. "Yeah, Jack," she said, then whispered, "I know."

"No, I mean we are in actual danger. Right now," I said in a barely audible voice. The last two words I mouthed in silence.

"Why are you not talking?"

I walked forward and cupped her ear. "Someone may be listening."

She stepped back from me. "Don't be ridiculous," she said loudly. Then added, "If anyone is out there. We need help!"

"Claire," I said, now in a normal voice, "someone has been to my place. They took the notebooks and the thumb drive. That means they know that we know. They probably know that we are infected too."

She walked across the room and sat on the sofa. "So?"

"So you think they want this getting out? They either want to contain the virus or the information. Don't you think?" The picture of a man's twisted face with a bag over his head popped into my mind.

Claire lay her head back on her couch. "Let them come."

"Let them come?" I repeated. "You can't mean that. They're not coming to help us. They mean to harm us." She looked spent, resigned to her fate. I fought against a similar feeling. "Look, we need time. We may not be the only ones in danger here. They may come for our friends and family."

Claire stood up from the couch and paced back and forth. "You really think they can hurt us more than they have already?"

"Yes. Besides, we've been careful the past couple of days, but what about before that? Who else do you think we may have unknowingly infected?"

Claire sat back down. "Well, they can't kill all of us," she said and laughed.

"I wouldn't be so sure. This thing was sealed tight. Only a few even knew about it, and even they didn't know much. My guess is they designed it to be cut off at a moment's notice."

"Cut off?" asked Claire.

"Yes, dismembered, along with any other loose ends. We have to go." I needed her to snap out of it.

"I need to warn Mia, my parents, everyone," said Claire, taking out her phone.

"We don't have time," I said, looking out of her window at the street. "Throw what you need in a bag."

I waited as she went into her room to pack. She rolled a large suitcase into the kitchen where I was going through the pantry. "What are you doing?" she asked.

"Getting anything we can use. We can't exactly go to the

grocery store. People will be looking for us everywhere. Besides, we don't want to infect anyone." I frantically loaded items into a box: candles, water bottles, duct tape. The internal clock in my head warned me that we had been there too long.

Once on the road, we headed north. We drove in silence. I checked the mirrors at least once every twenty seconds.

"Where are we going?" Claire demanded.

"North," I answered.

"North is not an answer."

A red pickup truck followed us ever since we started driving. He would alternate at least two, maybe three, cars back. I could see the driver was male with a black beard and sunglasses. I pulled into the right lane and slowed my speed to fifty-five mph. I waited. There was no sign of him. My heart pounded. A tail for sure. I eased down to fifty. The car behind us pulled within two feet from my bumper. Finally, the red truck whizzed past in the far lane.

"Hello? Jack? Hey!"

I glanced at Claire who was glaring my way. She was breathing heavily, nostrils flared.

"Oh, sorry, yeah."

"Son of a bitch, I feel like I'm being kidnapped!" she snapped.

"Calm down," I said in a shaky voice of my own. The red truck had unnerved me. "We're in this together. We just need to get away from people. The north part of the state isn't very populated."

"Who do you know there?"

"Nobody," I answered. "The last thing we want to do is go to someone's house we do know. Let's just get some distance between us and the city."

I pulled the car into the left lane and accelerated to seventy-five. Less than an hour later, mountains were visible on the horizon. The temperature was fifty-two, and we had another good two hours of daylight.

We drove through a handful of small towns. Some quaint and some dying at their core. I could sense Claire's anxiety. From the corner of my eye, I could see her rubbing her hands together and chewing the side of her mouth.

"Maybe we should go back," she said.

"We decided it's not safe," I answered.

"I don't remember deciding anything," she said. "This," she raked a hand through the air, "driving without a purpose—is not a plan."

We hit a dead zone between towns, a forgotten stretch of crumbling asphalt. For miles all we passed were dry fields, rusted trailers, and an abandoned service station. "I brought enough warm-weather gear and food for us to stay off the grid for a while. There's plenty of places out here to pitch a tent."

Claire's breathing became heavy. "Pitch a tent? You don't mean camping?"

"We can't exactly stay in a motel," I answered. "We're trying to avoid being seen. And avoid spreading whatever the hell this is."

I could see her hands begin to shake. "No," she said. I shot a glance in her direction. Her eyes were wild, shifting back and forth. "I'm not camping."

"We have limited options right now. Just a couple of—"

She forced her door open while the car was traveling at sixty miles per hour. "Claire, what the hell are you doing?"

"Let me out!" she screamed.

I slowed the car, pulling over beside a rusted, barbed wire fence. She jumped out before we came to a complete stop. "Are you crazy?"

I put the car in park and opened my door. Claire was already ten yards down the road. The air smelled of dry dust and manure. "Wait," I chased her down. "We don't have to camp." She didn't stop walking. Didn't turn around. "Did something happen to you while camping?"

She spun in my direction. "That's none of your damn business," she yelled. She turned back around and began walking away, faster than before.

I ran in front of her and put my hands out. "Hey, just take a breath. No camping, okay? There's nothing out here. Just get back in the car."

Her eyes welled. She stared across the hardpack field. "Then what?" Tears rolled down her face. "Then what?" she repeated, softer this time.

"We'll figure it out, together," I answered.

Claire looked at me and then to the empty road. I could see her hands still balled into fists, her nails dug into her palms. She said nothing. Eventually she walked slowly back to the car. She opened the door and sat back in the passenger seat.

We drove down the road again in silence. "There's all kinds of empty cabins further north," I finally said. "Second homes that are rarely used. We could watch one for a while. Once we're sure it's empty, we can hole up a few days to figure out a plan.

Claire nodded and murmured, "Okay. Sorry about that back there. It's just—" She didn't finish the thought.

"Don't worry. You don't have to tell me," I said.

"It's just the last time I went camping, I almost drowned. I got my foot stuck in this rock, and the current just kept coming... out of control... I felt so helpless... it—"

"Claire, really, you don't have to relive it." I could tell the memory rattled her.

She cleared her throat. "Anyway, Amy was the one who saved me. We were just kids. It was stupid and a long time ago. Nothing to dwell on these days."

"Sure," I agreed. But now our minds dwelled on everything. Our smallest fears were magnified. I wanted to say something else, but I could think of nothing helpful. We drove in silence for the next thirty minutes until we came within miles of Blairsville, Georgia.

"How about up there?" Claire pointed to some cabins perched on a ridge.

I shrugged. "I don't see any cars from here. Or any smoke from the chimneys. Let's have a closer look."

CHAPTER TWENTY

It was a steep, twisting road up to the homes. The first cabins we saw were fronted by massive oak and stone columns. They looked like ten thousand square feet of prime real estate. "Too expensive. These places probably have some kind of video surveillance," I said.

Further up, the road narrowed, becoming smaller and smaller until it was just a measly line of gravel. A small driveway on the hilltop bent away to a modest cabin. It wasn't in disrepair, but neither was it the grandeur of the ones below. We pulled over close to the drive to wait.

"How long is the stakeout?" asked Claire.

I shrugged. "What do you think?"

"Couple of hours. I don't see any cars under the port."

I nodded. "Couple of hours then."

We stared at the empty drive until the last bit of the sun sank below the mountains. It was quiet. A kind of quiet you didn't get in the city.

"Maybe we should just give up," Claire said.

"Come again?"

"Why fight it? We can't outrun this. You can't solve this," she answered.

She's right, you know. End of the road. "No," I said, as much to the voice as to her. "We can't."

She leaned back against the headrest. Her deep sigh cut through the quiet. "I'm tired, Jack."

"That's what you're supposed to feel. This virus is designed to make you feel tired. It's designed to make us want to give up." I let my window down, and the cool air seeped into the car. "One thing about Miles, he was the best at what he did. Yeah, he was secretive and a little strange, but when it came to this game, I mean science and virology, he was a genius. If anyone could design a virus to hijack your brain, he's the one."

Claire's eyes shut. "Comforting," she said.

"But see, he wouldn't design something he couldn't control. Miles had to know the antidote. He just ran out of time."

"And now we're on the clock," said Claire, looking out her window.

"But we have to keep fighting," I said. "We can't let the virus win."

She turned to me and reached out her hand. "Maybe you're right, Jack. Whatever is worming through our heads is going to work from the inside. From my counseling experience, it's not the monsters outside us that are the real threat—it's the ones already in our minds. This 'weapon' is likely to somehow use our own fears against us."

"So then, Claire, what are you fighting for?"

"Hmm, what am I fighting for?" she repeated in a whisper while looking out the window again. "My parents. After Amy died, I don't think they could take it if I was gone. They don't deserve that kind of heartbreak."

Outside, the last remaining light disappeared, and with it

the temperature dropped. I raised the window. "Tell me a happy memory of your parents?"

Her eyes opened. "Jack, I'm the therapist."

"Right," I answered, "then you know how this works. Can two thoughts occupy the same space at the same time? Negative and positive? Just try it."

"Fine. I guess the county fair when I was a kid."

"Go on."

"Well, I grew up in a small town outside of Macon, Georgia. No more than ten thousand. This county fair was big for Amy and me. My sister liked the funnel cake and the two-headed goat."

"Two-headed goat?"

"This was a while ago," Claire answered. "I liked the weird goat, and the rides, and the funnel cakes, but most of all I liked my dad to carry me on his shoulders. I was the shortest in the family, but on fair days I was taller than everyone. All day I felt like a princess parading around in the air. He didn't even complain when I dumped ice cream on his head. For about two weeks after fair days, Dad would walk with an obvious limp. The old witch, we called it." She laughed.

It felt good to hear her laugh, even if briefly. "The old witch?" I asked.

"That was the name I gave his right knee. He called it 'an old son of a bitch.' I thought he said 'old witch.' Turns out he got the old witch replaced six months later." Her eyes welled. "It always gets me—thinking of all that pain he must have been in but still refused to set me down."

The fact that her brain could still conjure a happy memory was a good sign. She stopped talking, and it was quiet again. I let the window down and strained to listen for any movement. Nothing. Just a faint rustle of leaves from the wind.

"What about you, Jack? Do you have a favorite memory of your father?"

My father. "Get help, damn you. You dumb little shit." His last words. Dying words breathed with venom and sweet breath. *Tell her how you let him die, Jack. She'll love this story.*

"Jack?"

"No," I answered. "I mean my father's dead."

"Oh, I'm sorry. Gosh, I should have known by your reaction. I'm usually better at this. Your mother then?"

My mother. The addict. Of course, there was a time she wasn't an addict. A time when I thought everything in the world would be right if it was just Mom and me. *Yeah, you really saved her, dumb little shit. Turns out you killed her too.*

"She's alive," I answered. "Favorite memory?" I tried to shift my thoughts from the years of dark memories. Domestic beatings, drugs, and broken promises filled my mind.

I could hear Claire ask softly, "Jack, you okay?"

I forced my thoughts back to a memory etched in my brain from long ago. One perfect memory, still untouched from the virus.

"I remember when," I said, trying to ignore flashes from old traumas, "Mom and I were alone for a week." I focused on a time when my mother's face wasn't weathered by lines from drug use or swollen from a fist. "We were coming back from visiting her mother when our Volvo broke down in Clarkesville, Arkansas. Quite a backward little town. The car repair was supposed to take a day, maybe two, but it was closer to five." My mind drifted to the townsfolk and the old mechanic's face, a man probably no older than forty but looked over sixty with thinning hair and a mouth caved in from no teeth. That mouth was wrinkled into a fixed point at the center—*like a cat's anus*, my eleven-year-old self told my mother. "Jack, that's awful," she scolded, then giggled like a teenager herself. "Going to be another day, folks," the wrinkled mouth would say each morning.

"This town had a fair too." I said. "True carnies. A scary bunch."

The faces of fair workers popped into my mind, one in particular—an older man with a nose misshapen by mounds of red humps. Rhinophyma, I'd later learn. *You can't leave until you try the darts,* he hissed in a voice stretched thin and tight. Wiry, gray hairs wormed their way from his ears and nostrils, and even from the center of his bulbous nose. *Lucky darts,* he hissed. Twenty dollars later I left with a Rubik's Cube missing a yellow sticker.

"We went to a movie one night," I said. "The town square had this historic theater with a balcony and stars on the ceiling."

I thought of the excitement in my mother's eyes when she looked up. *Honey, look. Stars.* Her face split into a wide grin. A perfect grin before my father's fist punched her right canine loose.

"*Crimson Tide*," I said, still remembering the movie. "Walking back from the square, we passed rows of caged roosters. My mother said they must be cock fighting. We took turns giving roosters their ring names: Spike, Thunder, El Nino. On our last night in Clarkesville, we drank Moosehead beer."

The bitterness of the drink had shocked me, but I forced it down my throat. This is what grownups drink, I told myself. What irony, I thought. I tried to hold on to positive thoughts, but my mind drifted. Alcohol sure screwed up my family. I knew the flame of evil was already there, but alcohol was the great accelerant.

"Jack?"

"Uh, yeah?"

"You okay? It looks like you went somewhere else there for a minute."

"Oh, yeah, fine," I lied. "Well, by far the best part of Clarkesville was that there was no old man. No screaming. No fist. No fear. Just the two of us."

"It's a nice story, Jack," Claire said softly, her eyes closed again.

An image of my mother with her head in a toilet bowl entered my brain. Her unkempt gray hair falling forward, collecting toilet water and chunks of vomit. "Jack, this is my life... my miserable life," she complained. More than a decade of using had aged her at least thirty years. Her once smooth face was like a road map of bad decisions. It was full of countless wrinkles, little scabs, and jagged cuts. The same bright eyes that looked at the stars on the theater ceiling were now flat and sad. They pleaded for help but never accepted any.

In truth, I'd given up and said goodbye to my mother years ago. The woman who raised me, the woman I loved, wasn't coming back. I wasn't fighting for her. At this point, I knew it was Claire who kept me going. Something was pulling me to her. I'd only known her for a few weeks, but it seemed like years. Was it the virus? No, it only destroyed life. I wanted to protect her. "Claire?"

"Hmm?" she answered.

Go ahead and tell her how you feel, Jack. My hands cupped my ears, thinking it may actually muffle the voice inside my head. *Save her? Don't you mean kill her, like you did your old man?*

"What is it?" she asked, staring at me now.

"Nothing. I think it's probably safe to go in now. You agree?"

"As safe as breaking into another person's home can ever be, I guess," she answered.

CHAPTER TWENTY-ONE

I pulled into the gravel drive of the cabin and out of sight from the road. We crept to the back of the house, stopping every few steps to listen. Our only source of light was from a half moon. We walked up three stairs to a side door on a small porch. We paused. I heard leaves rustle from the wind, Claire breathing, and the distant sound of an owl but otherwise silence. "What now?" she asked.

I reached my hand onto a flat ledge above the door frame. I blindly ran it across, pushing dust and breaking spider webs.

"What are you doing?" Claire whispered.

I felt the side of my hand push something to the ground. A pinging sound followed like a hammer hitting a nail. "What was that?" she asked.

"A key, I hope," I whispered.

We both knelt down in the dark to feel the wood floor. My hands ran over some loose rocks.

"Maybe it was this?" Claire held up an old, bent screw.

I shrugged. "Probably." I looked beyond the door stoop to the gravel below. It was too dark to see. Taking my phone from my pocket, I walked off the porch and shined its light onto the ground below.

"Jack, what are you doing?"

"I just have to be sure," I whispered back. I ran the light behind and under the small porch. I saw dirt, rocks, an old beer bottle, and the stub of a cigar. Aha, something reflected in the light—only a beer cap. I was about to give up when I saw a brass key on the rocks with its teeth in the air. I bent to pick it up, then heard something directly behind me. I snapped back. The crown of my head smashed into something hard.

"Ohhee, what the hell, Jack!"

I spun around to find Claire holding her chin in both hands. "Oh, sorry, Claire. You scared the shit out of me. You okay?" There was no need to keep whispering.

She swept a few fingers into her mouth then examined the blood on them. "I bit my tongue."

"Dang, sorry. I'm on edge." I looked down at the key in my hand. "I did find this, though," I said, holding it up.

She nodded, still looking at her fingers. "Was it just out here in the gravel?"

"I think it's a key I pushed off the ledge over the door."

Claire lowered her bloody hand. "Well, let's go in then."

The key slid in the hole easily enough but got stuck in the turn. After the third attempt, I was able to swing the door open. The cabin was dark and smelled of earth and stone. I blindly felt the wall until my hand hit a light switch. I flipped it on. The space was cold and still. I had a sense it had been empty for some time.

I scanned the main room. There was a large stone fireplace with kindling bundled nearby. A dried hide with war horses around a colored sun was stretched on a wall. It looked like an old piece of Native American art. Heavy pots and pans hung over a butcher's table in the kitchen.

"I'm going to wash up," Claire said.

I nodded. "I'll have a look around." I turned another light on in a bare hallway. I went down the hall to the first bedroom. In the center of the room was a queen bed covered by a quilt with a bold turquoise, red, and yellow print. Over it were two spears. They had crude flint tips. Colorful feathers hung from their long wooden shafts. A small bathroom was tucked away in the corner of the room. Its counter was bare except for a bottle of Listerine, a quarter full. There was very little in the bedroom closet: a vacuum, a flannel shirt, a blanket, and a spare pillow.

I took a look in a second smaller bedroom. A twin bed was pushed against the wall. On the wall hung a heavy glass frame containing a collection of old arrowheads. A hatchet with a sharp iron edge was mounted beside it. On the opposite wall hung a white stone that had been chiseled to a crude point. It was bound to a painted wooden handle by thin leather straps.

"Jack?"

I heard the door to the hall bath shut. "Yeah?"

"Everything okay?" Claire asked, standing in the hall.

I could see she had pulled her hair back. "Yep, looks empty. How's the tongue?"

"I'll live. I hate the taste of blood, though." She stuck out her tongue. I could see a small cut in its center slowly oozing blood. She swallowed. "Nothing like that iron taste."

"Sorry," I said, apologizing again.

"Really, Jack, I'll live." She turned back to the main room. "What now?"

"It's cold in here," I answered. "Maybe we should make a fire."

"You think that's a good idea?"

I shrugged. "I don't know, but I saw some stacked wood under the carport." I walked outside to the woodpile I saw earlier. It looked mature and dry, good burning wood. I unloaded two bundles beside the fireplace, then reached up to find an open flue, which powdered my hand with soot. I used a long-handled lighter on the mantle to light it. After it took, I pushed my body close to the flames. The heat brought some life to the cold, stagnant air.

"Nice job," Claire said. I turned around to face her. "Cupboards are pretty bare. I did find this," she held up a bottle of red wine. "Don't suppose this can spoil. Should we?"

"Absolutely, they already have us on a B and E here." Claire cocked her head. "Breaking and entering," I said.

"Oh, right," she answered.

I took the wine from her while she sat on the couch by the fire. "Are you hungry?" I asked while opening the wine. "I have some canned food in the car."

"Too tired to eat," she answered. I brought her a full wine glass and placed mine on an end table. She held her glass in the air. "To staying out of jail," she said.

And the morgue, I thought, reaching for my glass. "To a cure," I answered, and our glasses clicked. The wine was more sweet than bitter. It smoothly slid down my throat. We listened in silence to the crackling fire.

"Is this a date, Jack?" Claire joked.

"Weirdest date I've ever been on," I answered.

"That is true," she said and ran her finger once more over her tongue. She inspected it in the air.

"Still bleeding?"

"Just a little. Enough to ruin what's probably a nice bottle." She leaned closer to me, resting her head against my shoulder. "You know, Jack," she said, still watching the fire, "I wish we met before all this." She took another sip of wine. "I mean before the virus. I feel like a broken version of myself."

Her hair smelled fresh against my shoulder. "Me too," I answered.

"You really think you can fix us?"

There is no fix, just a slow death. I ignored the dark thought. "Yes, I just need time to think. And access to a computer."

"It feels safer with you," she said.

Her eyes were closed, her lips slightly parted. Any other time in my life I would try and kiss her perfect lips, even long for a full night of passion. But she was right—we were broken. My body ached in every joint. My head felt squeezed. Inside it, a sinister voice poisoned my thoughts.

Claire drifted to sleep. I watched the embers glow in the fire. No longer did it have a flame. I could feel myself fading off to sleep. I dreamed of a field of tall grass by a river. The sky above was an open blue. The river was a dark-brown color, full of fast-moving mud and silt. Claire was on the other side. I yelled to her, but my voice wouldn't make it across. I watched as she walked slowly, but deliberately, from the far bank. The water covered her shins, then her knees. Soon it was to her waist and pulled her under. I tried to reach her, but a force held me back.

The force pushed my head into the water. Cold silt filled my mouth. I pulled my head out and gulped the air. On the surface of the muddy water, I saw the blurred face of a man behind me. The steel-edged hatchet gleamed in his right hand. He forced my head under again. Floating chunks of large gravel entered my mouth. No matter how hard I tried, I couldn't stop the dirty water from pouring into my throat. The water was thick enough to chew. And chew I did.

CHAPTER TWENTY-TWO

FOX

Fox felt pressure from teeth pinching into his leather gloves. It didn't hurt, but he didn't want to deal with a human bite either. Too much risk of a nasty infection. He needed the man to calm down. Too much noise had been made already.

"I'm going to take my hand off your mouth. I'm not here to hurt you," he said. Fox had to fight the instinct to slide up the man's face and pluck out an eye. The first time Fox enucleated an eyeball, he was shocked by its simplicity. It slid out of its socket like a pea from a pod. Once an enemy lost an eyeball, they were easy prey—disorientation and panic set in, giving Fox plenty of time to finish them off. But he needed this man whole. In fact, he needed this man at his best.

Fox removed the gloved hand from the mouth. The man breathed heavily.

"Who the fuck are you?" Jack panted.

"Relax, name's Fox." He noted the woman was gone. He was sure she had gone to get a weapon. He was equally sure she was not a threat. Seconds later he could hear a nervous shuffle behind him. She must be working up the nerve to use it, he thought. Fox kept his eye on Jack sitting on the couch while swinging his hand backward. It collided into the woman's outstretched arms. She let out a short cry, and something rattled to the ground.

"What the hell was that?" Jack asked.

Fox glanced to assess the situation. The woman stood shaking and rubbing her hands. A handgun lay on the ground. From the looks of it, a .45. "Gun," he answered.

"I thought you said you weren't going to hurt us," said Jack.

"I'm not," he answered. Fox's own piece was still tucked in the small of his back. "Not mine."

"Then whose gun is it?" asked Jack.

"Mine," Claire answered, her voice shaking.

"Claire, what are you doing with a gun?" Jack asked, his voice also cracking.

Claire stood silent, rubbing her hands together. Her eyes scanned the room, darting wildly from side to side. Fox had been in enough tense situations to know these two were unraveling.

"I'm not here to hurt you," Fox repeated. "Why don't you sit down?" he asked Claire.

She stood frozen in place, eyes roaming wildly.

"Then why are you here?" asked Jack.

Fox walked around and sat in an empty chair. He took off his gloves and placed his bare hands on his knees, trying his best not to look like a threat. "In truth, I was sent here to eliminate you."

One of them let out a short, high-pitched squeak.

"But?" asked Jack.

"But I got infected," Fox answered.

The woman's rigid posture softened.

"Now, I want to help you," he continued. "I need to help you."

Jack rubbed his neck. "And how are you going to do that exactly, by suffocating us?"

Fox could feel his patience waning. "If I wanted you dead, you both would be cold already. We," he calmly eyed them both, "need to help each other."

Jack stood up and began to pace. "And how do you plan on helping us?"

"For starters, by keeping you alive," Fox answered. "I'm only one of a team assembled to tie up loose ends."

"Loose ends?" Claire asked in a quivering voice.

"Anyone presumed infected by the virus. They want them gone to neutralize the threat. Ultimately, to bury its existence. So I keep you alive, and you keep me alive."

"Who are these other loose ends?" Claire asked.

Fox didn't need her even more panicked. If he told her the truth—her friends and family—she was sure to shut down. "Let's focus on you two right now. Tracking you was easy." And it was damn easy. Not only had one of them left a digital trail, they took a known car. They were loud and sloppy. Even the weakest member of Fox's team would have no trouble finding them. "Can you cure this thing?" Fox asked.

"I don't know... no... yes... maybe," answered Jack.

"Jack, I thought you said—"

"I need things," Jack said, cutting Claire off. "I would need my notes back, need access again to the lab. Also a computer with a decent internet connection."

"I can get you those things," Fox answered.

Jack sat down and let out a heavy sigh. "Really," he said, more a skeptical statement than a question.

"First we have to leave this place," answered Fox. "I've got your data with me and know of a safe place a few hours from here with a secure internet connection."

"Tonight?" asked Claire.

Fox nodded. The woman looked tired and frightened. "You two are safe from my team for a little while. Actually, the next couple of days may be the safest you're going to be. The colonel, my contact, will think you two are dead. Once I don't report, though, he'll know the truth."

"So we are safe? For now, anyway?" asked Jack.

Fox looked at the stretched hide on the wall. "I'm assuming this cabin choice was random?" He didn't wait for an answer. "So we have no idea when, or if, the owner will show up. From the looks of the old Indian war weapons, this guy seems like someone who may want to mix it up." Before he had subdued Jack on the couch, Fox had a look around the place. He concluded the owner was an old man with a penchant for weapons and outdoor living. A man like that wouldn't surrender his cabin easily. "We don't need another dead body."

"Another dead body?" asked Claire.

Fox ignored the question. His mind was executing their departure. "We scrub the place. Take any essentials. We can take your car as far as down the hill, but we need to ditch it. We'll take my truck to a safe house two hours from here." Fox had spent the better part of a decade working on his safe house. Most of it he had constructed himself. Other parts he hired out to random workers, drifters. Never the same man twice. He surveyed the few workers to make sure they had left the area, kept drifting. He could think of only one man who knew of the place.

Fox had been a weapon of the US military for years. He knew most of his actions were off the books. Fox was under no illusion that his superiors would protect him. In fact, in the event of a scandal, he would be dismembered, left alone to take the blame. So the safe house was a natural product of his survival instinct. Even though he would never show it, until today, Fox was proud of his work. The place was off the grid. It ran on solar power, a massive generator powered by natural gas, and a smaller one by petrol. Any connection to the outside world was secure and encrypted. There was a weapons safe, a panic room, and enough provisions to last twenty-eight months. Its land was fertile and supported all manner of crops. Water was pumped from a deep well. Through the years, Fox had purchased the surrounding acreage using different identities. It was a place where he could hide from the world. If, by some rare chance, Fox made it to a ripe retirement age, he may live out his last days there in peace.

"Where are you taking us?" Claire asked.

No one knew of his safe house, and Fox wasn't going to divulge it tonight. In fact, he was still debating on whether to blindfold these two. "You will know when we get there," he answered.

"What about that?" Jack asked, pointing to the .45 on the floor.

"That's mine," Claire snapped.

"That gun belongs to Miles," Jack answered.

"Miles is dead," she said. "I need the gun."

"Why? So you can shoot someone? Maybe yourself?"

Claire reached over and picked the gun off the floor. "You're not taking this from me," she said, shaking it in the air.

Fox thought for a moment that she may point it at Jack, maybe even both of them. Fox had been focused on protecting them from outside threats. The fact that there was a deadly virus already killing them internally factored less into his immediate plans. Fox had remembered the desperate recordings of the last days of Patient Zero, Miles Chambers. It was true the virus was to be feared as much, or more, than the colonel and his team of assassins. But Fox needed to gain their trust. He wasn't sure of the mental state of either of them, but he had to trust them. "Let her keep the weapon for now," he said. "We need all the protection we can get."

CHAPTER TWENTY-THREE

COLONEL STINE

Stine worked from home for the fourth day in a row, which was fine by him. Most of what he had to accomplish didn't call for an in-person dialogue. He brought a second cup of coffee to the back of his house, to what used to be called the sunroom.

The addition was the idea of his second ex-wife, the plant enthusiast. It faced east and took the full brunt of the sun's rays, scorching by noon. But it was still early, 0700. The room's floor was a laminate in the style of a rich hardwood. The windows were double panes on every wall, including most of the ceiling. The room was once full of exotic plants and teeming with life, including two green parakeets. Stine hadn't realized how high maintenance the room had been until Loraine left. It took four short weeks for every living plant to die and for him to release the parakeets to the outside air.

Now he had nothing to maintain. The space was simple—a desk facing the woods, two large leather chairs, and faux wood. A good room for the dogs. One easy swipe of the laminate floor to wipe clean any pile of canine piss or worse. Stine sipped his black coffee and focused his thoughts. The glass room, he now called it, was one of the few spaces in the house where he felt comfortable. Every other angle in the home reminded him he lived alone in a typical suburban neighborhood complete with PTA moms and HOA fees.

Stine knew he should move somewhere more fitting for a single man. But staying put was a rare luxury for a military man. And he found the occasional peace in the glass room. His dogs, two muscled rottweilers, patiently waited by the door. Smith and Wesson, ages two and three, had been the topic of more than one HOA conversation. This was an irritant to Stine, seeing how his dogs had been nothing but obedient. He knew a different choice of breed, say golden retrievers or even Yorkies, would have gone a long way toward putting his neighbors at ease. Hell, even naming his dogs something like Max and Sammy, instead of Smith and Wesson, would have sat better with the suburbanites. But that wasn't Stine. Once Loraine left, the place settled into what he was, namely a soldier. Smith and Wesson, like most things in his life, were controlled weapons ready to be deployed at his command.

The colonel glanced at the secure message he received from Fox about six hours earlier: "Both threats have been neutralized. Mr. Clean." Good, Stine thought. Maybe they still had a chance to corner and kill this thing. The message from Fox was generic enough to withstand any outside eyes. They could be talking about the threat of a bad tuna salad, for all anyone knew. But to Stine the code was clear: Jack Baker and Claire Long were dead and disposed of in standard fashion. Neutralized, eliminated, killed—whatever the term, it was a concept he was comfortable with. A kill was clean, a finished product, predictable. Working with this virus was anything but that.

The colonel knew little about viruses. He never trusted the word. A virus always seemed like some bullshit answer a doctor would say when they didn't know the cause of something. Now it was a primary weapon under his command. Only it was unpredictable, messy, and a total mystery to Stine. The worst part, by far, was that the weapon was accidentally deployed before the antidote was finished. The scientists, with the exception of Miles, possessed only a partial knowledge of the project. Not only had Miles Chambers had a full understanding of the operation, but he was their most capable asset. With him gone, chances of finding an antidote before an unacceptable rate of viral contamination was not good.

Stine would put his trust in what he knew: killing the enemy. In this case the enemy, the virus, had been attached to Jack and Claire. Their elimination was a good start but only the beginning. Like any malignancy, the margins had to be cut clean, which would require a wider net. Even Fox would likely have to be in that net.

Casualties were the reality of any operation. He didn't even know how high in command this operation reached. The fact that Stine received his orders from an anonymous source made it likely that in the event the operation failed he, too, would be a casualty.

Stine opened the door to let out Smith and Wesson. He watched as the dogs chased each other around the fenced yard. Smith stopped short of the fence and began to claw. "Quit your damn digging!" he yelled. The dog released his nails from the dirt.

Wesson stopped and cocked his head at a noise in the woods. Stine had high fencing installed on either side of the yard to block his neighbors' view. Behind him was a long stretch of untamed woods, so he kept that fencing low. Wesson let out a guttural growl followed by a deep, full-throated bark.

Stine followed the dog's gaze into the woods. "What's out there, Boy?"

He tucked the phone with the encrypted message from Fox back in his pocket. It was unfortunate Fox would likely be eliminated at the operation's end. Stine knew Fox would be considered a loose end, and the order would be handed down. He didn't feel great about a loyal soldier like Fox being terminated.

Stine sipped his black coffee, now lukewarm. In a rare moment, he reflected on his thoughts. He felt for Fox. His two ex-wives had agreed on one thing: Stine didn't feel anything. But that wasn't true, he thought. He felt hunger and pain like any man. He felt cold and hot, and now he felt disappointment for Fox. It was odd that Stine, being emotionally detached, was now in charge of a virus that primarily targeted feelings. Maybe it was because the weapon—the virus—like Stine, destroyed and perverted the feelings of its victims.

"Get out of there!" Wesson and Smith had now both decided to dig. Stine turned the hose on them. They were obedient dogs, but he preferred to discipline them at a distance if possible. The colonel had seen too many good men come close to losing an arm by surprising a dog at the wrong time. The dogs stopped digging and snapped their white fangs at the incoming water.

He killed the hose. "Down!" Stine yelled. The dogs obeyed, crouching on all fours. He then let them back in the glass room where he spread an old blanket out for the dogs to dry. The time was early, but still Stine was itching for a shot of bourbon. The next few days would be unpleasant. They would need to trace, and eliminate, all known recent contacts for Baker and Long. The longer the list, the harder it would be to keep it quiet. After that round would come the termination of the terminators. That was an unpleasant reality of any operation with this level of exposure. That round of elimination would likely include Fox, most of his team, and any other people in the know. The thought of Stuart and his lackey being killed was a bright spot for Stine. In fact, that may be an indulgence he saw personally.

CHAPTER TWENTY-FOUR

CLAIRE

The blindfold smelled like gas. Two hours ago I had my hand on a glass of wine and my head on Jack's chest. Things were far from perfect, but I had Jack, and I had the gun. The .45 was my way out. An indelicate exit of this new cruel world to be sure, but an exit nevertheless. I squeezed Jack's hand tightly.

"You okay?" he whispered.

The question almost made me laugh. I was blindfolded, being tortured by a weaponized virus, and carted off to an unknown location. But I wasn't alone. Jack was in the same position.

"I guess," I answered. The gas smell made me nauseous. Was he going to ditch our bodies and burn us? "Smells like gas," I said, louder than I intended.

"Yeah, sorry about that," Fox answered. "That's for the generators. I only have so much natural gas."

We took a sharp turn, and my body leaned into Jack, close enough to feel his warm breath on my cheek. It was slow and steady. Was he not worried?

"We're only about an hour away now," Fox said. "Sorry about the blindfolds. No one knows where this place is exactly. It's better for you this way."

"We understand," Jack said.

I started to say something, but nothing came out. No one knows where we are. That's good, Claire. Unless, of course, something goes wrong. I was tired but couldn't sleep. The motion of the car, especially when blinded, was making me nauseous. I fought against an urge to vomit. I fought against outright panic. My body was on the edge of a full-blown anxiety attack. I pressed against Jack, trying to absorb some of his apparent calmness. I could feel his steady breathing, his rhythmic heartbeat. If only I had the gun, I thought. That helped keep me calm.

I felt the car climb. The incline made the engine whine. Hard turns slung my body from left to right. My ears popped. My mouth watered, and I felt moments away from being sick. I bit my lip in frustration. "Can you pull over?" I asked. "I think I'm going to be sick."

The driver said nothing. I felt out of control. What time was it? Where the hell were we? Who the hell was Fox, anyway? A flood of adrenaline and nausea came over me. I shook. This was bullshit. This guy Fox was scary, but I didn't care what happened to me—this blindfold was coming off. I pushed it off my head.

The dashboard lights lit the figure of Fox. His cleanly shaved head was an odd blue shade in the panel of lights. It was the same head I held a .45 against just hours ago. "No worries," he said, still staring at the road. His head rotated on his thick neck just far enough to glance at me. "We're close enough now." His large hands squeezed the steering wheel, causing a series of muscles in his forearms to bulge. "You can take your blind off too, Jack." The car eased off the road to a turnout. "You need a moment?" Fox asked.

I sprung the car door open, jumping out to the cool night. I breathed the outside air. This was better. Out of the blindfold, away from the gas, and free to run. Clouds covered the half moon. I had no food, no water, a thin jacket, and no cell service. I looked at Jack, who was still seated in the back of the car. His blindfold was off, but he hadn't moved. Fox was in the same spot behind the wheel, looking in his side mirror with his square jaw clenched.

"You coming out, Jack?" I asked. I studied Fox. His eyes were narrow and cold above high cheekbones. A jagged scar ran just outside one eye all the way down to his jaw. The face of a killer. If he wanted me dead, I'd be dead. He's infected; he needs us. Well, he needs Jack, I thought. I am expendable. "Jack?"

"Only about fifteen from here," Fox answered. "You two can leave the blinds off now."

"I'm good," Jack answered. "Take as much time as you need."

I sucked in the crisp air. The nausea subsided, some. My joints still ached as did my head, which was the same for days. I stared into the dark woods. I wouldn't make it for a day out there. In the car an assassin waited. I could say the same about the inside of my head. I was out of options. "Can I have my gun back?" I asked.

"You don't need it," Fox answered.

I'm a grown woman, and that's my fucking gun, I thought but said nothing. The way he answered, he wasn't going to argue. I took one last look into the dark woods. "Okay, let's go."

I climbed in the back seat. This time, despite the cold air, I cracked the window. The next ten minutes were sharp turns and rolling hills. The only light outside was from our own car. A clock on the console read 2:30 in blue light.

Fox pulled off the road into a gravel lot and to a stop. He jerked the emergency break up. "It's the Kubota from here," he said, hopping out of the car.

Alone with Jack in the back seat, I asked, "What's a Kubota?"

"No idea. I just hope it doesn't hurt," he answered.

"Hurt?"

"I'm kidding," he answered.

Fox walked in front of the car's headlights to a corrugated metal shed. It was about the size of a two-car garage and tucked tight in the woods, like a section of the forest had been sliced out for that very purpose. Tree limbs reached over the roof and grew into one another. We waited while Fox unlocked it, then pulled its large front open. The headlights hit the entrance at a side angle, showing only a black void. Fox disappeared into its mouth.

"Should we go in?" I asked. Jack said nothing. Fox had accomplished one thing, I thought: I had no idea where we were. Less than a minute later, an engine started. A four-wheel vehicle with a hardtop pulled out.

"Go ahead and throw your gear in the back," Fox yelled out. "Need the four-wheeler from here."

We loaded up the open back of the four-wheeler. The vehicle wasn't big but looked like it could drive over almost anything. The four-wheeler's body was wrapped in a camouflage pattern and lifted high off the ground. The tires were thick and had deep treads. Jack threw our bags in the back next to a rifle and three jugs of gas. A crossbow was tucked just behind the driver's seat.

Fox pulled the door to the shed closed while we waited in the four-wheeler. I sat in the middle of the bench seat. Fox's heavy frame to my left and Jack to my right. We drove down a dirt road full of potholes and overhanging tree limbs. There was little space on the road and less for my body. I felt closed in. Not having my phone made me feel even more trapped. My claustrophobia only intensified the further we cut into the dense woods.

"How much further?" I yelled, louder than I intended.

"Not far now," Fox answered. The headlights gave little warning of what was ahead. Fox narrowly dodged holes in the ground, deep enough to flip us. A few more blind turns, and we stopped just short of an iron gate. Fox got out and punched in a code. On either side of the gate was a stone wall, a few heads taller than Fox. We waited as the gate inched open. I followed the stone wall as far as I could see until losing it in the darkness.

"How long is this wall?" I asked.

"Surrounds the entire property," Fox answered. "No one is coming in this place."

"Or out," I said as we drove through. My chest and throat tightened. I suddenly felt like I couldn't get enough air. "I can't do this. I can't stay here."

"Claire, we're safe here," Jack said.

The iron gate slowly closed behind us. I heard it lock into place. It felt like the bars to a prison cell. "Let me out." My heart raced, thumping in my ears. "Fox, let me out."

"There's nothing good out there," he answered. "It's 3:30 in the morning and pitch black."

It felt like someone was on top of me, pinning my shoulders to the ground. "I'm serious!" Jack put his hands out to calm me, and I swatted them away.

"Code is 38406," Fox said. "There's more than the colonel's men out there that can kill you."

I pushed Jack off the seat so I could climb out. I walked to the gate and found the box. I blindly punched a number, and the screen illuminated. I entered the code. Once again, the iron gate began to swing.

"Come on, Claire," Jack said behind me. "You don't know where you're going."

I heard him walking to me from behind. The gate was almost fully open. I could see nothing ahead, just the narrow road to darkness.

"Stay tonight and get some rest. If you feel the same way in the morning, I'll go with you," Jack said.

I looked at the dirt road ending in blackness. Another opportunity to escape into the woods. But escape to what? The open gate did allow my throat to open up. I took a few gulps of air. I wasn't leaving Jack. At least I had the code. Maybe I could find the gun later.

"Okay, I'll stay tonight," I said, still facing the road out.

I walked with Jack back to the four-wheeler. It was a short drive up a moderate grade to the cabin. Two sensor lights came on as we came to the front. There was a large covered porch that wrapped around the side of the house. A stacked stone fireplace rose in the home's center. Fox walked up the stairs and unlocked a heavy oak door in the front. He went inside and began turning on the lights.

"I guess we go in?" asked Jack.

"We're not staying out here," I answered. We grabbed our bags out of the back of the four-wheeler and walked up the front steps to the open door.

Inside was a warm wood tone. The floor plan was open with plenty of windows. A second fireplace made of round river rock was centered on the back wall. Large wooden beams accented the ceiling in parallel rows.

I sat my bags down and walked left into the kitchen. The appliances were a shining stainless steel, and the cabinets a light, natural wood. I ran my hand over a middle island.

"You like it?" asked Fox.

The countertops were covered in a gray granite with stunning veins of gold scattered throughout. "I love these."

Fox laughed, deep like thunder. "I'm not quite the savage you thought, huh?"

I took my hand off the counter and looked at him. The scar down his face formed a giant keloid, thick and raised from his temple to his jaw. His predatory eyes studied me. He stood a full foot over me, with shoulders twice as broad as my own. I tried to smile, even laugh, but couldn't.

"Where should we put our bags?" Jack asked.

"There's a guest bedroom to your right," Fox said.

Jack nodded. "Just two bedrooms?"

"Yep, one more than I usually need," Fox answered.

I walked in the living room in front of the large fireplace of river rock. Inside was clean. If it had ever been used, it was some time ago.

"What's back here?" Jack asked. He thumped on a wall, which made a hollow noise.

"Four inches of reinforced steel," answered Fox. "Some people call it a panic room. Complete with separate provisions, ventilation, bathroom, and a generator. Even a bunk bed."

"Is that door one piece?" Jack asked.

"Yep. And all four sides are welded together. Probably weighs as much as the entire house," said Fox. "That steel box will be here hundreds of years from now. It was installed before any of the rest of the house. Don't think a crane is coming back here ever again."

Jack stood looking at the wall. A small number box was next to it, similar to the one at the front gate. "Same code?" he asked.

Fox shook his head. "No. Let's hope we don't ever need to go in. But I've got plenty of weapons stashed in there if we do."

"How long did it take you to build this place?" asked Jack.

Fox's eyes shifted as if he were calculating. "Too long. I spent over two years just on the outside wall." Fox rubbed his eyes, then ran his hand over his bald head. "You've got some extra blankets in the back closet. Take what you want from the kitchen. I'm going to get some rest."

"Wait," I said. "I haven't been able to reach my friend Mia. I have to warn her."

"It may be too risky," Jack said.

I wasn't going to let Mia be some kind of sitting duck to a military operation that was "tying up loose ends." I opened my mouth to tell Jack as much when Fox spoke first.

"It's okay. I have a couple of virgins here and blank SIMs," answered Fox.

"Virgins?" asked Jack.

"Phones never used. They're safe."

Fox walked to the other room. "What did you think he was talking about?" I asked Jack.

Before he could answer, Fox returned with a phone.

"When do you think this colonel will come looking for us?" I asked.

"Couple of days, most likely," Fox answered. "The less Mia knows the better. Just tell her to lay low. Maybe get out of town for a while."

The less she knows. I wasn't sure she would believe me anyway. There is a virus making people crazy which was created in secret by our own military. Oh, and by the way, there is no cure. Did I mention they may be trying to kill those infected?

"You can dial straight out," Fox said.

I punched in her number and listened to it ring. I pictured Mia asleep. Her phone was probably in the other room or on silent. Ever since one of her patients got her number, she had been careful not to pick up unknown callers. Come on—nothing.

"I'll try in the morning. Maybe I'll call the office."

Fox took the phone. "Try and get some sleep. This place is safe."

Jack came out of the spare bedroom carrying a pillow and blanket. "I'll take the couch," he said.

Fox had already disappeared to the other room. I didn't want to be too forward, but I didn't want to be alone. What would he think if I wanted him in the room? Would he think I wanted to do more than sleep? Would that be so bad? My body felt wrecked. It was hard to imagine ever feeling good again. It was hard to imagine wanting to feel someone's skin again.

"Jack, why don't you stay in the bedroom?"

"I'm not letting you take the couch out here," he answered, tossing the blanket down.

"It's okay. I don't bite." Ugh, that was a cheesy line. I wish it was two months ago. Or better yet five months ago. Back when Amy was Amy, carefree and laughing too loud at everything. When my only worries were my sick patients. Now I was coaxing a man I'd known less than a few weeks into a bedroom. For what? Sleep? Companionship? Protection?

"Good to know," Jack said, bringing the pillow and blanket back into the room. "If I snore you have my permission to elbow me gently in the ribs."

"Good to know," I said. I had just enough energy left to find my toothbrush, brush my teeth, and wash my face. I crawled under the sheets with my pajamas on. I drifted off to sleep while wondering what to do if Jack reached out to touch me.

CHAPTER TWENTY-FIVE

JACK

You're not making it out of here. The voice in my head woke me. Only it was now distinctly my father's voice. I looked next to me to see Claire still sleeping. She looked peaceful. I hoped she felt some peace. The world as I knew it was turning from gray to black. This woman was the only bright spot. *You think you're going to protect her, like you did your mother?* Mocked my father's voice.

I watched her chest slowly rise with each breath. I tried to stay still. At the moment, she looked perfect. Her angelic face even had the hint of a smile. *I think you should kill her, like you did me. End her suffering. Hell, killing may be the only thing you ever did worthy of respect.* I curled my pillow around my ears and pressed, trying to will the voice away.

It's not real; it's this damn virus. Why did Miles have to be so fucking good at his job? This virus, this thing, is only doing what it's designed to do. I thought of his notes. This was the perfect storm in the brain. Depression, anxiety, and eventual psychosis. *It's going to get worse, little Jack. Dumb little shit. End it. End her, Killer. Hell, you may be my son, after all.* I squeezed the pillow against my ears again in desperation. "No, No."

"Jack?"

I released the pillow, opened my eyes, and saw Claire looking at me. "Oh, sorry, I think I was having a nightmare."

"You didn't look like you were asleep," she said.

"Well a daymare then."

"Daymare?"

"Um, nightmare during the day," I answered. My dad's voice laughed.

Claire brushed her hair back from her face with her hands. "Right, I guess this whole thing is a daymare."

I lay back again and shut my eyes. *She's amazing, Jack. And her hopes are in you?* My father's voice laughed until he wheezed and coughed. *Funny, the country's fate, the world's fate, in your hands.* Another wheeze. *A born loser.* "Fuck you," I said into the air.

"Excuse me?"

"Oh, sorry, not you," I answered. A small crease formed between her brows. "It's just," I hesitated. *I'm a killer, Claire,* the voice finished. "It's my father," I answered. I waited. There was silence in my head. Maybe this was how to shut him up, I thought. My father was a coward. If I called him out, he would hide. "I need to tell you something I've never told anyone."

She nodded.

I then proceeded to tell Claire things I'd kept silent since I was twelve—namely, how I found my father dying. Then how my mother blamed herself. I left out a key detail: I didn't just stumble on my father dying. I left him for dead. At the time, an act I thought would save my mother. Save us both.

Recounting the story out loud, I could almost smell the blood and rain from that night. When I finished, there was silence. Claire had not spoken since I began the story. Neither had my father's voice. It was working. Just call him out. But it was my father's voice that broke the silence. *That's my boy*, he laughed. *Keeping the juiciest parts to himself.* I cupped my ears and closed my eyes. I wasn't sure how much more of this I could take.

"Did you hear me, Jack?"

I took my hands off my ears and opened my eyes. "What?"

"You're not a killer," she said.

"What? How did you—"

"Jack, I've been doing this a long time. I'm not an expert in many areas of mental health, but cognitive reframing is one of my strong suits. When I said our brains would use our worst fears against us, I meant it."

"Yeah, but how did you know that—"

"I've counseled some difficult patients. True, psychosis is not something I counsel regularly. But there can be delusional thinking in severe depression, bipolar disorder, and acute stressful events—all of which I see plenty."

I felt a weight being lifted. But still, I felt I needed to say it. "My father, I, um, left him to—"

"It doesn't matter, Jack," she cut me off again. "You were just a child."

I nodded and braced myself for my father's voice.

"You're a good man," she said.

I listened. Tried to believe her.

"I'll tell you something else." She put a hand on my shoulder. "You are nothing like him."

Bullshit, his voice said.

Claire bent her head down to look me in the eye. "It's true."

I lay down on the bed, head on the pillow. Claire's voice was like an angel talking. I was shocked how much those words meant. Words I had no idea how much I needed to hear.

"Jack?"

"Uh-huh," I answered, still lying flat.

"I've got some pills I took from Miles's medicine cabinet upstairs."

"Oh no, Claire." I sat up. "Listen, we're going to get out of this. We can still find a cure. We don't have to—"

"Jack, I'm not talking about hurting myself. The pills are clozapine. They're antipsychotics, used for schizophrenia. They may be useful to prevent these delusions."

"I don't know, Claire. I'm not sure this virus is going to slow down with standard medications. I mean, remember how ketamine didn't even work for you weeks ago?"

"It won't hurt to try." Claire held up a pill bottle and shook it. She opened it, spilling four pills in the palm of her hand. "Here, take these."

I took the pills from Claire's hand and went to the bathroom. I popped them in my mouth, freeing my hands to collect water in the sink. I drank from my hands, swallowing the pills. "Any side effects I should be aware of?" I yelled from the bathroom.

"Like any you don't have already," she answered.

"Good point." I splashed cold water on my face. I looked at myself in the mirror. Damn, I hope this works. From somewhere inside my head, my father laughed.

CHAPTER TWENTY-SIX

COLONEL STINE

The colonel stepped on broken glass and old nails on his way into the abandoned warehouse. When he entered the room, he was met with the smell of burning flesh and human shit. The two men for hire were on either side of the Korean girl, whose head was hung in her lap. He walked closer to see if she was moving.

"I think she shit herself," the shorter man of the two said, grinning.

Stine struck the man's jaw with the back of his hand. The force almost toppled the man over. The colonel waited for him to react, hoping he would. But the man stood silent, four feet away, rubbing his jaw.

"What a cluster fuck," Stine said, scanning the room. His blood was running hot. Whenever he got like this, unloading it in the form of a verbal or physical assault was the only way for him to relax.

"She don't know anything, Colonel," said the tall man.

"Of course she doesn't know anything, you ignorant sack of monkey spunk," he answered. "She doesn't have any thumbs."

"You want us to give her the Versed?" asked the short man.

Stine rubbed his temples. If the man had been closer, he would have knocked a tooth out. How were these two morons assigned to his service? No wonder Fox liked to work alone, he thought. "First, it's too late to inject Versed. That window has closed. Now, she'll have a perfect recall. Second, and I can't believe I have to say this aloud, she doesn't have any fucking thumbs or," Stine looked closer at the woman who was unconscious, "half an ear."

Versed was a drug they used at certain times during an interrogation. If given at the right time, it produced a retrograde amnesia of events. If not a complete memory loss, it fogged the brain enough to make details impossible to remember.

"What do you want us to do, sir?" asked the tall man.

"Reboot," Stine answered.

"Sir?" he asked.

Stine ignored the question. Reboot was the term they used to make a person disappear. It was when other options were exhausted. Stine had been in enough dirty business around the world to make a death look like anything from a heart attack to a suicide. He wasn't even sure where the term reboot came from. If the scene couldn't be made to look accidental or natural—if the subject had no fucking thumbs—reboot came into play.

The Korean woman started moaning. Stine could hear her labored breathing quicken.

"She's waking up, Colonel," said the short one. "Anything you want to ask her?"

Stine ignored his question too. He pulled his Smith & Wesson handgun from his back and shot the woman between the eyes. A five-inch steel silencer suppressed the sound to a low thump. He then fought against dropping the two morons. But he knew he had to give an account to his superior for every life taken. And each body came with its own complications. Coworkers, debt collectors, neighbors, loved ones—all wanting to know where that person was. Someone would miss even these two lowlifes.

"We'll get rid of her, Colonel," the tall one said, staring down at the perfect hole between the woman's eyes. He approached to move her.

"Don't touch her," Stine warned. Reboot was a process, a meticulous process. These two clowns had no idea how to properly scrub a body from this earth. Stine looked down at the dead face, thinking. He believed she knew nothing of their plans. There were better, more sophisticated, ways of obtaining information than cutting thumbs. But dismemberment did have a way of making people talk. If Claire Long were alive, Stine figured she would have contacted Mia. Unless of course she wasn't alone. Fox had been in the wind for nearly seventy-two hours now. Stine figured Fox wouldn't let Claire contact anyone. So she was either dead or with Fox. Even a lack of information could, ultimately, be information.

"We can't just leave her here," said the short man. He walked over and bent down to drag her arm.

Stine twisted to level his firearm at the man's head.

"Hey, whoa, I'm just trying to clean up."

Normally Stine would never point a gun without pulling the trigger, at least once. In this instance, it was a mere reflex. He wasn't going to shoot the man. The colonel was a soldier and had been his whole life. Soldiers followed orders. He was ordered to kill only those infected. Killing was part of his profession. Only amateurs killed out of passion. He wasn't about to break his professional code for this piece of shit. Besides, he would have to answer to his superior for every kill. Annoyance wasn't a logical reason, even if these men were sloppy.

"We're pretty sure she wasn't infected, sir. She really didn't know anything about that," said the tall one. Stine ignored him. "My brother, sir, he works in a meat factory. No one's there at night. We could grind her up."

Stine closed his eyes and took a deep breath. He rubbed his temples and counted to five Mississippi, just like his first wife had asked him to do. The fact that these two bozos had ever been in uniform was a disgrace to Stine. He kept his pistol by his side and spoke in a low, calm tone. "I want you to hand me the rest of the DNA. By that I mean the body parts. And no, I don't want to spew the rest of her DNA through your brother's meat grinder. What I would like, after I collect the two thumbs you cut off—and the half ear—is for you both to leave my sight. Clear?" The two nodded but didn't move. "The body parts!" screamed the colonel.

The short one collected the thumbs and ear and handed them to Stine. "Thank you. You may leave." They stood still. "Now," Stine said, squeezing his grip on his side arm.

The two left the warehouse through a steel door on the left. Officially they were on US property. An unknown space to the general public, five square miles used for training exercises. Unofficially, it was a place where acts off the books occurred.

Stine opened his hand and looked at the dismembered thumbs. They were neatly painted a cherry red. He wondered if Mia would have spent the time to manicure her nails if she knew they would soon be cut off her body. Or better yet, her body cut off from this earth. Stine had seen so much death that he rarely thought much about life. They were both equally common events.

He held the thumb up to his own and was surprised that its length was almost the same. Hers was slender and clean, except for the bloody stump, while his was round, calloused, and had pits in the nail. He wondered if he could use the thumb to lure

Claire out of hiding, if she were alive. He twisted it over in his hand, thinking about the question. Where would he send it?

Probably better to clean everything, he thought. He was undecided. Stine threw the half ear and one thumb beside the body. He tucked the other thumb in his pocket. Out of his other pocket he pulled his encrypted phone and called for a clean, a reboot.

After he completed the ten-second call, he felt an emptiness. It was the thumb that got to him. All the care she had taken to file it, to polish it, to paint it—and for what? Then he thought of the two morons who had just left him. Someone had spent a large part of the prime of their life caring for those two degenerates. Bathing them, dressing them, feeding them, making sure they didn't run out in front of a car—and for what? So they could put ladies with fancy thumbs in a meat grinder?

Stine didn't allow himself to reflect for long, never did. He had a job to do. Fox was out there. And it looked bad on Stine. Fox was his man, and now he was in the wind. If Fox was out there, he must be infected. That was the only reason he wouldn't report to debrief. Fox was smart. He was sure to have taken the two to find an antidote. That's what Stine would have done. But what the colonel knew, and what Fox had to know, was that he was running out of time. Fox, as well as Stine, had been briefed on the virus. From what little Stine did understand about the nature of the viral weapon, pretty soon those three would be going mad. It was only a matter of time before they killed themselves. Or each other.

CHAPTER TWENTY-SEVEN

CLAIRE

I smelled something before I saw something. Like a whiff of spoiled meat. It came and went, just around the corner. It was the same smell from Miles's house. It would linger for a moment, then vanish. But finally, I saw her. First the back of her head. Her blond hair was matted in dreadlocks, missing in chunks on a pale scalp. I knew that head, even without its usual straight, golden locks.

Then for a day the smell was gone. There was nothing. But the next day the smell was rank enough to burn my eyes and cause my mouth to water. That day I saw her face—pale and blue. Rotten flesh peeled off her bones like old tissue. Amy, what's happened to you?

In the beginning she came in flashes. She'd give a cold stare or flash yellow teeth in the shape of a grin. It was never a look that the live Amy would give, the twin sister I knew and loved. Gradually the flashes of dead Amy stayed longer and longer, until she finally spoke.

Bet you didn't plan for this.

Those were her first words. Garbled but clear enough. Her

voice sputtered and cracked like she was choking on dry earth. At first I ignored her. She was clearly a delusion, and I wouldn't engage. I closed my eyes, turned the corner, and she'd leave. For a while, anyway. But she began to follow me with her trail of rotten flesh.

You know there's only one way, Claire.

That was the second time she spoke. This time in a deeper voice.

"What do you mean?" I asked, breaking my promise not to engage with a hallucination. She laughed, then disappeared. One way for what?

The moments I didn't smell her, or see her, I was trying to help Jack. He had been busy working on genetic models to create an antidote. I was no help in the world of virology, but what I could spot was when Jack was in trouble.

It was the change in his eyes. They would go from a focused, concentrated look to one of troubled introspection. It was like a tell. "Don't listen to him, Jack." I could see him snap out of it for a minute. "You can do this," I would remind him. "You are not him. You are not a killer." Those last two truths I repeated like a mantra. If his father was trying to work a black rut in his brain, I would do my best to fill it in. The human mind worked in phrases. I wanted him to hear those words so often that he believed they were his own. I wanted those words to drown out his father's words by twenty to one.

And sometimes it worked. He would snap out of it and go right back to the computer. Other times I could see his eyes retreat again to the delusion. I continued to feed him the words, the medications.

"Five pills this time?" he asked.

I nodded. "Down the hatch." I knew the psychosis would worsen. Our only hope was Jack cracking the code. And his only hope was staying sane. I was dosing him three times over the recommended amount already. But I knew as the virus replicated, we drifted further from reality. If the medication was going to help at all, it had to block enough dopamine to overwhelm the virus. It was a gamble. The difference between risk and benefit at this point was a razor's edge. I didn't prescribe clozapine, but I knew enough about the psychiatric drug from my patients. I knew if I pushed the dose too high, it could fry his liver, cause a seizure, or even obliterate his bone marrow. But do nothing, and Jack may succumb to his delusions and never find the antidote.

"I don't get it," said Jack, staring at the computer after he'd taken the pills.

I put my hands on his shoulders, closed my eyes, and breathed in his scent. I was hoping to rid the sudden smell of rotten flesh that filled my nostrils. "Don't get what?" I asked.

"Miles had the entire viral genetic code. He knew the virus inside and out. I mean he created it." Jack leaned back and turned his head to crack his neck. "The antidote was in front of him the entire time. It just doesn't make sense why it wasn't activated."

"Maybe he ran out of time," I suggested. "I mean maybe he was about to before—"

"Before he went batshit crazy," Jack finished.

"Got infected, I was going to say."

Same thing, I heard a low, graveled voice. The smell of decay intensified. I looked up to see her standing there, left of the computer. *I can see why you like him*, dead Amy said, reaching out to him with her rotten flesh. *He's sweet and smart.* She pulled her cracked lips back, flashing her yellow teeth. *If you really cared about him, you would end his suffering. Did you figure it out yet?*

I closed my eyes and leaned into Jack, so close I almost hit the back of his head. I breathed deep, inhaling mostly Jack with only a slight whiff of dead flesh.

"You okay?" asked Jack.

"Yes," I answered, my face inches from his head. I was afraid to open my eyes. Why couldn't I see any resemblance of the real Amy? This virus was trying to ruin the memory of my favorite person.

Jack pulled away, turned around, and looked at me. He smiled. "You sure?"

I opened my eyes. My rotting twin sister leaned close to Jack and smiled. A few of her yellow teeth had sharp end points. *You need to take back control, Sis.* The dead Amy raised her arms high and brought them down in a chopping motion on the crown of Jack's skull. *So easy*, she hissed.

The tomahawk, I thought. It was the first thing I grabbed when Fox took the gun from me. I couldn't believe he hadn't searched my bag. It didn't give me the same control as the gun, but at least it was a weapon.

"Yes, Jack," I lied. I shut my eyes. I couldn't look at the corpse of Amy pretending to bury a hatchet in the head of my only hope left on earth.

"I don't believe you, Claire." He stopped his work and turned fully around to look at me.

"Well, the truth is I think I heard the voice of my dead sister."

"Okay," Jack said.

Heard? Amy laughed.

I wasn't going to get into it. Not now. Jack was close. At least I hoped he was close. The fact that some zombie version of my sister was tormenting me wasn't going to help the cause.

"Have you been taking the medication you're giving me?" he asked.

I nodded. Another lie. I probably needed the medication.

Well, I definitely needed the medication. But I'd done the math. The dose Jack needed didn't allow enough for me. And I was worried about Fox. He hadn't come out and said anything, but I could see a shift in him. He was the one with training, the one with a gun. The last thing we needed was a 250-pound paranoid soldier with a cache of deadly weapons.

Jack nodded. "Good."

I had to try and get away from the smell, and sight, of the corpse of my sister. I walked outside to get some air. Fox was in the yard. He was shirtless, doing what looked to be some kind of martial arts. His movements were fluid and delicate. His hands glided gently through the air. Like the rest of his body, his hands were thick. How many lives had those hands ended? My eyes followed to his powerful forearms and then to his muscled neck and chest. His whole body looked like a weapon.

CHAPTER TWENTY-EIGHT

FOX

Fox was experiencing something he hadn't felt since the age of thirteen: fear. It was the same fear he felt those nights walking alone in the projects. Before he knew how to defend himself, before he had killed a man.

It made no sense. Fox had training. He had a stash of at least twenty weapons in the cabin that could quickly end a man. But even the high walls didn't ease his anxiety when it came washing over him in waves. It was an old feeling that something, or someone, was behind him, or at the next turn. If there was any feeling Fox couldn't tolerate, any feeling he despised, it was vulnerability.

That weakness, that fear, was purged the night he saved his brother, Nate. Gone as soon as that lead pipe struck the man's temple. No longer did he ever feel he might puke just walking the streets. No longer was he looking for an escape path in every ally.

Fear was a luxury for civilians. As a soldier, Fox couldn't afford to feel it. Now his thoughts were clouded. Shadows stalked him in his own cabin. Inside the walls of his own safe house, he felt like that thirteen-year-old boy in the projects.

Of course, it only came in waves. When he felt like himself, he cleaned his weapons, punished his body with his usual routine, and planned against his enemies. Today he was doing tai chi. Fox needed to gain his balance. He had studied every fighting discipline on the planet. Fox knew he couldn't run from his fear. He had to be supple, like flowing water. But also like water, he had to be strong, able to kill.

"Is that tai chi?"

Fox stopped to see Claire watching him. "Yes, it is. Good eye."

She nodded. "I had a friend who used to practice."

"Care to join me?" he asked.

She shook her head. "No, I'm afraid I wouldn't know where to start." She looked at him intently. "Is this something you do a lot of?"

Fox shook his head. "Actually, no. I'm trying to find some balance."

"Balance?" asked Claire.

"To overcome any enemy, you must embrace it," Fox answered. He wanted to be alone.

"Is that what you're doing, overcoming fear?" she asked.

"No," Fox snapped back through clenched teeth. His brows lowered and eyes narrowed. "Fox, it's okay," Claire said, smiling.

Fox didn't like it. He felt like his thoughts must be broadcasting. "Why would you think that?"

"Relax," she answered. "You said 'it,' so I assumed it wasn't a person. Besides, it's all coming from the virus. It's producing fear in us all. Maybe your fear is just *having* fear. I imagine that's difficult for a soldier."

Fox stopped his movements. She was too close to the mark. It was strange. "How do you—"

"Look, Fox, I'm a therapist. I can't protect us like you or write an antidote in genetic code like Jack. What I can do is read people. Anything the virus uses to attack us is going to be something already in our heads. Have you seen anything that's not there? Or heard any voices?"

Fox didn't need a therapist, but this lady *was* in his head. She had him pegged the minute she walked outside. His eyes shifted. A wave of adrenaline flooded over him. Maybe he should get a weapon.

"Look, Fox, I'm just trying to help. This virus is designed to fuck with our heads. It makes us paranoid and feel like we can't trust each other. But you can trust me. In fact, you need to trust me."

Damn, this woman was good. Could he trust her? "No," Fox answered. "I mean I haven't seen anyone not there. Or heard any voices, for that matter."

Claire nodded. "That's good."

"I guess," he followed, "it's more of a feeling."

"Go on," Claire said.

Fox had never been in therapy. He wasn't used to talking at all, yet alone about his emotions. But at this rate, this woman was likely to read his thoughts anyway. "Well, it's a feeling I had when I was young. When I lived in the projects. I guess I felt like a target."

"You were scared," she said.

Fox didn't comment on that. He wasn't going to be defined by that thirteen-year-old boy.

"Listen, like I said, it's the virus, Fox. It's trying to twist your mind. That fear isn't real. It's in your head. Remember that."

He nodded.

"I've got some pills that help. I gave some to Jack already." She pulled a bottle from her pocket. "They'll help you keep track of what's real and what's not. Think of it as helping you find your balance."

"Are you taking them?" he asked.

Claire nodded. Lying for a second time. The truth was she should be taking them. If only she had enough. But Fox wouldn't need as high a dose as Jack. He hadn't been infected as long. The virus wouldn't numerically explode in his head for another week or two.

"Okay," he said. She handed him two pills. He swallowed them dry. "Thank you." He started back with his tai chi movements. She was about to leave when he asked, "Just what is it that you're afraid of, Claire?"

She shrugged but soon looked frightened just by a thought. "I'm going inside, Fox."

CHAPTER TWENTY-NINE

CLAIRE

Dead Amy answered the question for me. *You know what you're afraid of, Sis. And you know what you have to do too.* She was behind Fox now, doing tai chi herself. She mirrored his movements, reaching out her arms and mocking his motions. Her flesh sagged, peeling in sheets.

I told Fox I was heading inside and quickly left the sight of my sister's corpse. I went into the bedroom, then the bathroom. I locked the door and sat on the closed toilet seat, breathing heavily. My chest tightened, and my heart raced. My hands trembled. I felt dizzy, nauseous. I inhaled deeply through my nose and exhaled from my mouth, trying to control my breathing. Slowly my adrenaline began to fade. My heart still pounded but slower. I heard the door move against the lock, then a knock.

"Claire?"

Jack was outside the locked door. "Just a minute." I unlocked it.

"You okay?" he asked. "I saw you rush inside. Did something happen with Fox out there?"

I shook my head. "No. But it's...I don't know. It's getting worse."

Jack nodded. "For all of us. Look, Claire, I'm close. We just have to test a few of the models in the lab now."

I nodded, wanting to believe him. I sat on the bed, Jack beside me. After I calmed down a bit, he went back to his work. I was alone until Amy appeared. As usual, her dead scent preceded her. Each time she came, her dead flesh sloughed from her body more and more. Those areas of skin she picked at when alive were now coming off in chunks. Some areas were clear to the bone without the cover of muscle, fat, or skin.

Did you figure it out yet, Claire? she needled me in her groveled voice.

I closed my eyes. I wasn't going to look at her or answer her.

She laughed. *Claire,* she hissed, *you can't ignore me. I'm in your head.*

I kept my eyes shut and didn't acknowledge her.

Some brilliant therapist you are. Know thyself—didn't they teach you that in school? This is a softball. You try to solve everyone else's problems, but you don't know your biggest one?

"Shut up," I said out loud. My eyes remained shut. My heart raced again, and my breath quickened. My sister's corpse quoting Socrates, bullying me, it's—

It's what, Claire? Too much for you?

I squeezed my temples with my fingers. She *was* in my head.

Where did you think I was? Open your eyes. I opened my eyes. She stood over me. So close I could feel her hot breath. There was a rancid odor to it, different from her rotting flesh. *You know...say it. Say it,* she hissed.

"Fine, control," I said.

So now you get it?

I didn't answer. It was hardly a revelation. I had struggled with control my whole life.

Such an analytical mind. How are you going to use your logic now? Don't you see?

I said nothing. Challenging the logic of each thought was one of my therapeutic cornerstones.

You can't use what's sick to heal itself. You have only one move left. You know it?

How do I fix these twisted thoughts by thinking? I shuddered. I knew the answer but wouldn't say it out loud.

Yes, that's right, dead Amy said in a whisper. *You have to destroy it, that brain of yours. And if you care about Jack, you'll kill him too.*

I shut my eyes tightly, then opened them again, and she was gone. All night I braced for her return. I waited for her low, gravelly voice and the smell of her rotting flesh. In each corner, I expected to see her peeling corpse. But she didn't appear again until I was asleep.

That night I dreamed of a river. A dark, fast mass of water. There were objects floating, bobbing up and down in the current.

They're all in the river, Amy said.

The objects surfaced. I looked closer. Heads. They were all human heads. People of all ages. Mouths open, eyes fixed. Some bald, some with long, stringy hair. They were floating into each other, sucked underneath the current then pushed back to the top. A few bodies rose to the surface, turning over to expose their ghostly white, bloated flesh.

Amy stood next to me on a cobblestone street. *Everyone is in the river,* she repeated.

I woke up gasping for breath, sure I would vomit.

"Hey, whoa," Jack said. "What do you mean they're all in the river?"

"Oh," I answered him, "nothing, just a dream."

He studied me, then rolled over. "Okay."

I was up, thinking for the next few hours. The river, the street—they seemed familiar. I couldn't place it, but I knew I had been there before. After being up most of the night, I drifted to sleep again.

The sound of Jack's voice woke me. "Mia's dead?" he asked.

"What?" I said, groggy.

"Mia is dead. That's what you said."

I tried to process that. My head pounded. The memory of my last bit of sleep returned to me. My dead twin had spoken to me again. *By the way, you know Mia's dead*, she said matter-of-factly.

Jack was propped on a bent elbow, looking at me. "I don't know," I said. Where was Amy getting this information? There is no Amy, I thought. Your sister is dead. This is all coming from your head, Claire.

Jack got up and went to the desk to work. I could hear him talking to Fox. I walked over and stood in front of them. "What is it, Claire?" asked Fox.

"Is Mia dead?" I asked him.

"Who?"

"You know, my partner, Mia."

He studied me for a moment. "Sorry, I don't know what you're talking about," he answered, then turned back to Jack.

I didn't move, just looked at the back of their heads. Dead Amy appeared next to him. *He's lying. It's all over his face*, she said. I couldn't believe they couldn't smell her rotten flesh.

Fox turned back to me. "Claire?"

Liar, dead Amy said.

I walked away. Back to the bedroom. *You have to end this*, said Amy. *They're all dead.* She let out a sigh, blowing her rancid breath in my direction. *But they're free. You need to free yourself too. You and Jack.* I felt trapped. Trapped in the cabin, trapped by Amy, trapped in my mind. *Coward,* Amy hissed.

"Fine," I said and followed her to the corner of the closet. There I pulled the tomahawk free from the bottom of my bag. I ran a finger slowly over its steel blade, almost cutting my flesh. Still deadly sharp. I grabbed the leather handle. Feathers fell from the neck, tickling my hand. I walked methodically into the other room. Jack was now alone, still sitting at the desk.

Dead Amy walked beside me, coaxing me. *That's it, slowly,* she said.

We walked behind him and stopped. She bent down next to him. *There's no reason he needs to suffer,* she said. *Either of you.* Dead Amy ran her rotted hand inches from the top of his head. *One swift motion to the center, and you can end this.*

I stood behind Jack, frozen. I took steady breaths, waiting for him to hear me. Waiting for him to turn around and stop me. But he didn't. His eyes were locked on the computer screen. His round head looked as ripe as a melon. I closed my eyes, wishing it all to go away.

Coward, this is never going to end, said Amy.

I gripped the tomahawk with both hands. I opened my eyes and lifted it high above my head. The corpse of Amy grinned at me with her sickly, yellowed teeth. I brought the blade down with all my might onto the top of Amy's skull. The tomahawk hit her square on the crown. It traveled straight through her body, like she was a mere mist. The sharp edge bit into the wood and stuck in the desk.

CHAPTER THIRTY

FOX

"What the hell?" Jack yelled.

Fox heard it from the other room. He quickly rounded the corner to see Claire standing next to Jack who was seated. They were both looking at a hatchet that was embedded into the top of the desk. Jack's mouth was open. Claire was shaking, rubbing her hands.

Fox's first thought was to secure the weapon. He moved in between them. The hatchet had a leather bond handle with feathers attached by the blade. The tomahawk from the cabin, he thought. He gripped the handle and freed it from the wood. "Just what happened here?" demanded Fox.

Jack said nothing, only stared wide eyed at Claire.

"It's me," she said, her voice trembling. "I've been seeing things, specifically my dead sister. She made me—" Claire stopped and wiped tears from her cheeks. "I thought I may be able to somehow get rid of her. I don't know." She shook her head. "I can't believe the two of you can't see her. Can't smell her."

Fox did a mental inventory of all the Indian weapons on the

wall of that old cabin. Most of the other items were bulky. Surely he would have seen a bow and arrow. But he let a twelve-inch war tomahawk slip past him. Stupid.

"It's okay, Claire," said Jack. "It's like you said. The virus, it's doing things to us all."

"Jack. I'm so sorry. You know I wouldn't—"

"I know, Claire," he said.

But Fox wasn't convinced. Claire's eyes were shifting around the room, like she was tracking something that wasn't there. They were all unraveling. Just last night Fox had slept in his panic room. And still he felt like a target. But Claire, he had thought she was the stable one of the three. She had been the one talking him down. Keeping him grounded. But she clearly seemed to be losing her grip on reality.

The tomahawk hung heavy in his thick hand. The blade was sharp enough to bite into at least a full inch of the wood. That would have split a man's head straight down the middle, he thought.

"You need to lie down?" Jack asked her. "You said you didn't get much rest last night."

For a man who almost had his skull cracked, he was acting pretty calm, thought Fox.

Claire bit her lip. Her hands still shook. "No, I mean yes, I didn't get much sleep. I think I will lay down." She avoided their eyes as she walked slowly to the bedroom.

Once she was out of sight, Fox let out a low whistle. "She's starting to unravel, Jack." Jack looked down at the desk where the tomahawk had been. He ran his hand over the break in the wood. "Let's go outside and talk," said Fox.

Fox pulled an unopened bottle of Cognac from the shelf and poured them both a glass. They walked to the porch. Jack sat on one rocking chair and Fox the other. Jack swirled the brandy in his glass. He took a long sip and winced. "What's on your mind, Fox?"

"Did you know she was that bad?" Fox asked. Jack answered with a shrug. "What the hell is that?" Fox copied him, shrugging his own massive shoulders. He rested his thick forearms on the porch railing and stared at the distant river. Sunlight flashed on the water like a Morse code. His cabin was built on the highest point for six square miles. This way Fox could see over the wall encircling his house. Sure, he had cameras outside, but he liked to see with his naked eye.

"Did I know the virus would shift to activate certain receptors that cause psychosis? Yes, I did. You read the notes from Miles, right?" Jack took another swig of brandy. "It appears to be on the mark."

Fox put his own drink down untouched. "Well, it appears that mark just might kill you." If Jack died, the antidote would die with him. Fox swirled his brandy, then tossed it over the deck. This wasn't the time to take up alcohol. He was already on edge.

"You shouldn't waste good brandy," Jack said.

Fox waved his hand, dismissing the comment. "How close are you?"

"Actually, I think I've finished what I can do here," answered Jack. "Everything else will have to be tested in the lab."

"Are you having delusions, Jack?" Fox asked.

He finished the brandy and answered, "Um, yeah, a little. I hear my dead father's voice from time to time."

"And how's that?"

Jack's eyes shifted. "It's good, you know, mostly positive. He was a great guy." Bullshit, thought Fox, watching the way Jack's body tensed. "Actually, Claire was, um, helping me with that," Jack continued. "She even gave me some medication, which may have slowed things down." Fox nodded. "And yourself? You in trouble, Fox?"

Fox shook his head, a lie of his own. The truth was Fox was in deep. His only help had been the girl. "Listen to me, Jack. I still have a contact who's inside the colonel's operation. I want you to submit what you have. I can trust this guy."

"Is this the same guy who killed Mia?" Jack asked.

"I told you I don't know anything about that," answered Fox.

"Oh yeah? I know a bullshit answer when I hear one," said Jack.

Fox was impressed. "Kind of like those cozy moments with your dead father?"

Jack gave a slight grin.

"But the answer to your question, Jack, is no. He wasn't in on that." Where were they getting their information? "How did Claire know about that?" asked Fox.

"I don't know. She said her dead sister told her in a dream."

"Hmm," said Fox. The kill was recent, less than two days ago. "What else did her dead sister tell her, besides to split you open with a tomahawk of course?"

"So he does have a sense of humor," Jack said. "Something about a river. They're all dead in the river."

"What river? This river?" Fox pointed to the river beyond the walls.

"I don't know. I don't think so."

They're all dead in the river. The phrase meant nothing to Fox. But it made him nervous. The girl had been right about everything. Just yesterday, it felt as if she could read his mind. And she somehow knew about Mia. His own paranoia was closing in on him. Less than twelve hours ago, Fox almost unloaded a magazine of hollow point bullets in the panic room. That would have been a disaster. Six bullets deflecting in a steel box. Fox would have never survived such an idiotic move.

Fox found it difficult to trust anyone. That trait helped keep him alive for the past twenty-eight years. He wanted to trust Claire. Without her, his grip on reality would probably already be lost. But she was clearly losing her own mind. If she killed Jack, that would be the death of them all. As for Jack, he couldn't totally be trusted. Who knows how bad his delusions were? He was obviously lying to Fox. "We need to give my contact everything you have on the antidote. He has connections in the lab, people who worked with Miles before. He can pass the genetic code to them to build the antidote."

"So we just wait here then?" asked Jack.

"Well, we're not safe in the general public," answered Fox.

"How do we know this thing is not already out there spreading? We're just holed up here when we should be out there informing the public. Telling them who's behind this."

Fox was waiting for this. "First, my man on the inside has been tracking any cases. So far, he knows of no one else infected. Second," and closer to home for Fox, "is that I'm behind this. You go public with this, and my ass hangs out to dry. You think the government is going to take ownership of this thing?"

"So get out in front of it. Tell your side of the story first. Put pressure on the brightest minds to end this thing."

Fox laughed, the first time in weeks. "This ain't some 'he said, she said' story I'm going to clear up on *Dateline*. This is an unauthorized, biological weapon created to destroy a nation, currently our own. Get out in front of it," he laughed again. "That's good."

They were silent.

"Okay," said Jack, "I'll send him what I have for the antidote."

CHAPTER THIRTY-ONE

JACK

Fox was right—the window was closing. The ax whizzing by my head was proof enough. But as much as Claire was losing her grip on reality, I wasn't far behind. My father's voice was now as much a part of my inner dialogue as my own. Every thought, every action of mine, he mocked.

If you weren't such a pussy, you would have got ahold of the tomahawk before that big Black fella. "I don't need a weapon," I said under my breath. *Like hell you don't. You don't think Ms. Crazy won't come at you again?*

"You're not real," I told him, and myself. My father laughed. I walked back to the bedroom to check on Claire. She slept. Good, I thought, she needs the rest.

I walked to the computer, picking up where I'd left off. My work had not changed in days. I was stalling, worried what might happen when I finished. My ability to produce an antidote may be the only thing keeping Claire and I alive. What would we be to Fox without it? *Expendable.* This time I agreed with the voice of my father.

I looked at the genetic code I created to target the viral core protein. Fox's contact instructions were written in block letters beside the keyboard. I followed his instructions to a secure site and keyed in his contact. I paused, looking down at the keyboard before sending the document. The divot in the wood to my right was still fresh. I ran my fingers into its splinters and suddenly wished it had been my head that was split. Enough, I thought, and hit send. The speaker made a swooshing noise.

Swoosh, my father mocked the noise. *Swoosh, now you're no use to Fox. Swoosh, like the sound of a throat being cut.* He laughed. I looked through the window at Fox, seated on the porch. His massive back spanned almost a foot on either side of the chair.

You're never leaving this cabin, at least not alive. This thought made me angry. It wasn't the idea of dying. Ridding my father's voice would come as a relief. It was the idea that no one would be held accountable. Someone had produced a weapon to torture us all and just may get away with it.

Maybe it was better this way, I thought. If we were cut off from the world, dying out here alone, it meant the weapon was dying with us. What are the odds we are the last ones infected? I thought of Mia. She didn't deserve to die. Who else would they come for? Animals.

I watched Fox and felt trapped. He was the only one who knew where we were. The only one with weapons. The only one trained to kill. And he was infected at least two weeks after Claire and I. Could he be losing it yet?

Mia was innocent. We were all innocent, I thought. Amy, Miles, Claire, myself. The truth had to come out. Who could I tell? My mother definitely wouldn't know what to do with the information, even if she did check her email. Ken would be my best chance. I wasn't sure if the same secure site would let me contact him. Fox had so many damn firewalls on this thing. I entered Ken's email and started typing. I didn't look at the screen or to the keyboard, only at Fox. As soon as he moved, I would have to hit send, regardless of what I'd written. I typed as fast as I could, knowing my thoughts were rambling. I shared as much as I could remember.

Fox stood from his chair. I raised my finger to hit send, but he only stretched and sat his bulk back on the seat. I still had time. I spent the next few minutes detailing the antidote and adding the genetic diagram. Fox stood again, this time leaving his seat for the door. There was no time to proofread. I hit send, repeatedly.

Fox walked behind me. He looked over my shoulder at the home screen, one of a few not blocked by his firewall. "Is it done?" he asked.

"Yeah, it's done," I answered, not turning around. I watched him from the reflection of the monitor. He brought his thick hands together. I braced myself for them to squeeze my neck, shutting off the blood and air to my head. Instead he cracked his knuckles, slowly, one by one.

"Good," he said. Then he repeated the word almost like a grunt, "Good."

"What now?" I asked. I wanted him to spell it out.

"Now, I'm going to get some rest myself," he said.

He disappeared into his bedroom. The cursor on the computer screen blinked. It was quiet, too quiet. The kind of strange peace that only occurs before something awful. *If you weren't such a waste of space, you'd find that tomahawk. Bury it in that big boy's chest.* "No," I murmured. "I'm not a killer." *You could have fooled me all them years ago*, my father's voice mocked.

"What now?" I asked again, this time to the empty room. My father's voice said nothing. Was it really my father's voice? If he was a delusion, then who was it thinking of burying an ax in the chest wall of my host?

My stomach grumbled. The thought of another can of food didn't sit well. Fox had plenty of meat frozen, but all the sides were canned. Each one packed enough sodium for an entire week. Four days on the cans, and I could hardly see my ankles.

I looked out the window. Plenty of light was left in the day. I could make it to the river, which had to lead to somewhere, someone. Then what? "I'm Jack, nice to meet you. By the way I'm carrying a deadly virus that will hijack your brain in a few weeks. Oh, but don't worry. I sent the blueprints out today for the cure."

I suddenly wanted to call my mother. I wanted to tell her to let go. Tell her it was my fault he died, not hers. I left him there to die, alone in the rain. *That's rich of you, Jack.*

Fox wasn't going to let us out here. I thought of the people I wouldn't see again and all the things left unsaid. I guess you never get to pick your final moment. I heard someone behind me and spun around. Claire stood five feet away. Her face was pale, and her eyes were wild. She started to speak, but her voice only cracked.

"Calm down. Calm down. Tell me, Claire, what is it?"

"It's... it's—" Her voice cracked again. She closed her eyes and took two deep breaths. "The river."

"Okay, what about the river?" I asked.

"Amy, she came again. The cobblestones. The bridge. The floating faces. I know them." She put her hand over her mouth. "I know...all of them, Jack."

I tried to follow but couldn't. "I still don't understand. What river? What faces?"

"It's my hometown. It's the Savannah River. Those bodies are my friends, people I grew up with." Her body shook. I stood up to hold her. "Oh no, Jack, I can't. It's terrible." She buried her face in my shoulder and let out a muffled scream.

"It's just a delusion, Claire. It's not real."

She pulled back. "No, Amy must have visited my parents while she was infected. She was trying to tell me, to show me."

Fox walked out from the bedroom. "What's going on?" he asked.

I told him what Claire said and what she saw. He listened intently. "When was this?" he asked.

Claire didn't answer.

"Fox, it's a delusion. A dream she had just now. What does it matter?" But I knew what he was thinking—Mia. Hadn't she heard about Mia from her dead sister? "Anyway, I thought you said no one else was infected?" I asked him.

"Yeah, I did. As far as I know." He studied Claire while cracking his knuckles, one by one. "Let me check the feed," Fox said. He took my place in front of the monitor. After passing one of his firewalls, he went to a search engine. Fox typed in "Savannah River" and "deaths."

A wheel in the center of the screen spun. The first hit was from a day ago. An article entitled "Savannah, Georgia: Something in the Water." Fox clicked on it, while I looked on.

Something in the Water
by Joyce Miner

The Savannah River is known for its scenic backdrop to boutique shops and restaurants like The Cotton Exchange Tavern. The body of water that forms a natural border between Georgia and South Carolina is now a reservoir for dead bodies. The death count is up to six, including a fourteen-year-old girl.

"I've never seen anything like this in my thirty years of policing this city," said Sheriff Tom Hunt. "The first two bodies were a shock. Now we are holding our breath, hoping not to find a seventh."

Early autopsy reports indicate the cause of death to be drowning. What isn't clear is the reason.

"I know these people," Hunt said. "They're good people. What would cause a perfectly normal fourteen-year-old girl to suddenly jump in the river?"

The rest of the people in town are equally confused. Tristen Anders, a neighbor of one of the deceased, Sam Young, says just that: "It just doesn't make any sense. I knew Sam. He was a happy-go-lucky guy. We had dinner with him less than a month ago."

But some others have a different memory of the recently departed. "Nicholas (one of the bodies found) wasn't himself these past few weeks," said a coworker at the Pink House. "He seemed to be struggling with something. Very quiet, withdrawn, which wasn't like him at all. After a while he stopped showing up for work altogether."

These conflicting reports, and the mystery behind the bodies, beg the question: Is it accidental, or a suicide pact?

"We aren't taking any explanations off the table," says Hunt.

Until more of this tragic event is known, we aren't either.

I felt Claire grip my arm. "Jack," she squeezed, "my parents. It can't be... my parents."

CHAPTER THIRTY-TWO

COLONEL STINE

"Of course, you could warn your friend. Maybe he slips the noose. And of course, there's always your pension to consider. And your freedom." Stine slowly ticked off the reasons why Stinger may want to reconsider protecting his friend Fox.

Ryan Stiper, known to everyone as Stinger, sat in the colonel's office and said nothing. He just stared a hole into the wall. It had been exactly one hour since Stine intercepted correspondence from Fox to Stinger, his inside man. "I just don't know why you thought I wouldn't be monitoring all channels?" Stine shook his head. "You think you could outsmart me? Is that it?"

Stinger didn't move his head. He was loyal. Of course, the colonel thought Fox was loyal too. Stinger had been in the shit with Fox more than once. Stine knew personally that spilling blood together made for a tight bond. He didn't really expect an answer to his question. The fact was Stinger was smart. And like Fox he, too, was a killer.

"Yeah, you could go with your friend Fox. Of course you

wouldn't have a home to come back to," the colonel said, trying to soften him up. "Or a country," he added. Stine stood over the soldier, who still looked dead ahead. "It would be a shame—putting your life on the line for all those years with nothing to show for it. You're what, five years from full pension?" Still nothing. "I don't suppose your parents would age well either. Yep, they can forget growing old in Jupiter, Florida, in peace."

Stinger's eyes turned from the wall and bore into Stine, killer eyes. The colonel didn't mention Stinger's daughter—he needed the man focused, not crazy. "Yeah, that's right. Deportation is a tricky business." The colonel did his homework on all his men. The visas for Stinger's parents from El Salvador had expired years ago.

"Now that I have your attention," Stine continued, "I'm going to need you to track down Fox and his companions in whatever hellhole they're hiding in. Who knows, maybe your buddy might even volunteer his whereabouts."

The colonel leveled his gaze back to meet the man's glare. Stinger's eyes stayed fixed, but his body twitched. He was a twitchy sort. Where Fox was powerful and methodical, Stinger was a quick and wiry weapon. He grew up learning combat in the world's most dangerous streets, where missing boys were never found or even reported. "Are we clear so far?" Stine wanted something besides the murderous stare.

"Clear, Colonel," Stinger said.

"Good. Now I'm going to need you to lead Beavis and Butthead in with you." The two morons used in the Mia job who the colonel refused to call by their given names anymore. Stine debated ending the two outright, but they may still have some use—if only to serve as a distraction for Stinger to get to Fox and the others.

"Now I want you to know something, Son," said the colonel. "These three ain't going to make it, even if you have nothing to do with it. You've seen how this virus works. So," he cleared his throat, "I suggest you abide by the ten-foot rule. No close kills. This virus needs to die with them. Are we clear, Soldier?"

"Yes, sir," Stinger answered.

But there was a pause first. And there was the glare. Stine didn't like it. Should I bring his daughter into it? he thought. The colonel wasn't thrilled with his team: Stinger, Beavis, and Butthead. But there had been enough leaks in the operation already, and he didn't want to brief anyone new. Besides, his superior wouldn't understand, whoever he was. First, Fox went rogue, now Stinger. That would look bad on the colonel, very bad. No, he needed to convince Stinger.

"Of course, we wouldn't want anything to happen to your daughter, Camille," said Stine.

Stinger moved like a cat from his seat. Twitchy. His forearm pinned the colonel against the wall within seconds. "You listen to me, Motherfucker. Anything happens to that girl, and you'll beg to die."

Stine was surprised by the speed. He also had combat training and even anticipated a strong reaction, but nothing that fast. He tried to speak but realized he couldn't breathe. Not wanting to give Stinger the satisfaction, he just smiled as broad as possible. Finally, the forearm eased off his throat. He hungrily sucked in the air as casually as he could. Stine didn't want to gratify the man by gasping.

"Go ahead. Finish me off, Stinger. I've got a man on Camille right now. Her and your parents." It was a bluff, but one he could easily make happen with a few phone calls. Stinger dropped his forearm and sat back down. "Now, are we clear? Motherfucker?"

"Clear, Colonel," Stinger answered. This time a quick answer to Colonel Stine's own satisfaction.

CHAPTER THIRTY-THREE

FOX

Fox wasn't surprised to learn the virus had leaked. How couldn't it? He had been infected from just shuffling some papers. But he was surprised that Stinger had missed it. Fox spent the next few hours sifting through news feeds, trying to find any further outbreaks. It was tricky. In its beginning, the virus mimicked any other illness—fatigue, joint aches, headaches. By the time it caused mental distress, it had replicated numerous times. And nobody thought to look for an infectious cause for mental illness, much less one manufactured in a lab. Of course, when people start jumping into a river en masse, it garnered some attention.

"Anything?" asked Jack.

"Apart from the Savannah mess?" Fox answered. "No, nothing obvious."

"I guess this changes things," said Jack.

Fox looked at the monitor and said nothing. "How's Claire holding up?" he finally asked.

"Not great, last I checked."

Fox spun his large, bald head, making a half turn. The

muscles on his neck bulged under his shirt. "Maybe you should check again."

Jack went to the back room and returned seconds later. Fox could sense something was wrong before Jack spoke. It was in the way he rushed back. The increase in his breathing, the hint of panic. "She's gone," Jack said.

"Gone?"

"Yep, gone." Jack buried his face in his hands for a moment. "I checked the bathroom, did a quick look out the window. Nothing."

Fox pushed back from the desk and stood. "You remember your last conversation?"

Jack looked down. "Not exactly. Just more ramblings about the river. How everyone was in the river." He bit his bottom lip and looked up to Fox. "'I belong in the river.' I think that was the last thing she said."

Fox looked outside and repeated the phrase to himself, "I belong in the river." Fox had his handgun with him. He released the clip to check the magazine. Satisfied with its load, he pushed it back, then pulled the slide to chamber a round. "Let's go to the river then."

Jack asked, "Do I need a weapon?"

Fox tucked the gun in the small of his back and studied him. "No."

Truthfully, Fox didn't think he needed a weapon either. It was more of a habit than anything else. He rarely left the cabin unarmed. As an afterthought he grabbed the tomahawk as well.

They left on foot. The gate was cracked open, an obvious sign Claire was gone. Even more obvious was her trail. Fox was an expert tracker. He'd been in remote places on plenty of operations. Left alone in the bush, with his only mode of survival to track his enemy and track his food. Equally important was not being tracked himself.

Claire's trail was like following a painted line. Her steps were heavy, wide, and, to Fox, frantic. At times her trail would spread out, causing Fox to stop.

"What is it?" Jack asked.

"Nothing," he answered. Then, "It looks like she fell here. Or purposely laid down, hard to tell. It picks up again just over there," he pointed to more footprints.

They were a few hundred yards in, a few hundred still to the river. Fox knew every detail of these woods. He'd walked them in snow, rain, and dark, moonless nights. He was familiar with the animals—their scents and their noises during each season. He felt something was off, and it wasn't just Claire.

Fox sensed something else. He had been this way hundreds of times. Fox knew the rhythm of the forest, so much he felt a part of it. When the forest was too quiet, or too noisy—when the rhythm was off—he knew that too. He wasn't sure what was in front of him, maybe just Claire, but he was sure there was someone behind them.

He leaned in closer to Jack. "You go on, alone. The river is dead ahead, about a quarter click, three hundred yards. I'll catch up."

"Where are you—"

"Shhh," Fox put one finger over his lips. "Just stay straight."

There was a drop ahead. Not much, but enough to blind someone following for a moment. When they moved forward far enough, he skirted to the side. Fox knew which ground made prints and which didn't. He was careful not to bend weeds or break branches. His trail would be a weak one, at best. He was betting they would follow the wide and obvious prints from Jack. And during that time, Fox would double back to see exactly who was following.

Fox moved through the forest, then stopped quickly.

Suddenly, he felt like the target—the one being watched. A tightness seized his chest, and he dropped to one knee.

He took rapid, shallow breaths, which made his head feel light. His mouth watered. Fox sat down, resting his back against the trunk of a tree. It was a stupid place to stop. Open to three sides. Fox closed his eyes and tried to right his mind for battle. But that same defenseless feeling from childhood suddenly overwhelmed him.

Fox thought he heard movement. He opened his eyes to level his pistol toward it. A squirrel jumped on a branch, causing him to whip the gun backward. Then a crow called overhead, making him jerk the gun to the sky.

He closed his eyes again to focus. Sweat ran down his spine. His hands shook with the gun in them. Fox felt trapped. An unacceptable feeling. He thought of eating his gun. A quick way out.

It's not real. Claire had said those words. She also warned him it would only get worse. Fox felt a surge of anger. He wanted to kill the virus. But that meant eating his gun. He hadn't survived this long to die by his own hand. His anger shifted to those behind the virus. They created a bug to scramble his brain. But that wasn't enough; they were sending men to finish him off.

Fox thought of the colonel. He knew how casually Stine gave the order to kill. Fox was sure the call for his own head was given with similar ease. As the anger in Fox rose, his fear faded. Soon his body relaxed, and his senses sharpened. No longer did he jump at the harmless noises in the forest. Fox then made a decision: whatever happened from here, he wasn't going to make it easy. The colonel was going to get his best.

CHAPTER THIRTY-FOUR

Fox stood up and started walking. He took his time, stopping frequently to listen. Whoever it was, they were sloppy. Their gait was loud and too cumbersome for professionals, he thought.

He relaxed a little, thinking it may be only a lost hiker. Fox slipped past a lone figure, catching a brief glimpse of the man. The face was turned away from Fox. Not a hiker. Not the way he was stalking the trail. The fact he had one empty hand and the other holding a chrome pistol made his motive clear enough. Fox kneeled, peering through a thick underbrush. He moved in closer, timing his approach with the man's footsteps. He crouched again, this time close enough to hear the man breathe, even smell him. The man stopped and assessed the woods, looking right past Fox.

He recognized the man immediately. He had been on the team the colonel had assembled. Jinx, they called him. The tall mouth breather who liked to work with a short, equally dim companion. How did they find him?

Fox didn't have time to contemplate that question. There

was plenty to do. He needed to quickly drop his tail, find any others, and finally find Claire. He assessed his weapons: the 9 mm, a folding buck knife, and the tomahawk. The pistol was too noisy. Jinx was clumsy, but he was still likely to get a shot off if Fox used the knife. That left the tomahawk.

Fox calculated the distance. He'd spent more than a few days throwing his hatchet into these very trees. He wasn't as familiar with the tomahawk, but it was roughly the same size and weight. The key was the rotation. Given the right amount of rotation, the tomahawk was sure to stick its target. The right distance was everything. If the math was right, Jinx was certain to have the business end of the old Native American war weapon in his back.

He waited for the tall man to start walking again. Fox calculated one revolution of the ax for every three paces. When the man was a full nine strides away, Fox stood. He let it fly, aiming for the middle of the back. Even if it wasn't a direct hit, the blow was sure to knock Jinx down.

The tomahawk rotated, its feathers trailing from the handle. Fox waited. Jinx moved his head slightly but not his body. The tomahawk sailed, like it had done in so many other battles. Fox wasn't sure if it would make the last rotation until he heard the groan.

Jinx fell to his knees. The blade of the tomahawk entered just lateral to his thoracic spine. Fox walked to the man. He was face down, grunting, trying to breathe. Fox pushed him on his back using the tip of his boot. Jinx's eyes were opened wide. He was moaning, gurgling, and choking on blood.

Fox leaned in beside him. "Who sent you?"

He gurgled, then gagged on a bolus of blood that he was too weak to clear. Fox tilted the man to his side to clear his airway.

Jinx coughed, splattering fresh blood on the ground. "The... the colonel."

Fox knew that much. He shouldn't have wasted a question. Given how fast the man was bleeding out, he'd be lucky to get two. "How did you find me?" he asked.

His eyes glazed over. Fox thought he already passed, when he let out one more agonal breath. "St... St... Stinger."

"Stinger?" Fox repeated. The man said nothing. "Where's Stump?" asked Fox. Stump was the name he called the short one. "Where's Stump?" Fox repeated, but it was no use. The light in the man's eyes was out. His gaze was flat and fixed.

Stinger, Fox thought. It made sense that Stinger would know where Fox was, maybe the only one. But why would he give up Fox's position? He pulled the tomahawk from the back of Jinx. The colonel must have something on him, thought Fox.

If Stinger led them to Fox, had he done it personally? If so, Fox had a lot more to worry about than these two clowns. He knew how dangerous Stinger could be. Fox had seen him kill, more than once.

Fox was silent for a moment, listening, thinking. Action was imperative for a soldier. But for a good soldier, action without thought was suicide. For the moment, Fox was still in the window of his former self, his mind clear between bouts of paranoia. If Stinger was here and wanted them dead, they would be dead already, thought Fox. They had been loud and sloppy walking through the woods after Claire. It would have been easy, too easy for a killer like Stinger. So why had he let Jinx go after him? And where was the short one?

The internal clock in Fox's head was telling him it was time to move. Jinx and Stump were both incompetent, but Jinx was the leader. He would have been in front, thought Fox. That meant the short one was either watching him or wasn't there yet.

As these thoughts went through his mind, Fox heard a loud

crack. A bullet brushed his left ear, exploding on a trunk behind him. He dropped into cover.

Fox lay flat in heavy vegetation and didn't move. He breathed in slowly, silently. The smell of iron from the tall man's blood filled the air. Through an open patch of sky overhead, a vulture passed. Fox knew the short man couldn't resist checking his friend. Also, he wouldn't resist checking for his kill. Fox had dropped the moment the bullet passed and hadn't moved.

Fox didn't have to wait long. Stump came loud and proud. Fox had his weapon sighted on the man before he closed within ten feet. Two rounds to the chest dropped him before he even got a look at Fox.

He stayed crouched for a moment. Once he heard no movement from the target, Fox stood and walked over to the man. He stared at the two bullet holes that dotted the chest. One in the middle of the heart and one in its apex—perfect shots.

Fox was still. The forest around him resumed its rhythm, the usual sounds. Fox had stood over more dead bodies than he cared to remember, but this time a new, strange feeling came over him.

It wasn't the earlier feeling of fear or paranoia. It was apathy. All those dead faces ran through his mind. There was no end to it. Surviving, killing—it was all Fox had ever known. And suddenly he felt tired of it. He felt like sitting next to the man with the fresh bullet holes. Taking a break from it all. The only man likely left was Stinger, who had been like a brother to Fox.

The colonel's face snapped him out of it. He promised to give Stine his best. To give him hell.

Finally, he moved on. He walked neither fast nor slow toward the river. He knew Stinger could kill. Fox had even counted on it before, more than once. But Stinger and Fox had principles. A soldier worthy of respect, especially one you spilled blood with, wasn't killed by sniping. If Stinger was going to kill Fox, it wasn't going to be a blind shot.

The rest of his walk was similar to a hundred others he'd done through these woods. If he discounted stepping over two dead bodies, no different at all. The air was a crisp forty-eight degrees with only a few wisps of clouds overhead. Trees along the trail showed colors of fall. No one jumped from undercover or slithered from the ground. There were no flying bullets or spinning knives. Until he reached the river, his only encounter was a lone buck.

Once the trail opened to the riverbank, Fox saw three figures. One standing, one kneeling, and one flat on its back. The first face that was clear was Jack. He was pacing and chewing at his nails. Fox could only see the crown of the head of the person kneeling. The hair was an unnatural blond and cut short enough to leave spiked ends—Stinger.

He was directly over a flat body, elbows locked and hands crossed. Fox had seen this image before—Stinger resuscitating a body—but it had been years ago. Stinger stopped pumping the chest and tilted the head back, Claire's head. He put his lips on hers, blowing in two quick breaths.

Stinger put two fingers on Claire's wrist. He raised his head and saw Fox approaching. Claire's lips were a dusky color, her body limp.

"I've got a pulse," Stinger said, "but it's thready."

Fox nodded.

Stinger took his fingers off her wrist and kneeled over her, once again locking his elbows. He started pumping her chest at a fast rate. "I found her in the river about ten minutes ago," he said. "No idea how long she was in there."

Fox knelt next to him and checked the pulse himself.

"Still weak?" asked Stinger.

Fox nodded. "But there."

"One thing is for sure," said Stinger, "this water is damn cold."

That may be some good news, thought Fox. Cold could kill but could also keep someone alive. He wasn't sure how, but Fox had heard this while in the field.

"That may protect her brain a bit," Stinger said. He stopped CPR and checked the pulse again himself. "Better," he said.

Fox looked up and saw Jack thirty yards away, still pacing. "What's he doing?" he asked Stinger.

"Beats me," Stinger answered. "Not helping. Mostly talking to himself."

Claire didn't move unless she was touched. "Is she going to make it?" asked Fox.

Stinger ran a hand over his spiked hair. "Maybe. Maybe not. She needs a hospital."

We all need a hospital, thought Fox.

"You take care of those two professionals with me?" asked Stinger with a hint of a smile.

Fox nodded. "Those two won't be making it."

"I figured they wouldn't be much of a threat in these woods."

Jack shuffled in closer, still chewing a nail on his right hand. "How is she?" he asked.

Fox looked down again. She was pale and limp, her lips a light blue. He said nothing.

"She doesn't have much time if she's going to have a chance. We need to make a decision," said Stinger.

"I'll pull the four-wheeler as close as I can. You and Jack carry her to the trailhead."

Fox moved much faster back to the cabin than he had away from it. He owed Stinger that much. It wasn't the first time

Stinger risked his life to save Fox. Only this time, he risked his life for a stranger. Once he put his lips on Claire, even touched her, his fate was sealed. Whether Claire lived or not, Stinger was infected.

As he ran back on the trail, Fox wondered if Stinger changed his mind. Did he come to protect Fox? Or was he here to kill him, but something changed?

The last time Fox had seen Stinger pumping a chest was ten years ago. It was a failed effort. The chest that he pressed that day—for hours on a dead man—was his close friend from home. It started in the field and continued on the chopper. They should have never loaded the man. He was twice as blue as Claire with an open wound split down half his gut.

"Don't you fucking die on me," Stinger yelled to the dead man. "Don't you fucking die." It went on the entire flight—Stinger yelling at his dead friend. When they pried the body from Stringer's hands upon landing, something in him changed. He never worked as a medic again. That day Stinger became a soldier. From healer to killer.

Once in his unit, Fox took the time to show him every combat technique and the nuances of a mission. In turn, Stinger used his knowledge of anatomy to teach Fox which areas on a man bled the fastest. Stinger was a relentless fighter, unleashing a pent-up rage every time he engaged the enemy. He was also a cunning fighter, with the quickest reaction time Fox had seen from anyone.

Fox hustled to the meeting point. Once there he saw Claire still unconscious, her head in Stinger's lap. Blood was smeared down the front of his shirt. Fox jumped from his vehicle.

"Did something happen?" he asked, pointing to the blood on Stinger's shirt.

Stinger looked down. "It's from earlier. I think she hit her head on a rock in the river. She has a gash on the back of the skull. Feels pretty shallow." He moved his hand behind her head, bringing it back with bright, fresh blood. "You know these scalp wounds—they bleed like crazy."

"Come on. Let's move. I got a kit in the shed," Fox said.

They climbed in, Fox and Jack in the front, Stinger and Claire in the flatbed. Claire's head was positioned in Stinger's lap with her legs folded. Fox drove as fast as he could while avoiding the potholes.

"Where are we going?" asked Jack.

"Hospital," Fox answered.

"All of us?" Jack asked.

Fox ignored the question. "Did you know the virus is loose in Savannah?" Fox asked Stinger.

"No," he answered, "but I'm not surprised."

"Yeah, people are drowning left and right. Claire's parents live there," said Fox.

The four-wheeler hit a large rut in the dirt road, lifting Claire's head then slamming it back. "Whoa, easy," said Stinger. "I think there's also an outbreak in Raleigh and maybe Atlanta. Hard to tell with this thing, but there is definitely some weird stuff going on in a few medical clinics."

"Did you tell the colonel?" asked Fox.

"I tried. You know Stine. All he's good for is a kill and cover," he answered.

"Is that why you came?" Fox asked. He jerked the wheel to avoid another large hole in the road.

"It's why I was sent," answered Stinger. "Not why I came. I had to make it look like I was hunting you down. He wiped blood onto his pants. "I didn't want those morons near you. But once I saw this lady in the water," Stinger looked down, "I don't know. I just reacted. I hadn't tried to save anyone since... since—"

"I know," Fox answered, relieving him of having to spell out his friend dying. They were close to the shed, one more turn. "Does the colonel have anything on you?" Fox asked. Specifically, your family or friends, he thought.

"I got my family to a safe place," Stinger said. He shook his head and spit out of the back. "Stine. I guess I shouldn't be surprised."

Fox turned the corner and parked in front of the shed.

"You never answered my question," said Jack. "Are we all going to the hospital?"

"You take Claire," Fox answered, looking straight ahead. "I'm going to pay the colonel a visit."

CHAPTER THIRTY-FIVE

COLONEL STINE

Colonel Stine sat in his office with the blinds shut, waiting impatiently for the newly enlisted soldier. The one he saw on the cargo net. A young cadet from Arkansas with auburn hair who looked like she could crack walnuts with her thighs. She was about four weeks out of basic training and needed career guidance. The only thing Stine was interested in guiding was his pecker between her rock-hard thighs.

He could use the distraction. Stine hadn't heard from his team in over twenty-four hours. Any explanation for that fact was bad. His thoughts were oscillated from the loss of communication with Stinger to that voluptuous backside from Arkansas. Each one frustrated him and ran his blood hot.

He paced the room, stopping to part the blinds. It was getting dark. Maybe someone had warned the girl that it may be inappropriate. Stine heard a knock on his door. He spun around and removed his hand from the blinds.

The door opened, and the wide body of his sixty-four-year-old assistant filled the frame of it. Stine felt immediate disappointment. "Sir?" she asked.

"Yes, Janet, what is it?" he asked curtly.

"You have a visitor. A Tess Underwood."

His momentary irritation left him. "Yes, yes. Send her in."

The portly Janet shifted to reveal the lovely, slender woman from Arkansas. The colonel was happy to see she wore a skirt, even if it was past the knee. He didn't like women trouncing around in those baggy cargo pants, at least not one with a body like Tess. She wore a green matching blazer, a white button-down, and no tie. Stine's eyes followed the buttons of her blouse down to her decolletage. One of his favorite parts of the female body—that area just below the neck before the breasts split. He even loved the sound of the word "decolletage." And hers was perfect—a soft, creamy shade of white. He wanted to bury his face in it.

"Colonel?" Janet broke his trance.

"Yes, Janet. Thank you," he answered, then added, "Tess, please come in."

The young woman smiled. Full, painted lips. She glided in the room, a slight shift in her hips. Damn, she was sexy, Stine thought. "Janet, you can go home for the night. Thank you."

Janet looked at the colonel, then appraised the young woman who was half the colonel's age and his subordinate by a dozen ranks. Her long stare voiced her opinion without speaking. Stine could care less. It wasn't the first time she had seen him court a female in uniform.

"Yes, sir," she finally said, shutting the door behind her.

Stine, happy to be alone, said to Tess, "Take a seat." He motioned to the sofa, well more of a love seat. Too big for one, and a close fit for two.

"Thank you," she said.

The Southern accent made her even more sexy to Stine. "Can I get you a drink?" he asked.

"I don't know, Colonel. Well, sure, if you're having one," she answered.

"Yes, I believe I'll join you." Damn right I'll join you, he thought. As he poured the two bourbons, she crossed her legs, making a low swishing noise. The colonel brought the drinks over, joining her on the love seat. He clicked his glass to hers. "To the start of a fine military career," he said.

She smiled and took a sip. The colonel watched her delicate neck as she swallowed the liquor. An image of Stinger's hands squeezing his own neck flashed in his mind. Son of a bitch, he was fast, the colonel remembered. How couldn't he sneak up on two civilians and a sick captain? Stine didn't expect much from Beavis and Butthead. They were mere pawns to allow Stine to move his real chess piece.

"Colonel, are you okay? You look distracted," asked the Southern accent in a slight husky tone.

"No, of course I'm fine. Nowhere else I would rather be." She adjusted her skirt and sighed, causing her ample breasts to move up and down. The colonel undressed her in his mind—her nipples erect, a delicious cherry red. If he was going to make that a reality, he had to get his head in the game.

Tess placed her drink down and crossed her arms. "Colonel, why am I here?"

The question, and her sudden change in posture, made Stine think this may be harder than he anticipated. That was okay. He once forged through waist-deep mud and pig shit for half a mile to meet a goal. For a taste of Arkansas beaver, he would do more than that.

"The military can be a tricky place for a young lady," he said. "Especially one as pretty as you." She straightened her back, pointing her knees away from him. "Of course you look like someone who can handle herself. A real ace in basic training." Her rigid posture softened.

"Thank you, Colonel."

"Of course, knowing the right people is the key to moving up ranks." Stine swirled his bourbon. "Maybe even leapfrogging ranks." He saw a slight curve of her lip. Ambitious, he thought; he could work with that. Whether he moved her up in the future was irrelevant. The goal was to have her stripped down on the love seat.

"Is that why I'm here?" she asked.

"Direct," he answered. "I like that." Actually, he preferred it left unsaid. This one could be trouble, he thought. But his motor was running. And he had done his homework. Tess was from Nowhere, USA. Not even a shit stain on most maps. If it came down to it, the colonel had enough money to pay a nondisclosure agreement. "This is just a friendly discussion about your future. Like I said, I'm impressed."

"I see," she said, the corners of her mouth tightening.

"Of course, it always pays to keep things open," he countered, sliding his hand just inside her knee. He could feel the warmth, or maybe it was his own blood heating up. Her creamy white thigh felt as smooth as it looked. Keep things open. Nice double entendre, he thought. He suppressed a chuckle, thinking how much of a clever bastard he was.

The colonel waited for her reaction. This was a crucial moment in the seduction. Then he felt it. It was slight, but it was there. The legs parted a bit. She looked at him, doe eyed. Her full, plump lips separated just a crack. This was going to be sweet, he thought.

Stine heard the door to his office suddenly explode open. Janet, he thought, enraged. Someone better be dead. He whipped his head around. In the doorway stood a man with massive shoulders. Thick, empty hands hung by his sides.

"Fox," Stine yelled.

"Hello, Colonel." Fox invited his big body into the center of the office. "Hope I didn't catch you at a bad time."

The colonel scoffed. He felt the stiff board in his manhood turtle back. "Just a friendly meeting," Stine answered.

Fox smiled. The scar down the side of his face caught the light and looked more gruesome than usual. "This meeting does have the looks of an impending promotion."

The colonel stood. His mind left the girl, switching into combat mode. He'd be damned if a subordinate was going to address him with that tone in his own office. "Where the fuck have you been, Soldier?" he demanded.

Fox's smile broadened. This aggravated Stine further. "Avoiding you and your hit team, of course."

"Son of a bitch, you took out Stinger?" he asked.

"You never were the sharpest knife in the drawer," Fox answered, then added a half-hearted "sir."

The colonel was enraged. He'd never seen such disrespect from Fox. He mentally assessed the situation. Was Fox empty handed? The colonel had weapons planted all over his office. The closest being a Swiss Luger in his desk drawer. More of a showpiece, but it could still put a hole in that wide forehead of Fox's. "I'll take that as a yes," he said, inching his way over to his desk.

"Colonel, maybe I should be going," said Tess from the love seat.

"Stay where you are," he shot back. Stine wasn't ready to give up on a witness being present, not yet. Maybe it was good for him, maybe good for Fox. He hadn't worked it out in his head.

Fox walked closer. "Stinger's fine. Can't say the same for those other numb nuts you sent."

The colonel assessed Fox. He could see no bulge hiding a weapon on his hips or his ankle. He had no line of sight to his lower back. The thick hands held calluses, nothing more. "You got a lot of nerve showing up here without a weapon, Soldier," said Stine.

Fox closed the gap between them before Stine had a chance to grab the Luger. "Colonel, you just don't get it," he said, now just a foot away. "I am the weapon."

Stine felt a sudden wet sting to his right cheek. Saliva from the mouth of Fox slid down the side of his face.

CHAPTER THIRTY-SIX

FOX

Fox laughed—it was the colonel's expression as the phlegm slid down his face. He had never seen the man this worked up. But Fox was just as angry and had been for a while.

"How does it feel to be wearing your prized weapon?" Fox asked.

The colonel made for his desk drawer. Fox knew about the Luger. He knew about all the weapons stashed in the office. When he lunged for the drawer, Fox leaned in, summoning his last bit of strength to shove the colonel. Stine sailed backward across the room. His head racked the wall. This gave Fox enough time to open the drawer and retrieve the Swiss Luger.

Stine felt the back of his head. He examined his hand, now covered in blood. Fox pointed the narrow barrel of the antique pistol toward Stine. "You didn't answer my question. How does it feel?"

This time Stine laughed. "I have no idea what you're talking about, Fox."

Tess, who had moved to the far corner, asked, "What is he talking about?"

"I'm afraid he's gone Section 8 on us, Sweetheart," the colonel answered.

She looked rattled. "Section 8?"

"Psychologically unfit for duty," Fox answered. "A term about as old as the colonel himself. And just like the colonel, no longer relevant." He steadied his grip on the Luger, keeping it pointed at Stine. Fox was exhausted. Pushing the colonel across the room took the last bit of strength out of him. Even though he had a loaded gun, one that hadn't fired in years, Fox felt vulnerable. It was the virus. Madness gnawed at the edges of his brain. Lurking, stalking him. He had seen it work on Jack and fully take Claire. All courtesy of the colonel's fucking bug. Fox squeezed the gun, telling himself he was in control. In the corner of his eye, he could see the young private leaving. "Wait," he told her. "You've yet to hear the story."

She stopped. "The weapon is a virus," Fox said. "Not one that causes sickness, although it does do that. No, it just starts out that way, first making you feel like dog shit—headaches, fatigue, nausea, joint pain. Then comes depression and paranoia. Not long after, psychosis. This virus, this weapon, was supposed to...how did you put it, Colonel?" Fox asked. Stine said nothing, just bore a hole into Fox with his eyes. "Oh yes, 'steal the soul of a nation,' that was it. Only," Fox chuckled, "he deployed it in his own country. And the best part," he shifted his eyes from the colonel to the girl, "is he has no antidote."

"You son of a bitch," the colonel said through closed teeth. "You're going down."

"No, Colonel, we are all going down, including this little friend of yours." Fox motioned to Tess.

"Wait, what?" she said.

"You want to know about Stinger?" asked Fox. "He's taking Claire to the hospital right now. Stinger is with me, Stine. He's always been with me. As for Jack, well he's alive too. And he's on his way right now to the press to deliver the story of the year to every news agency in the city."

"Fox," Stine yelled. "You're full of shit."

"Am I? This virus you created—I'm not giving you that much credit—the virus you unleashed, it's out. It is not contained. Just in Savannah you've got people drowning themselves in the river in droves."

Stine rose to his feet, clenching his fists and his jaw. His head bled steadily down his shirt. His eyes narrowed on Fox.

"You didn't know, did you?" he asked.

The colonel put his hand back to his head to stem the bleeding tide. "Fox, you've got just as much to lose in this as I do. You think if I go down, you walk?"

"Wait," Tess said. Her eyes shifted back and forth. She bit her bottom lip. "You mean this is true? Is what he's saying true?"

Neither of them answered. "Colonel, I don't care. You're going down." Fox realized that he meant what he said. For the first time ever, he didn't care. He was tired. Tired of running, tired of fighting, tired of surviving. He knew it was probably the virus, but he was spent. "You are a murderous bastard."

Colonel Stine laughed loudly. "Fox, please. You've killed more men than cancer."

"All under orders, Colonel. That woman you killed—Mia—she was no threat to you. The girl wasn't even infected."

"Save me your bullshit morality, Son."

Fox took a deep breath and steadied the Luger. "Colonel, I didn't come here to debate. I'm going to help where needed to complete the antidote. Count yourself infected now. You better hope we find a cure." Fox looked at blood still steadily oozing through the colonel's fingers. "That is if you don't bleed out first."

The colonel scoffed. "This is a scratch. I've been cut worse while shaving, Fox."

"Yeah, we need to get you healthy for the stockade, sir." Fox answered. Tess stood just out of reach of both of them. Her body was still frozen, only her eyes shifted between them. "You should come with me," Fox told her. She looked indecisive. Fox made for the door. From the corner of his eye, he saw Tess follow.

As he left the office, Stine yelled, "You'll be in the cell with me, Fox. Only this time, Stinger won't be there to save you."

CHAPTER THIRTY-SEVEN

Fox stumbled as he walked away from the military base towards his car. He couldn't remember a time when he felt this weak. That included the three days he spent walking through an Afghan desert with only one canteen. Once in his car and on the road, he checked his mirror constantly, certain he was being followed. He was plagued with a sense that something, or someone, just outside his line of sight was closing in on him. Fox locked eyes on every passing driver, even taking the time to scan the sky above. He tried to slow his rapid breathing and his racing heart. Traffic sputtered around him, choking him on either side. He cursed himself for being boxed in the center lane.

Claire wasn't there to talk him down. Fox weighed his immediate options, which were limited. It was best to lay low for the night in the safe house—a terrifying thought. There were far too many weapons available. Just thinking of his hand on the cold steel of a 9 mm made him sweat. The thought of a bullet tunneling through his cerebral cortex was equally liberating and horrifying.

Traffic crept around him up a steep overpass until it came to a stop, making Fox feel more claustrophobic. As he inched up the ramp, Fox expected to see a broken-down truck or a fender bender. Instead his eyes locked on two kids straddling a guard rail on the ramp. *They couldn't be older than twenty,* thought Fox. He brought his slow-moving car to a stop, parked, and got out. He left on foot toward the kids on the rail, certain it would be faster than the standstill traffic. The two were facing each other. The one closest to Fox had his back turned—a lanky frame of a teenage boy. Wisps of stringy red hair fell from under a skull cap. The face across from the boy was a young girl in a T-shirt and black leather jacket. She shifted her gaze from the boy to Fox. Her pale-blue eyes sent a chill through him. Fox picked up his pace to reach them in time, but the air felt thick, as if he was underwater. He opened his mouth, but it didn't seem to matter. The girl was in motion. Fox had seen her look in others—mostly in battle. It was not a look of fear or confusion. It was one of resolve.

She kept her blue eyes leveled on him. Slowly, but too quick for Fox, they both swung their legs over the ledge. She vanished, leaving a trail of curls from her head to an empty blue sky. From below, Fox heard tires screech, glass break, and the sound of metal hitting metal. He leaned over the rail. The girl was laying flat on the pavement, having missed oncoming traffic. A pool of blood leaked from her skull, blond curls on the side of her head soaked red. Her blue eyes were open but lifeless. The boy was embedded in a windshield at an angle only a broken body could make. The driver was likely crushed. A few people exited their cars. One man shouted into his phone for help. *No need,* thought Fox.

He walked back slowly, feeling the weight of what he'd just witnessed. Fox had seen plenty of bodies—enough to fill a small auditorium if he thought of them all. But not this kind of senseless death of the young. All from a sloppy, fucked-up idea from Colonel Stine, or Charles Stuart, or whoever was pulling their strings. Fox was shocked by a sudden feeling of nausea. He'd seen plenty of greenhorns puke at their first sign of a twisted body, but he never had. Not even as a private.

Must be the virus, he thought. How many other lives had been needlessly lost by this cluster of a mission? His fatigue and fear gave way to anger. A man behind Fox's parked car blew his horn and waved his arms in frustration. Fox walked past his own parked car and stood glowering over the man. The man was prematurely balding, likely in his thirties. An important man who couldn't be inconvenienced by a couple of teenage suicides. Fox ran his index finger over his keloid scar, a habit he was prone to while waiting for his targets to break. The man took his hands off the horn and put them up in the air. They trembled. Fox was weary. Before the virus, he likely would have dangled the man over the road below by his ankles. He took his phone from his pocket and dialed Jack, who picked up on the second ring.

"Fox, you okay?"

Fox answered his question with one of his own. "How's Claire?"

"Stinger took her to the hospital. I've checked in on the antidote."

"Any progress?" Fox asked. The man behind the windshield, now shaking badly, was saying something he couldn't hear.

"Yes, good news. As it turns out, they had quite a head start. I provided the final piece. They may be able to have a prototype as early as tomorrow."

One night, thought Fox. Surely he could make it alone for one night.

"Did you make it to the colonel?"

"Affirmative. He'll be in need of an antidote soon enough," Fox answered. "Did you get the story out?" Fox stepped away from the car. He had more pressing matters than this selfish prick. The man quickly pulled away.

"I asked them to hold the news story for forty-eight hours, until we can be sure we have the antidote. I don't know if you've looked around, but the world is not the same as we left it," said Jack.

Fox agreed as he walked back to his car, thinking of the girl's pale-blue eyes and her wasted potential. Those eyes should have seen another sixty years, not thirty seconds of thin air before hitting the hot asphalt. "I'm heading back to the safe house," he said.

"Good idea," said Jack. "I'll bring the antidote soon, hopefully within hours."

Fox shifted his car to drive and eased past where the two kids straddled the rail just minutes ago. "The path is a bit wider now. You should be able to make it through. I'll send the coordinates." Latitude and longitude were the easiest way to locate his safe house.

"Okay. And, Fox... um... don't—"

"You either," Fox said, not allowing Jack to finish the thought.

Fox drove to the cabin trying to ignore the dead stare of the girl with the crushed skull. Once he opened the gate, he started to feel pressure. The iron bars, there to keep others out, felt like a cage. He remembered how Claire reacted weeks ago to the gate closing. At the time it seemed odd, even histrionic. But now Fox was the one taking shallow gulps of air while trying to catch his breath.

Once out of the car, he bent forward with his hands on his knees and listened to his heartbeat thunder rapidly in his ears. Fox felt a tight squeeze from his rib cage. Sweat formed on his forehead and the back of his hands. His head was so light it made him stagger for balance.

You're safe. You are safe, he repeated the words from Claire. *You're a soldier*, he added. But he didn't feel like a soldier. Fox was unfamiliar with panic. His enemy had been outside his head, at least for the last two decades. He had no immediate defense against this internal assault.

Slowly his breathing and heartbeat decreased. His head cleared enough to make it inside the house. Once he shut the front door, the feeling of being trapped returned, pushing him against the wall. He slid to the floor, squeezed again by an unforeseen force.

His mind drifted back to dark nights in the projects of New York. One moonless night in particular, when at age nine he was sent alone to the corner store. He was two blocks from home when a gunshot ripped through the air. The shot paralyzed his movement. It sounded only yards away. Fox had no weapon—just his skinny, trembling nine-year-old body. His heart thumped wildly, making it hard to breathe. Nausea gripped him, causing him to vomit meatloaf on his sneakers.

Fox felt that same squeeze now. He rested his head against the wall. *You made it though*, he thought. And he had, eventually—tiptoeing the two blocks home, sure he would be cut down only weeks after growing his first patch of pubic hair.

CHAPTER THIRTY-EIGHT

Bleary eyed, Fox leveled his 9-mm pistol in front of him. He was about to fire two rounds into the shadowy figure in the doorway when a familiar voice rang out.

"Fox! It's me, Jack. Take it easy."

Fox rubbed his eyes. His shirt was damp with sweat. The figure in the door came into focus. It was Jack. Light spilled in the cabin from the open door. *How long had he been out?* The pistol was heavy in his hand, all rounds still in the magazine. The last twelve hours had been hell.

"Sorry, Jack. It's been a long night."

"I see that," Jack said, pointing to the open bottle of bourbon next to the couch.

"Yeah," said Fox. "I thought the booze may help with the feeling," he thought for a moment, "of being trapped."

"And did it?"

His head was pounding. *Boom, boom, boom.* Why did people do this to themselves? Fox thought. Mental clips from the night before flashed in his mind. He slept in shallow fits, like brief fever dreams. At two in the morning, he finally grabbed his pistol. Visions and noises came and went, nearly causing him to unload a magazine of bullets into the wall. He felt exposed, hunted with no place to hide. Desperation made him jam the cold steel of the 9 mm under his chin at one point. The taste of gun metal from just hours before was still on his tongue, making him want to vomit. Was he really that close? "No, I don't think it did help," he answered.

"Well, I've got some good news," Jack said. He waited, but Fox said nothing. "Okay, since you asked, I injected myself with the antidote before driving here. It's ready."

"Thank God," said Fox, knowing he didn't have another night like the last one in him. "Did you bring it?"

"Of course." Jack pulled a full syringe from his pocket. "I have to say I think it's already working. I'm not back to my old self yet, but I haven't heard my father's voice in hours. Before the shot, his voice was in my ear more than my own."

Fox pulled up his sleeve, exposing his massive bicep. "Let's do it, now."

"Impressive," Jack said, looking at the twenty-four-inch bicep. "But it goes in your glute."

Fox stood up and dropped his pants. "You had me at 'hello.'"

"Funny, Fox, surprised you still have a sense of humor. This won't hurt a bit." Jack cleaned Fox's right buttock with alcohol, then buried the one-inch needle and emptied the syringe.

"Now what?" asked Fox.

"Hopefully that's it. Now we wait."

Fox nodded. His head was still pounding, and his mouth was seriously dry. He had plans but was in no shape to carry them out. He needed rest, but the thought of drifting back into those fitful nightmares unnerved him. "I think I'm going to drink some water and take some ibuprofen. I may try to get some rest in the back room. Last night was—"

Jack nodded. "Sure, I'll hang out until you're up. You want some help pulling the sofa back?"

Fox looked at the sofa he moved to the hallway to monitor the front door. He stood up. "Just leave it. Oh, and help yourself to the rest of this poison." He handed what was left of the bourbon to Jack.

"Little early for me, Fox. Besides, it looks like it tried to kill you."

"Well, it had some help," Fox said. He went into the kitchen to guzzle two liters of water and pop four Motrin. He then lay on his bed. To his surprise, he fell sound asleep within an hour. Fox woke up eight hours later without a headache. In fact, he had no aches—the first time in weeks. His head was clear, focused. Fox walked to the front porch where he found Jack sitting.

"Good morning, Fox," said Jack. "How are you feeling?"

Fox took stock of his body once more. "Very good, actually. You?"

"I feel terrific," said Jack.

"I'll be damned—it worked."

"Sure as hell did," said Jack. "The antidote basically targets a core protein, the same one that is only later expressed on its surface. One of the only proteins in this clever virus that doesn't change. Anyway, the antidote stops the replication of the virus completely. We are pretty sure it can be used as a vaccine as well. The body's B cells should make antibodies to the surface protein once it's expressed."

Fox only heard bits from Jack but was glad to hear he was back on his game. He was even more happy to hear the antidote worked. But Fox had his own skill set, quite different from Jack's. He was sure the colonel would run and find the antidote when it was released. But Fox was also sure where Stine would hide out. Let him get comfortable, thought Fox. I'll come for him then. Charles Stuart was different. He may try to hide—money would help that endeavor. But Fox could track just about anyone, anywhere. Besides, until the news broke, Stuart wouldn't feel threatened.

Fox spent the next hour preparing his cabin for company. Luckily back in the lab, Jack saved three vials of his own blood before injecting himself with the antidote. Fox grabbed one of the vials capped with a blue rubber top, three zip ties, a burlap bag, and his 9 mm to meet Stuart.

Fox could still access military channels through Stinger to track Stuart, but there was no need. He called Stuart's wife, using an alias of course. She gave him up easily enough. "Charles is at the Figure 8 cottage for meetings," she told him.

He wasted no time in driving to the house where one of their first meetings about this disastrous operation occurred. Fox wasn't surprised to find Stuart's Range Rover alone in the drive. The only meeting Stuart was having was between the sheets. His wife's tone alone clued Fox into that fact. There was something in her voice that seemed happy to put her philandering husband in a sticky situation. This situation was going to be sticky indeed, thought Fox.

He eased his car to a shadowed part of the drive. It was close to midnight, but an upstairs bedroom light was still on. Fox shut his car off and took a moment for himself, breathing in the salt air. His senses felt charged, like some postviral hyper-acuity. Fox sensed his fast-twitch muscle fibers poised to strike. His vision was sharp, even in just a sliver of moonlight. The faintest sounds reverberated in his ears. Fox felt like himself—an apex predator.

In the passenger seat was the burlap bag, vial of blood, and the zip ties. The military ID he used at the gate lay on the center console. The night security guard was an old-timer, eager to chat about his unimpressive military record. He was just as eager to open the gate for Fox, almost breaking into a salute.

Fox placed his items in the burlap sack and crept toward the cottage. He quietly entered through a side window and followed the light upstairs. The door to a bedroom was cracked, spilling light into the hallway. Fox pushed the door open. A young blonde lying in a king bed gasped. She pulled a sheet to her chin, covering her naked body. Fox pulled his gun from the small of his back.

The bathroom door flew open. A naked Charles Stuart stood in the doorway. He didn't gasp. Fox pointed the gun to his face.

"Fox, welcome. If you told me you were coming, I would have prepared the guest bed," Stuart said coolly.

"This isn't a social visit."

The blonde in the sheets made a noise that sounded like a frightened grunt. "Charles, who is this...this man?"

"Oh, excuse me, Mrs. Stuart, my name is Fox. Charles, I didn't realize your wife was so young."

"Don't be a smart ass, Fox," he said. "What is it that you want? I assume you don't mind if I put some clothes on?"

Fox lowered the target of his gun to the man's groin. "Actually, I do mind. What I want, Charles, is for you to suffer the same fate as the others." Fox thought about the two kids jumping to the freeway. He pictured the girl in the pool of blood with dead blue eyes. He thought of Claire in the hospital, struggling to live. Finally, he thought about his own hellish journey trying to stave off a merciless legion of demons.

"Fox, don't be so dramatic. I'm sure we can come to an arrangement. How would you like to retire with six figures in your bank account?" Fox worked the slide of the 9 mm, chambering a bullet. Stuart laughed. "Hell, we'll make it seven."

"I'm out of patience, Stuart. In case you didn't know, it's a shit show out there from your virus and likely to get worse. But we now have an antidote."

"Great," Stuart said.

"Not for you. Put these over your wrists." Fox threw Stuart a set of zip ties he'd fashioned as handcuffs.

"Seriously, Fox, naked?"

"Put them on now, and I won't put a second tie around your nuts."

Stuart studied Fox for a moment, then picked up the zip tie and slid his hands through. "Now what?" he asked.

"Tighten it with your teeth," Fox told him.

Stuart did as he was told. "Can I at least put something on?"

"Sure," said Fox, pulling out the burlap sack. "I have just the accoutrement."

"You're not putting that damn thing on my head, Fox."

"Well, not yet." Fox emptied the other zip tie and the vial of blood from the sack to the floor. He picked up the vial and pulled the rubber cap off.

"What the hell is that?" Stuart asked.

"This is your baby. Your invention. I can testify that it's one hell of a ride." From his near photographic memory, Fox recalled one of Stuart's offhand remarks about containment of the virus. *I wouldn't worry, Cam. None of us are going to experience any of this horror.* He felt like crushing the vial into the bag to let Stuart choke on the glass and blood. Instead, he poured the blood out into the sack until the vial was empty. He walked toward Stuart who wheeled away from him. Fox rammed his fist into Stuart's gut, causing the man to double over and gag. He lifted him up by a fistful of hair and put the bag over his head. "It won't be long now before you can experience your investment personally."

"No way you get away with this, Fox," said Stuart, who then broke into a spasmodic cough.

"I can always tape your mouth."

"Sir?" The naked blonde spoke, still clutching the sheets to her chin. "I don't know anything. I promise. C-C-Can... I go?" she stuttered.

Fox was so engaged with Stuart, he forgot all about the blonde. "And leave your husband?"

"He's not—"

"Relax, I know. Yes, you can go. Just get yourself treated for chlamydia," said Fox.

"Very funny," Stuart said, his voice muffled under the bag.

"Last warning before you're gagged," said Fox. Stuart was quiet. "Good, let's go. I have a room waiting for you."

CHAPTER THIRTY-NINE

Fox kept Stuart tied and bagged in the back seat. Ten minutes into the trip, Stuart's muffled voice boasted empty threats.

"Fox, you'll be in prison before this virus so much as makes me sneeze."

He had no intention of listening to Stuart spout off for the rest of the night. Didn't he warn him already?

Fox pulled over. "Damn, you're hardheaded," he said. He weighed his options: knock the man unconscious, gag him, or place him in the trunk. He pulled the blood-soaked bag off and taped Stuart's mouth shut. "I don't think we need the bag anymore. Of course, I'm happy to put it back on and stuff you in the trunk if you don't shut the hell up."

For the rest of the trip, Fox heard only an occasional grunt from the back seat. He ignored the groans—Stuart was probably thirsty, had a full bladder, or was trying to yell profanity through the strip of duct tape. Whatever the reason, Fox didn't care. He was happy to be closing in on the safe house. Charles

Stuart's room was prepared in advance. It wasn't going to be his usual suite at the Four Seasons.

When the gate closed this time, Fox felt no squeeze in his chest. He felt only peace that the place existed. Fox needed a place to hole up for the next few weeks. The news of the virus was sure to go viral itself. There would be questions to answer, people to blame, heads to sever. He wanted the dust to settle before coming forward. The only ones who did know of this place were either in the hospital, on the run, or recent visitors—namely Jack and Stinger. Those two weren't talking about the safe house.

Fox led Stuart up the steps and into the cabin. He was happy to see Jack take his advice from his text and leave already. He didn't need to be involved. Once they were inside, Fox ripped the tape off Stuart's mouth, leaving a red streak across the bottom of his face.

"Son of a bitch!" yelled Stuart. "How about some fucking water?"

Stuart's hands were still bound with the zip tie. Fox slapped the tape back on his mouth. "That's poor manners for a guest," Fox said. Stuart protested a string of muffled shouts under the tape. "I wouldn't go to your house and behave like that."

Fox went over to the panic room and typed in a code. A thick metal door opened. The room was prepared. There was enough food to last months. Sheets on the double bed were fresh and folded. Two pillows and two towels were provided. Fox left a series of books and magazines out. A few items were noticeably missing: the weapons. Fox had cleaned out his various guns, ammunition, crossbow, and knives.

"You have everything you need to enjoy a pleasant stay," Fox announced.

Charles Stuart muffled something beneath the tape.

"Oh, apologies. Let me remove that and untie you." Fox cut the zip tie and removed the tape once again.

This time Stuart didn't yell. "A panic room, Fox? Is this supposed to scare me?"

Fox laughed. "What's going to scare you is what's between your ears," he said.

"This looks lovely," commented Stuart. "Correct me if I'm wrong, but aren't panic rooms designed to keep people out? I mean maybe I'll let you in, and maybe I won't."

"True. But this panic room has an option to reverse the settings. Currently the code is locked from the outside. In this case, it's me keeping you in."

It was now Stuart who laughed. "Whatever, Fox. I may be more sophisticated than you, but I've roughed it worse than this on many occasions."

"I'm sure. As you can see, there are video monitors set up for you to watch the property. You will be able to see no one is coming for you. Also, you can communicate with me on this feed." Fox pointed to one of the monitors.

"It looks like I have everything I need," Stuart answered. "Except of course, your ass behind bars for the rest of your natural born life. But that will come," Stuart warned.

"There is one thing you will beg me for eventually," Fox said.

"Yeah, and what's that?"

"You will see." Fox shut the door to the room.

Stuart was alone behind four inches of steel. Any noise he did make was sure to be trapped in the steel box. As for Fox, he didn't mind being alone. In fact, he was looking forward to restoring his mental and physical health. He had set aside a few classics he wanted to read, or read again: Sun Tzu's *The Art of War*, Ernest Hemmingway's *The Old Man and the Sea*, Jack London's *The Sea Wolf*, as well as a few passages from the Old

Testament. Weeks of suffering the effects of the virus had weakened his body, as well as his mind. Fox was determined to build his muscle mass back, maybe even pack on extra. That meant a daily regimen of calisthenics, strength training, yoga, tai chi, and hiking or running.

He had little communication with Stuart the first week. Charles made the occasional threat but otherwise didn't say much. Fox could tell from watching the monitor that Stuart was experiencing the first stages of the virus. It was obvious the way he clutched his head and kicked the sheets to a ball during sleepless nights. Fox remembered those first days of the virus, when its hooks sank in. There was overwhelming fatigue, nausea, weird headaches—all symptoms that would later seem like a honeymoon period to what was ahead.

On the days Fox left the gate, he would hunt for game or fish in the river. He only turned the news on once, and for only thirty seconds. The news ticker on the bottom third of the screen told him everything he needed to know. A virus causing psychosis grips America. Who's responsible?

"Please be advised the following images contain disturbing content," a middle-aged female newscaster announced. "We felt it was necessary to show some of these pictures to demonstrate just how dire the situation has become in some areas."

Fox watched a video captured on a cell phone of two people jumping from a subway platform onto the tracks in front of a train. He shut the television off and decided to text Jack. Fox had given him a secure phone before they went their separate ways.

Fox: Is the antidote out and working?

Jack: Yes, but it's been hard to produce enough of it. It's spreading so fast.

Fox: And the vaccine?

Jack: Yes, it looks promising. How is your guest?

Fox: Uncomfortable. How is Claire?

Jack: She's awake but doesn't remember anything.

Fox: That may be a good thing.

It didn't take long for Stuart to pace the steel box like a caged animal with a haunted look in his eyes. When Fox woke in the night or early morning, he would look in on Stuart from the monitor. Stuart was either fidgeting like a junky having withdrawals or grabbing his knees and shivering. One time, Stuart slammed his head against the steel wall. Only two and a half weeks and already unraveling, thought Fox.

Their conversations were brief. Stuart spent the first two weeks making empty threats. Then came empty bribes. Now he looked busy fending off whatever demons danced in his million-dollar head. Fox wasn't Claire. He couldn't predict what haunted the man, but he was sure Charles Stuart was being haunted.

Three and a half weeks in, and Fox heard a muffled noise from the panic room. He was surprised that any noise could make it out. He checked the monitor and spoke to Charles. "Everything okay?" he asked.

Stuart looked at him from the monitor. His face was hollowed out, cheeks sunken, eyes bloodshot, hundred-dollar haircut gone to shit. "Fox, let me out of here. I'll give you anything you want. Anything. Just let me leave with my life. You got the antidote?"

"There is only one question that I'm waiting to hear from you, Stuart?"

"Please, Fox. No riddles."

Fox stopped the audio feed. Stuart punched himself in the head with a balled fist and then slammed himself to the ground. He writhed in pain. Physical or mental, Fox wasn't sure.

Fox left to go fishing in the river. It was a fine afternoon. The sun was shining, and the birds were chirping. Any remorse for Stuart was eclipsed by the hell that he, Jack, and Claire had gone through. And there were the two teenagers he saw jump onto a busy freeway. Two wasted lives. Not to mention the numerous others who were suffering. Sure, Fox played a part in the virus, but he was following orders. He wasn't even familiar with the full nature of the weapon until it was between his ears. He wasn't some avarice prick who seized an opportunity to pad his own bank account. Besides, Fox had been part of the solution. They had created the antidote.

Fox knew guys like Charles Stuart never took the fall. It would be someone below him, if he was implicated at all. But justice was currently being served nearby in the four-inch reinforced steel box. And it was poetic justice, seeing how it was Stuart's own mind that was administering the sentence.

Fox was able to catch two nice-size trout, enough to pan fry a decent lunch in garlic and butter. He was back by sunset. Fox ate well and fell asleep reading an old military briefing. He woke to a muffled cry. Fox checked the monitor. The audio feed was so loud he had to shut it down. Stuart was screeching like a wounded animal. Fox pressed the feed again. "Tone it down, Charles."

Stuart looked at the monitor. "Fox, please. You have to help me. You win, okay? Just kill me. Kill me!"

"I'm not going to kill you, Charles."

"Fine. Then let me do it."

Fox had been waiting weeks for this. "What is it that you want?"

"A weapon, Fox. Please."

Fox went to the other room and retrieved a revolver with one bullet loaded. It had been sitting on the shelf since their arrival, waiting for this moment. He opened the panic room. It smelled like piss and fear. Fox could almost feel the madness trapped within the walls. Stuart was crumpled in a heap beside the bed. Fox threw the weapon beside him. "There is one bullet in there. Don't miss."

Fox wasn't worried about Stuart taking aim at him. He was too weak and too disoriented. Fox debated staying, watching the end unfold. Instead he closed the steel door. He walked back to the monitor and turned on the video feed. He then opened the front door to let the night air in. A minute later a shot rang out.

CHAPTER FORTY

CLAIRE

I woke up with a thick tongue, like a film was over it. I swung my arm out and hit a rail. I swung the other arm and smacked another rail. A hospital bed? Where was I?

I moved my arms and legs, making a quick assessment of my function. Everything responded normally. There was an IV in the back of my left hand, hooked to an empty bag on a pole. I ran my other hand down my body, checking for any other probes or lines. Nothing. No catheter, rectal tube, gastric tube, or any sort of drain.

I scanned the room. It was bare. As bare as I had seen any hospital room. No cards, flowers, balloons. Not even a television. Large coiled ducts lined the walls.

I adjusted the pillow behind me to sit up. I could see a private bathroom. A glass wall divided the room to a smaller anteroom. I had my own suite, I thought. But this was no luxury suite. I was being isolated. This hospital room was an island.

I could see someone in the anteroom dressed in a rubber gown and a hood. The glass doors to my room opened. There was a plastic shield in the front of the hood, but the face was blurry. The person ignored me, checking gauges, monitors, and the IV bag.

"Hello," I said. My voice cracked on the second syllable. "Where am I?" My voice sputtered and cracked again. I must have been silent for some time.

The hood whipped in my direction. A woman's face. She looked startled at first but then smiled. She was young with a heart-shaped face and almond eyes.

It was obvious there wasn't going to be any communication while she was in the hazmat suit. After the woman overcame her initial shock, she went about her duties. She recorded vitals and replaced the empty IV bag with a full one.

Her suit suddenly gave me the impression the air was toxic, that I was toxic. I took a few deep breaths to try and soothe myself. The air seemed fine. My lungs didn't burn. My head felt clear. Besides my muscles aching a bit and an empty stomach, I felt decent. I wondered when I'd last eaten. Would a hot plate of eggs contaminate anything?

"I'm hungry," I said to the masked woman.

Nothing. Could she hear me? Read my lips? I could feel panic rising. I looked around for a phone. Nothing. No phone, no television. No communication with the outside world. My only source of information was a woman in a rubber suit who couldn't hear a word I said. Was I trapped? I could feel my pulse begin to race.

Calm down, Claire. You aren't tied down. You aren't injured. They are protecting you. Protecting others. But from what?

The woman in the mask held up a finger. She extended her arms out with her palms up. One minute. And take it easy. I made an okay sign. I could also play this game of charades.

The woman left. One minute. Stay calm. At least I could

see through the glass to the anteroom. And I had a window. Having no catheter and my own bathroom, I assumed I was free to walk around.

It was a strange room. I followed the path of the large air ducts. They must be pumping air from this room to the outside. I knew hospitals had all different types of isolation rooms. I'd visited a few myself during psychiatric rotations. I remember wearing gloves and a mask but never a hood and a rubber suit. What exactly was this room?

It wasn't long before there was more activity in the little decontamination room. Another hazmat suit came through the glass doors rolling a video monitor attached to a pole. The monitor was wrapped in plastic. I got a look behind the plastic mask, the same pretty woman as before. She smiled and wheeled the monitor next to my bed.

On the screen was an older African American man with a gray, thin beard that fell in curls like Spanish moss. "Dr. Turner," I said.

"Yes, hello," he answered. "Can you hear me, Claire?"

"Yes, I can." Thank God, I thought. Let me get some answers. The woman in the hazmat suit gave me a thumbs up. "Can you tell her thank you?"

"You can tell her yourself, Claire," answered Dr. Turner. "She is going to give you a device. It works like a walkie-talkie. Just press the button on the side to speak."

The hooded woman handed me a device, which was also wrapped tightly in plastic. I felt the button on the side and pressed it in. "Hello?"

"Hello, Claire," came a female voice through my handheld. "My name is Adeline. I'm your nurse. You can reach me anytime through the handheld. If that doesn't work, there is a red button on the back of the bed that you can push."

I turned around and found the button. "Thank you,

Adeline. I'm Claire. I guess you already knew that." She nodded. "Where am I?"

"You are in Emory University Hospital in Atlanta, Georgia," she answered.

"My alma mater," I said. Adeline said nothing. Oh, I hit the button and repeated myself.

"Yes, we know," she answered.

"How long—" I stopped and pressed the button. "How long have I been here?"

Adeline's eyes shifted from my face to the floor. "I think it's best for Dr. Turner to answer. I'm going to let you two talk now." She backed out of the room. The glass doors opened and closed, leaving just Dr. Turner on the monitor.

"Dr. Turner, it's good to see you. It's been a while." The doctor rocked his head back and forth in response. "Something wrong?"

"Always good to see you, Claire. This is actually our fourth session since you've been in the hospital."

"Fourth session?"

"Yes, but don't be alarmed. You are making great progress. The first two sessions you didn't know who I was." He took off his glasses, wiped a smudge, and put them back on his face. "To be honest, in our first session, you didn't know your own name."

I said nothing; I didn't know where to start. So many questions. "How long have I been here?" I repeated.

"Almost three weeks. What else can I answer for you?"

What else can you answer? My whole life at the moment was a question. The only answer I had was where I was and for how long. My head swam with so many. Why was I even here, and in isolation? What was wrong with me? Where is everyone? What is this disgusting film on my tongue? "Start from the beginning. Tell me everything."

Dr. Turner adjusted his glasses and took a measured

breath, something I'd seen him do with other patients. "You know, Claire, they brought me in because I'm an old friend and mentor. But also because, like you, I'm a trained mental health professional. There is a lot to cover. Frankly," he stroked the Spanish moss beard, "most we have covered already. It may be a more productive use of our time if you tell me what you last remember."

I took my eyes off his face and looked at the ceiling. I thought back. I couldn't remember anything about this hospital. Not the smell, not the empty room, not the tiny bed or IV. I thought back to my life. I knew I was a therapist. I knew I owned a practice with my best friend, Mia. I lived in midtown with my sister, Amy. A hollow feeling shot through my gut. Amy, oh. I remember she was gone. The pills, the feel of her dead, cold skin. I tried to remember the funeral but couldn't. Did we not have a funeral? Actually, I couldn't remember much beyond her body lying in an awkward angle on our couch. An angle that no living person would rest in.

"I remember my twin, Amy, dying," I answered.

"Yes," the doctor answered, "I'm sorry. Is that the last thing you remember?"

"Yes."

Dr. Turner nodded. "You had a head injury, Claire. You are actually lucky to survive. You almost drowned." I winced. "Yes, I know drowning is a fear of yours. You were pulled out of a river and brought to a local emergency room. Eventually, you were brought here. And eventually, you regained consciousness. You appear to be suffering from retrograde and anterograde amnesia. Do you remember what those are?"

"Amnesia, how could I forget?" I asked.

He smiled. "Still have your sense of humor, I see."

"Retrograde amnesia is the inability to recall old memories, while anterograde is the inability to create new ones."

"I couldn't have said it better myself. You were my brightest student, Claire."

I smiled at his compliment, and he smiled back. He looked like a kind, wise grandfather. Anterograde amnesia, I thought, and shuddered. How many times would I suddenly remember the death of my twin sister?

"It's been just over two months since Amy's death," Dr. Turner said. "Some of the most memorable two months in our country's history. And you, Claire, have been in the center of it."

"What?"

"You are in isolation now because of the development of a virus that was weaponized."

"A what?"

"The military was experimenting with a virus to be used in warfare. It causes physical but mostly mental symptoms. The infected become depressed, anxious, paranoid, and ultimately psychotic, suicidal. It was never intended to be released."

A virus that attacks mental health developed by the military? I looked at Dr. Turner's face on the video monitor wrapped in plastic. I looked at the stark room, the ventilation system, the tiny glass room next to my own. None of it seemed real. It was like a science fiction book or the most expensive practical joke ever played. My thoughts drifted to Amy. Her suicide. That was no accident. My fear turned to anger.

"I guess Amy was infected?" I asked.

"Yes, I'm afraid so," Dr. Turner answered.

So many more questions. I fired them off, one after the other. Dr. Turner went through the mechanism of the virus, at least as much as he knew. It was a clever virus. "Who's taking care of my patients?" I asked. "How's Mia?"

Dr. Turner opened his mouth to answer but paused. It was enough. I knew something happened. Something bad.

"I'm sorry," he said.

I nodded. The anger building. "She was infected?"

The doctor took his glasses off again to clean them. Stalling. "How are you feeling, Claire?"

"Don't patronize me, Henry." He looked shocked. I rarely used his first name. "What happened?" I demanded.

He cleared his throat. "Claire, this may not be the time."

"I want to know."

"She was killed." He took off the glasses again, rubbing his eyes. "This wasn't the way I wanted this session to progress," he answered.

"How?"

Dr. Turner provided the information that he could. He didn't seem to hold anything back. "So they are just hunting people down and killing them now?" I asked.

"That would be impossible," he answered. "There are too many infected."

What was he saying? "So we are all doomed?"

"I haven't told you the good news."

Amy was infected with a virus from the US government that made her kill herself. Mia was tortured, then killed. The country, maybe the entire world, is now infected. And there is good news? "What could that possibly be?"

"You and Jack Baker, along with a guy named Fox, found an antidote. You are all national heroes."

"Heroes? Seriously?"

"Seriously. You had some help, but it was you three who pushed the cure out."

I shifted my weight in the small hospital bed. The IV dug into my hand a bit. I looked around the empty place. It was cold. Smelled of antiseptic. The exhaust ventilation hummed. I hated hospitals. "I don't feel like a hero. Besides, I have no idea who you are talking about. Jack? And Fox, what is that, a code name?"

"Actually it's Grady Jones. But evidently he only goes by Fox. He was hiding you three while you worked on the cure. You were all infected. He actually was part of the initial team that developed the virus."

"Great, hiding out with the enemy known as Fox."

"Not an enemy anymore. He's expected to receive a full pardon from the president."

Pardon. The word hit me wrong. What about my dead sister? And Mia? "I hope someone is going to pay," I said to the air.

"Of course. There is an ongoing investigation. There hasn't been a war crime like this in fifty years. You are not the only one who lost a loved one. The suicide rate has been up over 1,000 percent, over two hundred times higher than average. Up to 26,000 per day, some sources say. Savannah alone has lost a fourth of its population."

The pit in my stomach returned. Savannah.

"Don't worry, Claire. Your parents are fine."

A wave of nausea swept over me. The anger stayed. "So if there is a cure, then why do I feel like an Ebola patient here?"

"Well, you were one of the first ones infected. The cure is being administered across the country as a treatment and a vaccine. I guess, because your symptoms were so advanced, they are being precautious. The longer someone is infected, the more likely they are to transmit the virus. The replication at later stages reaches very high numbers. In fact," he raised his eyebrows, "no one who's had the virus as long as you and Jack is known to have survived."

"Who is Jack?" I asked. Dr. Turner told me everything he knew about Jack. I had no recall.

"I want to ask you the same question I did earlier. How do you feel?"

I took stock of my body. I was weak—that was a fact. I was hungry, also a fact. But nothing hurt. The loss of my sister hurt, as well as the loss of Mia. But I didn't feel terrible. "Okay, I guess, considering."

He nodded. "Are you hearing any voices? Seeing any visions?"

"You."

"Right, good."

"And someone walking around in a rubber Smurf suit. Is that a hallucination?" I asked.

"Unfortunately, that's real," he answered. "The fact you don't have any delusions is evidence enough you are cured. Of course, it's natural to be upset with all the news you just processed. I suspect they will come out of those Smurf suits, as you call it, soon enough."

"Don't they have a way of just checking a viral load or something?" I asked.

"I believe so. They brought you into this room in the beginning. No one was sure if you were going to make it. Like I said, it's been a process. Precautionary now, I would think."

I nodded. Dr. Turner turned a watch on his wrist over. "We've been at it for over two hours," he said. "Are you ready for a break?"

"Sure, when will we talk again?" I asked.

"Anytime you want. Just ask the nurse for me."

"Will you have to repeat everything again? Starting from 'There was a virus developed'?"

"If I need to," he answered. "But you are remembering more and more, so I doubt it. Our first few sessions you repeated the same questions multiple times. That isn't happening anymore. I think you will remember. I think you are remembering."

"Thank you. One more question."

"Yes, Claire?"

"Can I get something to eat?"

CHAPTER FORTY-ONE

Two days went by, and little changed, at least not to me. The staff said I was doing great, but I don't remember being ill. Adeline traded shifts with a male nurse, Jude. He was a bearded man who was probably midthirties with piercing blue eyes. He lost his father to the virus, who walked in front of an oncoming train. That wasn't even news anymore, Jude said. In fact, most companies put a halt on trains altogether until the crisis improved.

He shook his head. "Just last week some notable psychiatrist took a swan dive from the top floor of his fancy downtown office. It was the middle of the afternoon, and he just missed a couple strolling hand in hand on the sidewalk below. The guy was wearing all red, which looked pretty eerie surrounded in a pool of blood."

"Yikes," I said.

"Thankfully, though, it's getting better." He checked my blood pressure, pulse, oxygen level, and temperature. "Perfect numbers, Claire." He looked at his watch. "I'll be back in an hour. Just buzz me if you need me before."

Doing great, huh? My IV was out, which was progress. And the IPC on my legs was removed. That stood for intermittent pneumatic compression, Adeline informed me. A device to prevent blood clots. Now that I was up walking around, I could take these off. I kind of miss the hiss of air filling the device, and the squeeze on my calves. But walking around unencumbered, even in my weakened condition, was progress. And I was eating like a horse. I hadn't been this hungry since I was a teenager.

But the walls in my hospital room, my little island, felt tight. I had paced every inch of that room. I still had no phone, no access to media, and no contact with the outside world—except for Adeline, Jude, and Dr. Turner.

Today I was doing lunges. I was able to get six full lunges in from one side of the room to the other. After three passes, I was spent. The video monitor to communicate with Henry Turner hadn't left my room. I looked at the clock on the wall. I was thankful to have it. There was enough light from the window to tell night from day, but without the clock I would have no idea of the time. It was almost 10:30. Time for my session with Dr. Turner. Today, I was told my parents would join. At 10:28, Jude came in. He was still in the blue rubber Smurf suit.

He motioned for me to pick up the handheld. "Good morning, Claire," he said from under his hood. His voice cracked through momentary static on my device.

"Hey, Jude."

"How are we feeling?"

"We? Remember, Jude, I'm not crazy anymore."

"Right, just an expression. How are you feeling, Claire?"

I stood next to him, a foot away from the screen covering his face. I pushed the button and talked into my device. "I'm good, Space Ranger. When are you coming out of your NASA suit?"

"Ha, yeah, I hate this thing. You wouldn't believe how my beard itches under here." He tapped on the plastic shield like he wanted to itch his face. "If this keeps up any longer, I'm going to shave clean. With any luck though, your viral count will come back low enough to take these things off. Maybe as soon as tomorrow."

I punched the button on the side of the walkie-talkie. "Ten-four, Space Ranger."

"Someone's in a good mood today," he answered.

"I get to see my parents today. At least on the monitor."

"Yep, and I'm happy for you. Looks like it's already past 10:30. Let's get you connected." Jude powered the video on. He hit buttons until Dr. Turner's face filled the screen.

"Can you hear me, Claire?" asked Dr. Turner.

"Loud and clear. Good morning."

Jude said his goodbyes and left me alone with the video. "And how are you feeling this morning?"

"Good." I was anxious to move past the evaluation and talk to my parents. Dr. Turner did his usual assessment. Given his background, the medical team allowed him to be my communicator. Henry Turner was board certified in internal medicine, neurology, and psychiatry. My medical team included a neurologist, as well as an internist, but it was Dr. Turner who spoke for them. I wasn't sure if it was his background in psychiatry or our personal connection that led to that decision.

The next ten minutes followed what was now a daily routine: memory check, mood check, and a physical symptoms check. Dr. Turner said I was improving daily. There was still a gap in my memory. A deep gash that started with the death of my sister and ended in this hospital room. By Dr. Turner's careful approach to that gap, there must be plenty of trauma lying in it. My ability to read people's emotions was still sharp. Whenever I fished for my lost memories, the doctor's body tensed. Did I even want to remember the last two months? If those memories did return, Dr. Turner seemed poised to use every bit of his training.

Once done with his assessment, Dr. Turner said, "Great progress, Claire. I will inform your other doctors, Thomas and Paulson. Hopefully they can step down the personal protective equipment as early as tomorrow. I'm sure it would be nice for you to talk to someone in person not wearing a Smurf suit, as you call it."

I nodded. I loved Dr. Turner, but I was tired of our conversations. I was tired of talking only to him. I wanted to see my parents.

"So are you ready to talk to your parents?"

"Yes."

"Remember, Claire, a lot has happened to people on the outside. Even your parents have likely seen more tragedy these past few months than their entire lives. I know you're trained in trauma response, but I am concerned. Some of their, um, experiences may uncover some recent unpleasant memories of your own. If that happens, please contact me immediately."

"I understand."

"Great. Now let me patch them through. Matt," he yelled behind him, "let's get the Longs on now." There was a pause. "Bye, Claire."

The screen went blank. I thought the connection was lost until my mother's face filled the monitor. "Mom!" I was so happy to see her, anyone, I screamed.

"Claire-Bear. Honey, you look great. Oh," she moved back a bit, "here's your father."

"Hey, Claire. So glad you're okay." Dad's voice was even keeled as usual.

I stared at the screen, tongue-tied for a moment.

"When are they going to let you out of that room?" my mother asked.

"This glass cell? I don't know. They're checking the viral load in my blood now. If it's low enough, I think at least they can touch me like they won't explode."

My mother smiled, shaking her head. "We are so proud of you, Claire. You know you're a hero."

"So I hear. But I wouldn't know. I've been without any news here."

"You and that boy, Jack. I like him. Handsome boy. Man, I should say. Everyone seems like a boy to me." She hadn't stopped smiling since she got on the video.

"I don't know. I can't remember Jack."

"The doctors said as much," my father said. "Honestly, it may be better if you don't remember. The world has been... well, different."

"How?"

"It's been frightening. Some say it's the beginning of the end. The apocalypse. People walking out into moving traffic, trains. Neighbors jumping into the river."

"Stop it, Wendell," my mother scolded. "You said it yourself—she doesn't need to know." Her smile finally fell.

"I want to know, Dad. Tell me. I heard Savannah was bad. Anyone I know died?"

"Anyone you know? Hell, Claire, the whole town—"

"That's enough!" my mother cut him off, then softer, "Claire found a cure. That's what matters."

I looked at my father's face. The lines around his mouth and forehead were cut deeper than usual. I'm guessing, entrenched by weeks of worry. Even my mother, once her smile faded, looked exhausted. "Were you two infected?" I asked.

"Yes, we were, Dear."

"Right...from Amy." But it didn't make sense. If Amy infected my parents, then it must have been early, very early.

Even before me. And if that were the case, wouldn't they be, be—

"It wasn't your sister," Dad cut in. "We were actually in Florida when she came home. She came home and saw your cousin Beth. God rest her soul."

"Wait, Beth is what? Is she dead?" I took a sharp breath.

"What did I tell you, Wendell?" Mom snapped again. "Even the doctors said not to say too much."

My father's mouth tightened, lines cut underneath it. His eyes turned down.

"It's okay, Daddy. I need to know. Please, tell me what happened."

His mouth parted, but he said nothing. He looked at my mother and shut down. Two warnings and forty-five years of marriage will do that. "Please, I need to know." Still nothing, from either of them. "What happened to Beth?"

"It was over three and a half weeks ago," my mother finally answered. We were going to meet her to talk. She had been having a tough time. We weren't sure why. Remember when she used to take three showers a day? Always thinking she was somehow dirty?"

I nodded, thinking back to my cousin as a teenager. She was obsessed with cleanliness. Maybe OCD. "Yes, I do."

"Well, that got much worse. She was taking like eight showers a day. Some without hot water. And scrubbing her hands and apartment constantly. She claimed there were roaches, bedbugs, even maggots in her place."

The delusions, I thought. Dr. Turner said they preyed on existing anxiety.

"So we wanted to meet her. To help her. We met on River Street, right in front of River Street Sweets. She was wearing her...her—" My mother buried her face in her hands and sobbed.

"Perhaps it's better if we don't," my father said, putting his arm on her shoulder.

She raised her face and wiped her eyes. "No, I want to finish. She had on the peacoat I gave her for Christmas last year. The tan, wool one. She looked thin. The back of her hands were rubbed raw from scrubbing. She looked, I don't know." Another tear streamed down her face. "Troubled, I guess. Anyway, before we could get to her, she just jumped." My mother bit her bottom lip. More tears streamed. "If she hadn't been wearing that peacoat, maybe she would have come up."

"Mary, we've been through this," my father said. "It has nothing to do with the peacoat."

"But it was wool, Wendell. It was heavy. It may have pulled her down. She didn't have a chance."

My father pressed my mother to him and kissed her head. They were always a cute couple.

"Dad's right. It's not your fault. It's that deadly virus."

My mother shook her head. "It's just been awful, Claire. Just awful."

"I should have gone in after her," Dad said. "I had no idea she wouldn't come up."

"Don't be ridiculous, Wendell. That current would have taken you right under. Then I'd be without you and Beth. Ridiculous."

I could see the guilt in his eyes. "She's right, Dad. That current can be strong. And the water must have been freezing."

"Still," he said, looking at the floor.

"You tried to jump in, you remember?" Mom asked. "I had to keep you from jumping too."

"I could have gone in. You couldn't really have kept me from jumping."

"We've been married over four-five years, Wendell. I think I can keep you from doing a lot of foolish things."

"Guys," I cut them off. "I'm just glad you two are okay." I smiled.

"And we are glad you are okay," Mom answered. "Claire-Bear, our hero."

We spent the next few minutes talking about other people who were gone. Neighbors, old teachers, Mom's tennis coach. I didn't talk about Mia. I tried, but every time a lump in my throat formed, and I couldn't bear to talk about it. I knew they needed help. What they had been through. It sounded like classic PTSD. In fact, the whole country sounded like it was experiencing posttraumatic stress disorder. If I ever got back to counseling, I would be booked until the end of time.

After an hour, we said our goodbyes. We had both been asked by Dr. Turner not to talk for over an hour. An hour was enough for our first meeting since the accident, he had suggested.

CHAPTER FORTY-TWO

Two more days passed. I was so bored I asked for a copy of *Crime and Punishment*. If there was ever a time to finish Dostoevsky's classic novel, it was now. Besides if Dr. Turner sees me reading this book, maybe it will finally convince him that my mind is sharp

My viral load came back as no load at all, nearly undetectable. As a result, the hoods and rubber suits were replaced with thin plastic gowns and surgical masks. A step in the right direction, but I still hadn't felt another hand that wasn't gloved.

What I really wanted was out of the glass box. To breathe fresh air that wasn't negatively sucked from the room and pumped outside. I was told to be patient, and I would move in a matter of days. I guess the disappearance of the hazmat suits was the first sign that I may join the living again. But the real sign was that I was going to have my first visitor today. At least my first visitor who wasn't paid to take care of me.

In a perfect world, that visitor would be my twin, Amy. If not her, then my business partner and best friend, Mia. As it turned out, my visitor would be someone I spent the hardest weeks of my life with. Someone who knew my greatest fears and the things I loved. Someone who was a total stranger. How do I meet someone for the first time that I went through hell with? That I cheated death with? That I, supposedly, saved the world with?

Adeline walked through the room. Her plastic gown swished as she moved. "Are you excited to see Jack?" she asked.

"Meet Jack," I corrected.

"Yeah, I guess that's right. Meet Jack." Her voice was much softer than what had come through the handheld. "That's got to be weird."

I shrugged. "This whole thing is weird."

"Tell me about it," she said. "I've got news crews even mobbing *me* when I step out of the hospital."

"Isn't that a HIPAA violation?"

"You would think so," she answered. "Anyway, do you even know what Jack looks like?" I shook my head. "Well, let me tell you, he is easy on the eyes." Adeline laughed. "You two make a fine-looking superhero couple."

I took a deep breath. "Why does everyone keep saying that? We aren't a couple."

"Honey, it's the news. Even if you aren't, it makes for a better story."

"I guess."

"Well, he'll be here soon. I'll leave you to it."

Leave me to what? There was nothing to do but wait. It's not like I could fix myself up. I had no makeup and hospital gowns for clothes. I showered this morning, combed my hair, brushed my teeth. I was clean, but that was about it.

I stared at the ceiling for a while trying to remember anything about Jack. Nothing. I thought I may drift off to sleep from sheer boredom when I heard activity in the anteroom. I looked at the clock: 1:30. It was time. He must be here.

I don't know why, but I felt a nervous energy. What if I hated this guy? My superhero partner against the evils of this world. What if he was a jerk? Or just a total nerd? Nerd, I could handle. I mean we were just friends anyway, right?

I could see someone wearing a blue surgical mask putting on a plastic gown. A tall figure with dark, wavy hair.

He walked through the glass doors carrying a chair. I realized, for the first time, there was no furniture in the room besides my bed. He brought the chair next to me. My bed was folded into a seated position.

"Hey, Claire."

"You must be Jack."

"I guess you don't recognize me?"

I shook my head.

"It feels silly to be wearing this mask and this gown. I mean we had the same virus, and I'm out there walking around."

"I guess you never got admitted to the hospital?"

"Nope." He pulled down his mask. His skin was smooth, almost flawless. He had a strong forehead and jaw. I stared into his eyes—hazel eyes with long, thick lashes. "Anything?" He smiled widely.

"Nothing." I laughed.

"What is it? Does my face look that funny?"

"No, it's just I had this picture of you in my mind. It's like when you read a book and you can picture the characters. Then the movie comes out, and the person looks nothing like what was in your head."

"So this version of me," he pointed to his face, "movie version—better or worse?"

"Just different."

He blinked those impossibly long lashes, the only real delicate thing about his face. "Thank you for coming," I said.

He laughed.

"Now you're laughing. What is it?"

"It's just weird. I know I'm a stranger to you. But when I left you, after all we went through, I spent every day, every hour even, worried about you—thinking about you."

"And?"

"And when you said 'Thank you for coming,' I couldn't not come. I would have been sleeping on the floor in the corner for the past month if they let me."

I smiled. "Thank—" I caught myself, not really knowing how to respond. I looked over at the anteroom. Adeline made a motion for Jack to put his mask back on. "I think she wants you to put your mask back up."

He smiled, waved, and put the mask back on his face. "We're safe now," he said.

"Oh, definitely." I was a little disappointed. He had a nice smile. Even though I didn't remember him, there was something familiar about the smile. Everyone was gowned or masked but me. "So what's happening out there?" I asked, pointing at the window to the outside.

"Out there? It's crazy. Well, thankfully the craziness is settling some. But really, it's been sad."

"What's life been like for you?" I asked.

He shook his head. "Claire, I don't even know where to begin."

"I hear you're a hero."

"I don't feel like a hero," he answered.

"Well, you must be. One thing I can remember is that I know nothing about virology. I don't know the last time I even looked under a microscope. If there was a genetic sequence programmed to target the virus's core protein, it had absolutely nothing to do with me."

"For someone who remembers nothing, you sure do know a lot."

"Just what Dr. Turner told me."

Jack cocked his head.

"My old mentor from graduate school. He's also been my doctor here. They thought it would be easier for me to see a familiar face."

"Did he mention that it was you who saved us both? That you are the real hero?"

I smiled. "You created an antidote. Fox pulled me out of a river. I'm not seeing where I'm the hero in this story. If this was a movie, I hope they cast a pretty face for me, because that's all I seemed to contribute."

"Back to the movie? Seriously, Claire, if it wasn't for you, Fox and I both would have been in that river long before you. You were amazing. You kept us grounded. Even gave us medication." He leaned forward in his chair. "It's like you knew how the virus would attack our minds and talked us through it. If you weren't there, I would have totally lost my grip on reality. The same for Fox."

"Fox," I shook my head. "I keep hearing about him. Was he a bad guy? Is he a bad guy?"

"Fox?" Jack's eyebrows went up. "It's just so bizarre you don't remember. Fox started off that way, I guess. I mean he was with the team that created this godforsaken virus. But in the end, he found us. And he protected us. Without Fox, the colonel's men would have killed us for sure."

"Colonel?"

Jack took a deep breath. "This is a long story. Let's just say if you're looking for a villain, the colonel is the one."

"So Fox protected us."

"And you protected him," Jack said.

"And you, Jack, protected everyone."

"All that's left is the award ceremony," he answered, smiling.

"Whatever happened to this colonel?"

Jack shut his eyes for a moment, like the name stung them. "I think they're still looking for him. He's public enemy number one, that's for sure. But who knows? I'm sure he was getting orders from someone else too."

I tried to picture this colonel but couldn't. Tried to picture Fox and couldn't.

"Why are you smiling?" asked Jack.

"Oh, I didn't realize I was. I was trying to picture these characters. People, I should say. The villainous colonel, maybe Jack Nicholson's character from *A Few Good Men*."

"Yeah, he was a nasty piece of work," Jack agreed. "But I think he was a general. The colonel is a wiry guy with a thin white mustache. You haven't seen pictures?"

"No, I have had no media at all."

"That's good," said Jack. "You've been through a hell of a lot. The last thing you need is to relive that trauma. I hope you never remember. I like seeing you like this."

"Like what, exactly?"

"Um, carefree. Happy."

"You didn't like me before?"

His eyebrows pointed. "Claire, I loved you before." He seemed to gauge my reaction and pulled his head back. "Sorry, that was a little much. I liked how you were before. I'm just happy to see you not suffer."

I said nothing. It was strange—a stranger I shared so much with. Adeline came through the automatic glass doors. "Hey, I'm afraid time's up for today."

"When will I see you again?" I asked.

"As soon as you want," he answered. "Even though you don't remember me, I feel like we should get through these next steps together." He thought for a minute. "Like I said, it's pretty nuts out there."

"What about Fox?" I asked.

"Fox is, well, Fox."

"What does that mean?" I asked.

"You'll find out soon enough."

CHAPTER FORTY-THREE

Celebrity status. It was already painful. The good news was that I moved to a regular floor. The bad news was three nurses and two random patients had already taken selfies with me. I couldn't walk twenty yards down the hallway without someone stopping me for a picture or a story. I was gaining a whole new appreciation for the life of those stalked by paparazzi. On the bright side, maybe I could open a niche practice for counseling famous figures.

I had been on a regular floor for three days, which was a full eight days after my meeting with Jack. We had talked on the phone twice since our meeting but nothing in person. Another bright spot in my life was when I saw my mother. Not on a screen but in person. And for the first time, in a long time, I had real contact with another human being. A hug from my mother to be exact. It felt so good to embrace someone, especially her. Having lost Amy and Mia, I needed to know someone else was there.

It was so odd to me not having Mia or Amy to talk to. After meeting Jack, my mind was swimming. I needed to talk. With

Amy and Mia gone, it felt like my whole support system was gone all at once. Those big events that happened in my life didn't even seem real without sharing it with one of them. In truth, I still talked to them. I spilled my guts out aloud, even spooking the nurse one time who came to check on me.

"Don't worry," I said. "I'm just, um, praying out loud." The last thing I wanted was to alarm Dr. Turner. He was constantly asking me if I was having any delusions.

"Please, Honey," the nurse said, "I do that all the time. Sometimes I catch myself singing out loud in a meeting." She laughed. "Can I get you anything?"

I shook my head.

"Well, I knew you were glad to see your mother. Mine passed four years ago, and not a day goes by that I don't think about her."

"I'm sorry," I said. I could see the loss in her eyes.

"Thank you, Sweetheart. I heard you have another visitor today. Someone by the name Fox. One of the three, I guess."

"Three what?" I asked.

"Don't act coy with me. Three heroes, Honey. You know that's right."

I smiled. "Sure, one of the three," I answered.

"I'll leave you be then. Call me if you need me."

She walked out, leaving me alone in the room. Finally, I had a television, which was currently turned off. Next to it was a dry-erase board. It had today's date on it, the name of the nurse on shift, Venus, and the physician on duty, Dr. Sanders. Venus had been nursing for over thirty years, my most seasoned nurse to date. She had caramel skin, a smile to warm your heart, and ended or began most sentences with "Honey". She was the opposite of Dr. Sanders, who was pale white, cold, and laconic. At least he wasn't starstruck. No selfies for Dr. Sanders.

Visiting hours started at 9:00 a.m. At 9:05, an enormous

figure stood in my doorway. His shoulders almost touched either side of the door frame. He wore a short-sleeved green T-shirt and faded blue jeans. Giant biceps bulged beneath his shirt sleeves. His veins wormed just beneath his skin like buried cables. His right hand gripped a small vase of yellow lilies. The delicate flowers looked misplaced in his giant hand. At any moment, I expected the small vase to shatter in his palm.

"Hey, Claire," he said. His thunderous voice matched his overall presence.

"Fox?"

"Right, guess you don't remember me." He took one step into the room. "Can I come in?"

"Sorry, of course. Thank you for the flowers. Let's put them on the window sill." Before they explode in your hand, I thought.

He nodded and walked the lilies over to the window. The overhead light revealed a deep scar that ran down the side of his face, narrowly missing his right eye. The wound formed a large keloid that bubbled along a jagged course. On any other face, it would look shocking, even gruesome. But on Fox, it seemed fitting.

He took a seat in a bedside chair. "So you look great."

I couldn't return the compliment. It was the first time I remember seeing his face. "Thank you," I answered.

He shook his head and smiled. The smile was unexpected, breaking through his stone face. "I can't believe it. Here we are. Claire, alive and well. I wasn't sure if this would ever happen."

"Alive and well. Thanks to you, I guess."

"I only played a small role in that. It was my friend, Stinger, who actually pulled you out of the river."

He seemed like someone who wasn't used to attention or compliments. "Anyway, I heard you protected us. Um, Jack told me you had to stop some of the colonel's men." The stone face returned. "Kill some of the colonel's men, I should say." I took a deep breath. "That must have been hard on you."

Fox shrugged. "That hasn't been hard in a long time." He rubbed a large hand over his smooth, dark head. "Maybe it should be. It must be weird for someone like you to hear that."

"I don't know. Maybe."

"It's become mundane, like any other errand in life." He chuckled, a low, rumbling laugh. "A human life, it should be different."

His sudden introspection took me off guard. My years of giving therapy kicked in. "It must be your training. They make it routine. It's a matter of self-preservation. We call it compartmentalization in our business."

"Compartmentalization," he repeated. "I like that. Maybe you're right. Maybe it is my training. And maybe it's time to train to do something else. I'm tired of being the last face someone ever sees. They should be looking in the eyes of someone they love, or the face of God, not me."

His words took me by surprise. This massive warrior of a man sounded almost poetic. "I hear you're pardoned now. What will you do?"

He looked through the window to the outside. "I don't know. I have a lot of respect for what you do, Claire. How you kept me sane during our time together. I'm in your debt."

"So you think counseling?"

He laughed. His face looked so hard between smiles; each grin was unexpected. "I just told you I have no empathy for the people I kill. No, I think that career choice would be a stretch."

I laughed with him. "Fair enough."

"I know you don't remember, but you really did pull us through."

"Maybe you could go into some kind of security. You could even start your own security company." I had to change the subject. Taking credit for something I couldn't even remember doing felt disingenuous.

He stood up and walked over to the window sill. "No, too easy." He pinched one of the flower petals between his thumb and finger. "If I want to change, I need to stay away from violence. I need something more delicate."

"I understand."

He nodded and headed toward the door.

"Fox?"

"Yes?"

"Will we keep in touch?" I asked.

"Anytime, Claire. And you really should stay in touch with Jack. I know you don't remember him, but you two looked like you had something."

I smiled. He turned to go. "Oh, Fox, one more thing."

"What's that, Claire?"

"Whatever happened to the colonel?"

He shrugged. "He's on the lam."

"Maybe that could be your next project."

He shook his head. "That sounds like more violence."

CHAPTER FORTY-FOUR

Discharge day. Exactly six weeks after admission. What brave new world awaits? A world without Mia. A world without Amy. A world where I'm a celebrity.

I just hoped my five minutes of fame would run its course. Just the attention I gained from the staff on my hospital floor was enough to make me want to hide. Please, something big happen in the world. Nothing catastrophic, just something interesting enough to take the focus off the virus.

Now that I had access to media, it seemed like the only story covered. Who was involved? How do you know you're cured? Where is Colonel Link Stine?

Thankfully, my doctors had refused access from the news stations and late-night talk shows. If I could just dodge them for a few more weeks, maybe the world would look the other way.

I was being wheeled outside—hospital policy. A lousy policy if you ask me. Hospital patients should walk out standing upright, heads held high. Two volunteers saw me out. The one pushing my chair was an elderly man. He was audibly wheezing with the effort. He and I should switch places. Beside him a young girl carried a box of my fan mail. Hundreds of letters. Yep, I definitely wasn't ready for this new world.

We entered the elevator, just the three of us. The young girl dropped the box of letters on the elevator floor, the old man wheezed, and I watched the numbers.

"Someone special picking you up?" the old man asked. I nodded. "Parents?"

"Just a friend," I answered. I could have said Jack Baker. He probably knew him. Like Claire Long, everyone knew the name Jack Baker, at least for another few weeks.

Amy would be proud of me. Actually, Amy *is* proud of me. I was taking a chance. I could feel her with me since I woke up in the hospital. We were knit in the same womb. Her fearless approach to life was with me. It has always been with me.

The elevator doors sprang open. The front wheels creaked as the old man pushed me to the exit. Glass doors opened to a clear, brilliant sky. Outside for the first time in months. The full sun hit my face like a kiss from God.

"Claire?"

I turned and saw Jack, smiling broadly and holding a dozen roses. "That wasn't necessary," I said, looking at the flowers.

"You've finally been released. It seemed only fitting."

I stood and smiled. The old man wheeled the chair away, and the girl left my fan mail beside me.

"I'll pull the car around. You want to get some coffee?" asked Jack.

"Actually, I've been in this antiseptic prison for six weeks. I could use something stronger." He laughed. "What is it? What's so funny?"

He took my hand and smiled. "Nothing. Just reminds me of a person I used to know."

EPILOGUE

FOX

Fox gave it six months. The world moved on. Slowly, mankind was washed of its sin. No one had tested with any discernible viral load in weeks.

Fox forged through an unmarked trail and found the house with the faded terracotta roof. He cleared the sweat off his forehead with the bottom of his T-shirt. Damn, it was humid. But what did he expect in September in Costa Rica?

The house was just what he expected. It matched the colonel's drunken description from eight years ago to the letter. Ten miles south of Samara and a stone's throw from the sea. Tucked away in thick brush, surrounded by wildlife. A family of howler monkeys tracked him closely as Fox assessed the bungalow. The average size of the group was no bigger than an overweight house cat, but their cry was like a four-hundred-pound gorilla.

Their screams were good cover for his approach. A few mosquitos feasted on his neck as Fox cut through the undergrowth. His mind drifted back to the malaria fever spikes from ten years ago. That was the Congo, he thought, not to worry.

He broke through the jungle ferns and stopped in front of the porch. It was empty, except for a hammock strung between posts. Fox played the memory of Colonel Stine's drunken voice in his head. "I'm not fucking around with the elements, Fox. Concrete. Solid concrete. It's going to outlast all of us. Even those fucking tree rats, those Costa Rican monkeys, won't be able to touch it. They're practically giving that land away, Fox. Just over a dozen clicks south of Samara." The colonel raised his glass of bourbon in the air and toasted himself. "If and when I need to escape this world, I will have it. Not even my ex-wives can find me there. Damn parasites. And another thing, Fox," he steadied himself, "I can live on about a dollar a day down there. Hell, if needs be, I'll cook up a few of those tree rats."

Fox carefully approached the concrete home, painted a pine green. He doubted the colonel remembered his drunken speech. Not drinking alcohol had its advantages. Fox was never spewing information he held close to the vest. Of course, having a near photographic memory also had its advantages.

His boot on the concrete porch made little to no sound. Maybe the colonel wasn't here, thought Fox. Well, if he wasn't, Fox could camp out here until he did show up. He looked at the front door. It was wooden and hung slightly off. A sliver of light showed through a crack. Fox eyed the lock. It didn't seem like much of a threat to a boot with 250 pounds behind it.

Fox put the full weight of his right heel beside the door handle. The wood splintered at the frame, and the door exploded open. The colonel was seated on a small couch.

"Son of a bitch, Fox. You can't knock? The door was open." Fox said nothing. Stine rubbed his temples. A near-empty liter of whisky sat on the ground. He scanned the area around Fox. "How did you find me, anyway?"

Fox pointed at the whisky bottle. "You never were a quiet drunk, Colonel."

Stine's eyes followed to the bottle. He laughed. "Yeah, Fox, you got me there. You always were as sober as a fucking judge. Must have slipped up one night, huh?"

Fox nodded.

"So what do you want, Fox? You want a place next to mine? Cheap as dirt. Will keep your nose clean for a while."

"I don't need to hide, Colonel. I've been officially pardoned by our president. I'm sure you heard."

Stine picked up the whisky bottle. A few good swallows left. He turned it up, winced, then wiped his lips. "Yep, it's all bullshit. We do their dirty work, and they proclaim themselves clean. Absolved of the sin they created. But the dirt never does wash off, does it, Fox?"

Fox took a measured breath. He didn't come here to talk philosophy. "Some of us are more dirty than others, sir."

"What the fuck is that supposed to mean, Fox? And you can drop the 'sir.' I don't like the patronizing way it comes out of your mouth."

"It means, sir, that your hands like it in the dirt. The kind of hands that kill innocents, like Mia."

"Mia?"

"Korean lady. Claire Long's business partner. The one with the bullet in her forehead and no thumbs."

"Oh, that Mia." Stine laughed. "She wasn't very helpful." Stine stood up. "Come on, Fox. This world is ours." He motioned around him. "This is where we belong. It's the jungle. Society is done with us."

Fox rubbed his palms together. "Colonel, we are not the same."

"Bullshit, Soldier," yelled the colonel. "I knew you when the back of your ears were still wet. You are a survivor. It's what we do. We kill to survive and survive to kill."

Fox let Stine's words sink in. *Kill to survive and survive to kill.* "I don't even know what that means."

"It means we can't change what we are—born for war, killers."

Fox shook his head. "No," he answered and pulled his handgun from the small of his back. He pointed it at the colonel. "After today, I'll never kill again." He took aim and squeezed the trigger.

ACKNOWLEDGMENTS

First, I would like to thank you, the reader, for choosing *The Enemy Within.* Many early readers were helpful in shaping this novel and providing valuable feedback. These include: Pamela Hart, Brett Player, Suzanne Champion, Dale McGlothlin, and Kelsey Lucas.

I would like to thank Lisa Kastner with Running Wild for hunting down stories she believes in and sharing them with the world. Thank you to my beautiful wife, Jennifer, for giving me time and space to write. And I would like to acknowledge my two amazing daughters, Em and Kate—keep pursuing your personal legends.

ABOUT RUNNING WILD PRESS

Running Wild Press publishes stories that cross genres with great stories and writing. RIZE publishes great genre stories written by people of color and by authors who identify with other marginalized groups. Our team consists of:

Lisa Diane Kastner, Founder and Executive Editor
Cody Sisco, Acquisitions Editor, RIZE
Benjamin White, Acquisition Editor, Running Wild
Peter A. Wright, Acquisition Editor, Running Wild
Resa Alboher, Editor
Angela Andrews, Editor
Sandra Bush, Editor
Ashley Crantas, Editor
Rebecca Dimyan, Editor
Abigail Efird, Editor
Aimee Hardy, Editor
Henry L. Herz, Editor
Cecilia Kennedy, Editor
Barbara Lockwood, Editor

Scott Schultz, Editor
Rod Gilley, Editor

Evangeline Estropia, Product Manager
Kimberly Ligutan, Product Manager
Lara Macaione, Marketing Director
Joelle Mitchell, Licensing and Strategy Lead
Pulp Art Studios, Cover Design
Standout Books, Interior Design
Polgarus Studios, Interior Design

Learn more about us and our stories at www.runningwild-press.com

Loved these stories and want more? Follow us at runningwildpublishing.com, www.facebook.com/runningwild-press, on Twitter @lisadkastner @RunWildBooks

RUNNING WILD
RUNNING WILD PRESS

Made in the USA
Middletown, DE
29 August 2025

13213748R00156